A DC KENDRA MARCH CRIME THRILLER

FAGIN'S FOLLY

Book 2 of the 'Summary Justice' series

Theo Harris

ALEMAR
PUBLICATIONS

Fagin's Folly
Book 2 of the 'Summary Justice' series

Copyright © 2022 by Theo Harris
All rights reserved.

Paperback ISBN: 979-8-359896-60-3

Second Edition, © 2024

PRAISE FOR THEO HARRIS

'Couldn't put the book down. Loved it.'

'The pacing of the book was impeccable, with each chapter leaving me hungry for more.'

'WOW! I was not expecting much but totally surprised.'

'One of my favourite reads of the year, waiting for the rest of the series!'

'Really gripping storytelling that is clearly well researched and engaging,'

Cool gritty romp... Excellent lead character and plot - really enjoyed the story.'

Before AN EYE FROM AN EYE...
There was

TRIAL
RUN

An exclusive Prequel to the **'Summary Justice'** series,
free to anyone who subscribes to the Theo Harris
monthly newsletter.

Find out what brought the team together and the
reasons behind what they do... and why.

Go to **theoharris.co.uk**
or join at:
https://dl.bookfunnel.com/7oh5ceuxyw

ALEMAR
PUBLICATIONS

Also by Theo Harris

DC Kendra March - 'Summary Justice' series

Think you've gotten away with it? Think again!

CONTENTS

PROLOGUE

They lay in wait, two in the bushes and two behind the old oak tree to one side of the path. All four wore black garb, including beanie hats and snoods, which they pulled up to hide their faces, leaving just their eyes visible. They looked like ninja warriors from a television show, waiting patiently, biding their time, ready to strike at any moment. They had done this many, many times in the past year; it was something at which they had become proficient.

The darkness had arrived less than an hour earlier, partially concealing the poorly lit path that was frequently used as a shortcut from the busy eateries in Mare Street, Hackney, to the gentrified residential streets beyond London Fields, the park that the path cut through. The four ninjas had chosen London Fields as their focus for tonight, one of the dozens of venues throughout East London that they had carefully selected for their ambushes. They were careful to pick dark locations, where their victims would not be seen or heard, which had several escape routes, and where it would be difficult for help to arrive in any good time. They had picked their venues well, with significant – and increasing - success.

They didn't have to wait long tonight for their next victims, a couple in their late thirties out celebrating their wedding anniversary at their favourite bistro. Although not drunk, a relaxing bottle or two of wine had helped them disregard the dangers of cutting through a park so late at night. The husband, six-foot-three and stout, almost twenty stones, was feeling untouchable with three glasses of wine in his system. As they approached the bend that was overlooked by the gigantic two-hundred-year-old oak, the four ambushers used their now familiar hand signals to indicate that their quarry was almost upon them.

The couple, huddled together and enjoying each other's company, stopped suddenly as two of the masked strangers stepped out from behind the tree.

'Money, jewellery, and phones, now!' shouted one of them, brandishing a machete.

'Steady on, fella,' the man said, sobering up instantly as he recognised the threat. 'We don't have anything you want,' he added, extending an arm towards them, palm up, as if to fend them off.

'I won't ask again. Do it now or we'll cut you both. Bad.'

The second stranger wielded a large knife, which he waved in their faces.

'Look, mate, we've just been–' The husband didn't have time to complete his pleading as the man lunged at him and slashed the blade towards his arm. He instinctively stepped back, pulling his wife behind him. They did not notice the other two assailants sneak out from behind the bushes on the opposite side, behind them, both similarly armed. One of them sliced the back of the husband's leg with a serrated hunting knife that had been sharpened frequently, slicing through his left hamstring as a knife would slice through a piece of raw chicken. He screamed and collapsed to the floor, clutching the back of his furiously bleeding leg, trying desperately to keep his wife safe from the attackers.

'Please, don't! You can have everything!' the woman yelled in fear, handing over her handbag to the nearest attacker. He grabbed it but continued to slash her arm, eliciting a scream of pain.

'Here!' shouted her husband, handing over his wallet with one hand whilst holding the back of his blood-drenched leg with the other, weakening from blood loss.

The machete-wielder took a knuckle duster from his pocket and put it on his right hand, flexing his fingers as he looked lovingly at his pride and joy. It had raised bladed edges marking the letter 'E', measuring two inches by two, the back of the 'E' rounded and the middle line slightly longer, giving the impression of a claw.

'Next time, do what you're told, old man,' he said, before punching the man hard in his midriff, prompting a grunt as the breath left his body, leaving bloody slashes in the shape of the knuckle duster. He looked up just in time to see the attacker strike again, this time flush on the forehead, a blow that knocked him out cold.

The attacker turned to the woman and said, 'When you tell your friends this story, remember to tell them that you met the East London Consortium, and remember to tell them that we show no mercy.'

She nodded quickly.

'I'll tell you what,' he said, slowly approaching, 'let me help you with that.'

He placed the knuckle duster against her forehead. The woman whimpered, frozen stiff in fear, fearing for her life as the cold steel caressed her skin. She closed her eyes as the attacker pressed hard into her forehead, squeezing first upwards then downwards to ensure that the letter was clear on her skin, drawing blood, painful enough for her to cry in agony. She had been branded.

The four attackers then proceeded to rummage through their victims' pockets and stripped them clean of everything of value, including their wedding rings, credit cards, gold chains, and mobile phones. Within seconds they had taken their stash and vanished into the gloom. The woman opened her eyes and looked around, blood pouring from her wounds, not knowing what to do except scream for help.

It would be thirty minutes before the ambulance finally arrived, the police shortly afterwards. Her husband's injuries and blood loss were severe, and he would be in a coma for three days before finally gaining consciousness. Their painful injuries, especially the robbers' brands on their bodies, would remind them for the rest of their lives of their fateful walk in the park.

It was not an anniversary they would ever forget.

1

VIGILANTES

'Okay, listen up, everybody, let's make a start,' shouted Detective Sergeant Rick Watts, clapping his hands with authority as he moved in front of the magnetic board that he would be referring to during the briefing. The voices died down to a murmur as the Serious Crimes Unit turned to listen to their highly respected leader, the man who had recruited them. He waited patiently, shaking his head as the team took their seats in the briefing room.

'Come on, you lot. Honestly, it's like being back at school again. Let's get a grip here!' he said, eliciting smiles and giggles from his team. He grinned back.

'Before I start, I want to clear something up, as I know you're all champing at the bit waiting to find out what the hell is going on. We have been joined today — graciously, I might add — by our esteemed colleague, Detective Constable Kendra March,' he indicated to the smiling Kendra, who had taken a seat near the front. She shook her head, feigning irritation.

The rest of the team clapped and whooped enthusiastically, glad to see her back with them in a formal briefing. It had been a long time.

'Don't you shake your head, March, you know I have to do this,' Watts continued. 'Anyway, as you can clearly see, young Kendra here is recovering well from her injuries. It's taken a little longer than expected but she's getting there, right?'

Kendra nodded theatrically.

'And that's the good news. The downside is that she has decided to slow things down a little, which is understandable, and has opted to go part-time.'

This somewhat surprising announcement was met with silence, the rest of the team unsure how to respond.

'Now, as you know, we don't have any part-timers on this, the most elite of teams,' he said, noticing the silence and stepping in quickly.

'Come on, guys, we are elite, aren't we?' He extended both arms to his troops, prompting more laughter and applause.

'So, you may quite rightly be asking why she is here in this briefing, right? Well, we have managed to secure permission to include Kendra's honoured presence in our briefings and investigations as a representative of the Intel Unit downstairs. So, in a way, she'll still be part of the team, she just won't be able to get involved in anything exciting until she decides to come to her senses and come back to us full-time.' Watts looked directly at Kendra and winked.

'Anyway, that's enough of that. Kendra will still be around to help with stuff, so before you know it, we'll all be sick of her again.' More laughter.

'What about Andy Pike, boss? Any news on when he's coming back from sick leave?' asked Nick McGuinness, one of the longer-serving members of the team.

'Well, he hasn't been in touch much, as you know, but we have heard that his papers will be going through any day now, for him to be medically retired. I spoke with him a few days ago, he is still quite bitter and unhappy but seems resigned to his fate, which is an improvement on how he was. He is planning to take some trips and will probably then fade away; he doesn't want to engage with anyone at the moment.'

'Shame, that,' Wilf Baker said. 'He was a good 'un.' There were lots of murmured agreements.

Kendra did not respond in any way, knowing what she did about Andy and his current status. She didn't like to take credit for anything, but she had pulled Andy, her partner on the team, from the depths of depression and helped transform him into a Q-like figure from a James Bond film. His progress, from agreeing to join she and her father Trevor on the quest for justice, had given Andy a new lease of life, made all the more satisfying by their having found out that he had a genius flair for hacking and navigating the dark web, as well as the ability to procure almost everything they would ever need. Thanks to their joint efforts, and with the help of some talented friends, they had managed to secure premises and equipment, more than enough to deal with the types of criminals that had been getting away with their crimes for decades.

It was why she kept the emotion from her face as the team openly and enthusiastically showed theirs.

'Those Albanians have a lot to answer to, the bastards,' Pablo Rothwell said, still angry that the Qupi gang had never been brought to justice for their vicious attack on Kendra and Andy, which was the cause of Andy's subsequent retirement.

'If you will allow me to continue, I will explain what this

briefing is all about,' Watts said, taking back control of the conversation.

'You almost spoiled it for me there, Wilf, so thanks for that,' he said sarcastically. 'As you know, we were barred from engaging with the Qupi investigation, because those higher beings from the top floor thought it would cause a "conflict of interest",' he said, doing air quotes. 'But it didn't stop us from causing a few problems for the bastards, and the two ships that we sent information about were bringing over a ton of firearms and people that would have caused a lot of problems here in East London when they were seized. We did that, we caused a massive problem for Qupi, so well done, us.'

They all clapped briefly, accepting what was essentially a pat on the back, which would bring no official recognition as they had conducted their interference covertly.

'So, why this briefing?' Watts continued. 'Well, it seems that the Qupi gang have vanished from the face of the earth. Now we knew that seizing the ships and the cargo would cause them problems, but they were a solid outfit, so it doesn't make sense that they would just disappear.'

'What, you mean they've stopped their criminal activities?' asked Jillian Petrou.

'No, I mean they have completely vanished. Nobody has a clue where they are. There's no activity recorded at any ports; they have just disappeared. Their warehouse is empty, their houses are empty, their bank accounts are empty, their cars gone, no trace of anything anywhere.'

There was silence in the room as the team digested this news. It was very rare for anything like this to happen. With modern technology there was usually a trace of someone somewhere, so this had stumped them completely.

Kendra kept quiet, knowing that the Qupi gang were now

in deepest Africa paying a heavy price for their crimes, their wealth taken from them and ready to be used to fund operations against other criminals. Her team had done a grand job taking them off the streets, something the police had been unable to do. It was a pattern that was repeating itself many times all over London, and a pattern Kendra was doing something about, covertly and very much against the laws of the land.

'Well, that's good news, right?' asked Norm Clarke. 'Shouldn't we be happy that a bunch of nasty bastards are now off our streets?'

'If only it were that simple, Norm,' said Rick. 'Personally, I'm delighted they have vanished, but at the same time, I'm pissed off that we can't put them away for twenty years or more. Those upstairs have suddenly become concerned — how typical is that? One day they order us to stay away on pain of being sacked and the next they want us to investigate!'

'Sarge, if they've disappeared, then what is there to investigate? You've already said they've cleared everything out, including their houses and bank accounts. What do they actually want us to do?' asked Kendra.

'For one,' said Watts, 'they want to know where the money's gone, in case we can seize it under the Proceeds of Crime Act. And then there are the deaths on the ships of those poor refugees, so they're desperate for convictions, to show Europe that we are on top of these things. A lot of it is political so we just have to get on with it.'

'Understood.'

'So, for the next few days, let's put some intel on this board and start searching, people. I'll start the ball rolling with this fella.' Watts placed a recent picture of Guran Qupi on the magnetic board, writing *Where is Qupi?* underneath.

'Kendra, if you and the intel team focus on all UK ports against Qupi's goons in case we missed any trace of them leaving, that will be a good place to start.'

'No problem, I'll start on that today,' she replied.

'Let's crack on, then, team, let's find these people sharpish. Unless there are any other questions, you're dismissed.'

Nobody raised their hand or asked any questions, so the team rose from their chairs and left, typically in groups of two or three, discussing the next steps. Kendra held back to speak to Rick privately.

'Sarge, is there anything else that we can help with downstairs?' she asked.

'No, don't worry, K. I have asked for the Financial Investigations Unit to help trace the money, but I think it's probably all back in Albania now, paying for their mansions and swimming pools.'

'Okay, I'll let you know if anything comes up with the ports. See you later,' she said, turning to leave.

'It's good to have you back here, Kendra, you part-timer,' Watts said with a smile as she left.

2

CHANGES

'Well, that is interesting, isn't it?' Andy said, once Kendra had briefed him and her dad.

'Is there any chance they can trace that money back to us?' asked Trevor. 'It's just that you've gone and paid mortgages off and bought the factory, amongst other things. It's going to be tough to explain all that.'

'No, don't worry. They're good at what they do, but tracing money that has been transferred into crypto currency and then transferred between multiple overseas bank accounts numerous times is beyond them. What we may have to explain at some point in the future is how we came by the funds to set up everything over here, like the factory. And I've taken care of that, too,' Andy said, beaming. He was in his element and loving it.

'Go on then, Einstein, tell us how you've taken care of that too,' said Kendra, mockingly, but happy that Andy was enjoying life again.

'As I mentioned, the funds to pay for the factory and the mortgages for the gym and garage were made by the *Sher-*

wood Management Trust and *Loxley Investments*, two companies that are registered in the Cayman Islands. I've already registered you, Trevor, as an unpaid director of both companies, meaning that you won't be bothered by the tax man. The funds in their bank accounts, as I mentioned, were run through several other overseas accounts, in countries that will make it very difficult for anyone to get assistance with tracing the monies. It's too complicated and jumbled for them to make any sense of it. As long as we don't show off any of that wealth personally, we'll be just fine, so if we all carry on doing what we've always done, they won't ever find us. Once the businesses have paid their taxes as normal, they won't bother us.'

'None of that made any sense to me, but I'll take your word for it,' said Trevor. 'Worth the risk in any case, I'd say: expanding the gyms is taking more kids off the streets.'

'We'll be fine, Trevor, don't worry about a thing. Now, can we get back to the reason why we are meeting tonight? Kendra, what are your thoughts about this investigation, are we at risk?'

'I don't think so. Like you said, they are unlikely to trace the money back to us, and they won't find anything at the ports because the gang didn't leave by legitimate means, remember? There may be some crumbs from existing employees at some of the businesses, but I believe Dabbs is now taking them in hand quite nicely and treating everyone a lot better than Qupi was doing.'

Brodie Dabbs had helped them with their exploits against the Qupis by sending some men to help, in exchange for taking over Qupi's territories and businesses, such as the brothels and the gambling houses.

Kendra continued.

'Some of the gangsters may have had family here. We cleaned out the main players' houses and left no trace of them, but there are likely to be wives of some of the muscle who may report them missing. It's not anything we need to concern ourselves with. Remember, I'll be there in the office, monitoring things, so if by any chance they get lucky, I'll be able to get word to you quickly enough for you to be able to deal with it.'

'Don't you just love all this sneaky spy stuff?' asked Trevor, smiling broadly, 'and isn't it fun to see two decorated police detectives breaking the law so blatantly in the interests of justice? I am so loving this!'

He also loved pointing that out regularly, especially considering the irony of it, but deep down he was immensely proud of what they were doing. And especially proud of Kendra. They had gone from having a distant and cold relationship to being partners in crime against crime, and he wouldn't change a thing. He clapped his hands in delight, laughing.

'Lap it up, Dad, we get it. Just remember that it's all your fault,' Kendra said mischievously, knowing it would get an instant reaction.

'Wait, what? What do you mean it's my fault?'

It was Kendra and Andy's turn to laugh. Trevor looked from one to the other, waiting for an answer.

'I'm just kidding, but if you like, we can make something up. For example, we would never have gotten rid of the bad guys without you, which means we probably never had plans to take them on. Isn't that right, Andy?'

'Sounds about right,' Andy replied, 'so basically, it's your fault, Trevor. You should be ashamed of yourself, putting your daughter through all this.'

'Funny, both of you, ha-bloody-ha. I'm getting a beer,' Trevor said, shaking his head as he left the room.

'Love you, Dad!' Kendra said as he left.

'It's great that you are both getting on so well, K, I'm chuffed for you,' Andy said.

'Yeah, we have a lot to catch up on. I just didn't think it would be by taking down criminal gangs!'

'Listen, there's something I've been meaning to tell you,' he continued. 'I'm about to be medically discharged, and I've been doing everything we talked about, staying away, acting distant, blah, blah...'

'Go on.'

'I've done plenty of research and spoken to a few experts. Once I'm officially out of the Met I'm going to take some time off to get surgery on my foot. I just wanted you to know so that we could plan around it. I'll probably be gone for about a month, hopefully less.'

'What do you mean, surgery? What are you having done?'

'I'm having the foot amputated, K. It's a useless lump of flesh and doesn't work, and never will, the damage was permanent. If I have it removed then I can get a prosthetic, it will allow me to be more mobile and I really want that.'

'I understand,' she said, not knowing what else to say.

'It's fine, honestly, and for the best. I've been getting properly jealous while you lot have been going out having all the fun!'

'It hasn't all been fun, Mr Pike! And anyway, who will be taking care of the ops room while you're out having fun?"

'We'll manage,' he said. 'The joys of technology will help us. Maybe we can get a nice van kitted out, like in the movies?' He raised his eyebrows, suggesting that it was a good idea. And it probably was, but now was not the time to think about that.

'We'll cross that bridge when we come to it, Andy; for now, I just hope you'll be okay.'

Andy looked at her affectionately. 'I will be, K, it'll be fine and for the best, I promise. I'll be able to walk properly again, in fact I may ask them to add some bionic gadgetry so that I can run faster than any man alive!'

Kendra laughed. 'Fine, Steve Austin, you do that. I'm going to see if Dad has stopped sulking yet.' She gave him a kiss on the cheek. 'Whatever happens, we'll be just fine.'

———

SHE FOUND Trevor in the kitchen, rummaging around for some cheese to make a sandwich.

'You ok, Dad?' she asked. 'You know we're only jesting with you, don't you?'

'Yes, darling, of course I do,' he replied, laughing. 'It's keeping me on my toes, but I enjoy it very much. Are you ok?'

'I'm doing great, thanks to you and Andy. What we are doing has lifted my spirits and given me hope, so thank you again for having our backs.'

Trevor gave her a big hug, shaking her playfully from side to side. 'Remember how much you used to like me doing that?'

'That seems like such a long time ago now, Dad, and a lot has happened since, hasn't it? But yes, it's one of my favourite memories, and it's good for you to be able to do it again; your shoulder has healed well.'

Trevor flexed his arm and rotated his shoulder, where he had been shot by Qupi. The flesh wound had healed well, and his grimace was softening each day. 'It's getting there, love.'

'Good. And let's not have such a lengthy break from each other again. Deal?'

'I'd like nothing more, love,' he said, kissing her on the cheek.

'Anyway, enough of the mushy stuff, let's get back to Andy so you can update us on what is going on at the factory and the gym.'

They walked back to the underground ops room, where Andy was busy on one of the multiple keyboards he had arrayed on one of the desks.

'Just bear with me, folks,' he said, glancing up as they came back in, 'I'm just moving some funds around again. I think it's prudent to do it regularly now to make it impossible for them to trace.'

'Good call, Andy,' said Kendra. 'Go on then, Dad, tell us what's been going on these past few weeks.'

'Okay, to start with, I've had some of the boys working at the factory, making it fit for purpose, more comfortable, that sort of thing. We need a corporate look for the front, so they've been painting and buying some artwork and fake plants. You won't recognise it. I also have a gardening firm ripping all the weeds out and cleaning the whole site, they'll be finished in about a week and it will look great outside.'

'Have they fitted the CCTV yet?' asked Andy. 'Just remind them to send me the info so that I can log in and monitor it from here.'

'They've almost finished, there's a lot of them to put in but we're getting there. The false walls are in, too, so there's an acoustic barrier now between the front and the back of the building, where we're kitting out the rooms for our guests.'

'That's great, Dad, so we should be ready to go in a couple of weeks, right?'

'Sooner, if needed, but best not to rush. I'm also giving some of the lads a few training courses, so they can familiarise themselves with the security industry. I think the factory should be a consultancy, mainly in security. We may as well see if we can do some business that way, right?'

'Okay, didn't see that coming,' Kendra said.

'Look, sooner or later, someone is going to want to visit or speak to us, or whatever. It would not be a good idea to spend all that money buying the place, kitting it out, and then having nothing to show for it. I'm actually talking to some freelance consultants to work for us remotely. Andy, I'm hoping you can sort out a website and some email addresses, so that we can start networking. Honestly, I don't see how this can work properly if we don't look like a legitimate business. Don't you think?'

Andy and Kendra looked at each other and nodded, impressed with Trevor's forward thinking.

'Also, let's keep the knowledge of what we're doing to a minimum. The youngsters are all keen to help me, but I want them to think that what they are doing is legitimate, so I think we should employ them and give them real jobs at the factory – or company HQ, as we should start calling it. The less they know, the better. And I think you should work from here most of the time, Andy, and we should keep this ops room a guarded secret that only the three of us know about, again, just in case things go haywire.'

'You'll get no argument from me,' said Andy, 'and of course I'll help with the rest, including bank accounts and all the legal stuff.'

'What about the gym, Dad? Did you secure the new one yet?'

'Yes, that's all sorted, and Charlie is helping me with the new kit. That will be up and running any day now. I've already had a dozen kids asking about it, so it won't take long before we can help a lot more of them there. I've also found one for the single mums, not too far away from the other two. I want to keep them separate for now because most of them are vulnerable, but I'm sure they will be referring some young single girls too, who are just as at risk. I'm hoping you can come and talk to them soon, darling, so they have a fresh perspective on things.'

'Of course, Dad, happy to help whenever.'

'Some of the girls at the boxing club will be going over to train them frequently, and they've started bringing some friends they trust, to make up the numbers.'

'Great. There's still plenty to do but we're getting there quickly, so all is good.'

'On that note, I think I should bring my situation up now,' added Andy.

'What's that?' asked Kendra.

'A bed has been freed up at one of the hospitals I told you about, so I'm going to go and have that surgery sooner rather than later. It'll be weeks before anything major needs doing, so I may as well go now. I can monitor accounts and move things around on my tablet when needed, so I won't be completely gone.'

'Surgery?' said Trevor.

'I'll tell you later, Dad, it's all good,' Kendra said quickly. 'That's great, Andy, I hope it all goes as well as it can. Keep in touch in the meantime, okay?'

'I will. You have a key for my house so you can come in

and use the ops room as and when you need to. I may be out of touch for the first couple of days, but all being well, I'll be bugging you relentlessly after that!'

'We'll look forward to it, of course!' Kendra laughed.

'Don't think I won't slap you just because you're getting circumcised,' Trevor said, holding out his hand for Andy to shake.

'Damn, I told you it was a secret, K!' Andy said in mock alarm.

'Honestly, the pair of you,' Kendra said. She walked over and gave Andy a kiss on the cheek.

'We'll see you soon, okay?'

'Damn right you will,' he said.

3

A PATTERN

Kendra was back at work in the Intel Unit the next day. She was more than happy with how things were going with her covert operations, and Trevor had taken control of all the upgrades and the equipment. It was for Kendra to keep on top of any intelligence-related matters that were likely to overlap with what they were doing. Being involved, even part-time, was worth its weight in gold, and would always allow her to be one step ahead.

Sam Razey sat down next to her, shaking his head and rolling his eyes. 'This is doing my head in, Kendra. I'm not even sure what we're looking for anymore, the only records and sightings we have are those we already knew about. There's nothing at any port, nada. They have literally vanished. We told them this already, so what else are they expecting?'

'There's no point getting pissed about it, Sam, these things happen sometimes. All you can do is try, and if nothing shows up, then nothing shows up, so what? That's what you tell them upstairs.'

'Yeah, I guess, but you know they'll look down on us in disapproval, don't you? Especially that Watts, he always looks at you as if you've done something wrong, frightens the life out of me.'

Kendra laughed. 'He's not like that at all, Sam, you're making something out of nothing. Rick is one of the good guys, trust me.'

'I suppose. Anyway, have you found anything worth mentioning?'

'Nope, nothing, so don't feel left out, Mr Grumpy.' She laughed as he huffed and rolled his eyes again and walked off, hunching his shoulders and walking with an exaggerated gait as if to mimic a moody teenager.

Kendra was pleased the intel team was not having any success. She just had to make sure they were all seen to be trying and documenting their efforts so that Rick Watts would keep off their backs. She went through a list of checks that she wanted to document as being carried out, before switching to covert mode and looking through the crime reports.

It didn't take long to spot some stand-out crimes and patterns worth researching. There had been a number of burglaries and robberies in East London the past few months that were clearly connected to one particularly vicious gang, the East London Consortium. Each victim, whether from a burglary or robbery, had been violently attacked and disfigured in some way, typically by an unusually small, bladed weapon of some kind. Kendra studied each report and soon found what that weapon was – a particularly nasty knuckle duster. One had been used a couple of nights earlier and had left a brand on the victim's forehead. This cynical branding had escalated in the past six weeks and was becoming a big concern. There had been no evidence or clues left behind at any scene; the assailants were very well prepared and knew what to do to avoid detection, vanishing into the dark every time.

There was no pattern to where they struck, it seemed as though they were random attacks by the same brutal gang, and there was nothing further for the police to investigate, due to the lack of evidence and intelligence.

'Well, this seems like something we should look into,' Kendra muttered to herself.

LATER THAT EVENING, back at her flat, Kendra and Trevor shared a large margherita pizza and a bottle of red wine as they caught up. It was starting to become a ritual that they enjoyed very much, with both hoping that it would stay a long-term thing.

'It's weird not having Andy around,' Trevor remarked absently, 'I'm starting to warm to him.'

Kendra laughed. 'He's great, isn't he? When he's on form, he is the most charming and likeable person you will ever meet.'

'You like him a lot, don't you, love?'

Kendra was surprised at the comment, and it showed on her face.

'Of course, Dad, he's my mate,' she blustered. 'I mean my friend, not mate-mate, not like that, you know what I mean!'

Trevor laughed out loud. 'I'm only teasing, darling, but I see how you are around him and how you look at him. I want you to be happy, but also careful, okay? What we are doing isn't a joke, it's some serious shit that will be painful at times, you know?' He lifted his injured shoulder to emphasise his point.

'You think I don't know that? I was there when you were shot, remember? I was there when Andy lost his eye and the use of his foot. I've had two very badly broken legs, or did you forget? I know what I'm doing, Dad, and I know you're being protective but I'm a big girl who knows how to take care of herself.'

Trevor nodded in understanding. 'I won't ever forget, love, and I will never stop protecting you, either. So, I think we understand each other, right? Now pass me that wine, I'm parched.

'Changing the subject,' said Kendra, 'I think there's something that we should look at next.'

'What is it?'

'There's been a spate of violent robberies and burglaries where the victims have been scarred, almost branded, by a nasty bladed knuckle duster. The gang responsible are not worried about linking themselves to so many offences, it's as if they're advertising who they are and what they are about – which seems to be life-threatening violence.'

'They sound lovely, who are they?'

'They call themselves the East London Consortium. There's nothing at all in the Intel Unit, no links to anyone at all, so we're starting from scratch. Can you ask around some of the lads at the club, see if they've heard anything?'

'Sure, I'll do that first thing tomorrow. Now are you going to pass that wine, or not?'

TREVOR WAS INCREASINGLY proud of their recent successes but more so regarding the positive impact and progress that he had made with the boxing clubs. His original intention was to keep youths off the streets, keep them out of trouble, and give them the discipline and strength that comes from boxing training and the routines associated with it. That would also, simultaneously, give them breathing room from the 'gangster' lifestyle that was so prevalent on the streets of East London.

The youth, in the main, had given up on education, they didn't care for routines, they didn't have the patience to learn skills through apprenticeships or starting in lower positions at any job – they had no patience for the end game. They certainly didn't care for the types of jobs they considered demeaning. With that came a profound lack of respect for authority or anyone older that tried to teach them life skills that had been learned the hard way. They wanted everything now. Things that would typically take a person decades to earn – and they didn't care about the damage they caused along the way.

Trevor's clubs gave hope to a small number of well-intentioned youngsters and more so their parents, those that had been strong enough to influence their kids positively enough to try the boxing training. The parents saw an almost immediate positive impact and it cheered them up no end. Most of the youth had stuck it out and some had gone on to bigger and better things, away from the blighted area. Trevor didn't mind that at all; it was in the right direction and that's what mattered. There were a few who didn't last long, or who didn't have the strength to resist the lifestyle that was portrayed so attractively to them. Trevor had made efforts to change their minds but had failed in some instances.

Then there were those who were in between. Those who

didn't have the will or the affinity to train religiously every day but who had the strength of mind to stay away from the gangs and do something less 'criminal'. They were the youth that Trevor assisted in other ways, giving them jobs on the side, introducing them to others that could do the same, and training them in other ways accordingly, to contribute in some way to the venture with Kendra and Andy. They showed promise, and they had such loyalty to Trevor, which meant he would always have 'back up' for the trials and tribulations that lay ahead of them.

At one of the newly acquired boxing clubs, Trevor watched from the side as the youngsters were put through their paces by twins Mo and Amir, who had enjoyed the saga against the Qupis so much that they were thirsty for more, which had opened the door for Trevor to insist on the pair doing more to contribute elsewhere.

'If you want to do more, then you'll have to put in some work to help in other ways, otherwise I'll just call you up every now and again – if I ever need you,' Trevor had insisted.

They were reluctant at first but had since become proficient and, more importantly, they were enjoying the extra responsibilities that came with being a trainer. Trevor gave himself a well-earned pat on the back for that.

He glanced over to the far end of the club where two teenage girls were being put through their paces by Charmaine, the latest trainer he had recruited in his drive to become more inclusive. Although he had set up a separate club for girls, that was more for single mothers or vulnerable women who preferred to keep to themselves until their situations had improved. He had since integrated several teenage girls into a couple of the other clubs, and it had worked out much better than he had ever hoped. He was proud of their progress and achievements and saw great futures for them, which would be limited only by their ambition. He also saw a need for their secret team to be more diverse and could see the team being greatly enhanced with their inclusion. Despite his ever-present concern for everyone's safety, Trevor was more confident about the future than ever.

'I will train them all well, and harder than ever,' he had told Kendra and Andy. 'The more training they have, the more confident and capable they will all be.'

Charmaine was a prime example of what he was hoping to achieve moving forward. When it came to her own fitness, she took pride in keeping up with – and most times beating – the men.

She did not see girls as the weaker sex. Not at all, and woe betide anyone who got into that argument with her. Charmaine found ways of proving it many times when sparring with the men. She used her guile and her extensive knowledge of the human body, along with psychological techniques, to better almost everyone she fought.

Much of this she passed on to the young women she trained, focusing on mental strength. She was successful, and she was outstanding.

Trevor couldn't believe his luck when she agreed to take up a position with him.

'I like the way you think, old man,' she had said when he had explained his aims.

'There just aren't enough places for these kids to train and better themselves,' he had emphasised, 'and I aim to change that. And less of the old man,' he'd added with a knowing wink.

'When can I start?' she'd said.

'How about we start right now and you show me what you can do?'

Three minutes in the ring with her was all it took for Trevor to realise he had made the right decision taking her on. The bruising on his side had taken two weeks to go.

———

'Okay, everyone, let's gather round. You too, girls.' Trevor waved them over.

The frenetic activity stopped almost immediately and the noise level dropped to a quiet whisper as they all made their way towards the main sparring ring where Trevor had jumped up to speak to them.

'First off, it's good to see so many of you today, so thank you for making the effort. You're all working very hard, and it is starting to show, so well done.'

'What's up, Trev?' asked Amir, as he stripped off the binding on his hands.

'I need to ask if any of you have heard of the *East London Consortium*, or ELC as they are sometimes referred to. There's a lot of noise about them on the streets but nobody seems to know who they are. They're causing a lot of problems around here and I want you all to be aware and to be careful, they're a nasty bunch of arseholes, okay?'

There was a murmur from the group.

'I've heard something,' came a quiet voice. It was one of the girls.

'Quieten up, everyone,' shouted Trevor. 'What's your name, love?'

'It's Zoe.'

Trevor could see she was nervous, but he also recognised a determination about her that he found encouraging.

'What have you heard, Zoe? You have a great jab, by the way.'

'Thank you,' she said, her nerves easing. 'A friend of mine and I were at the Hanger club last weekend and witnessed a nasty fight between four men. It was three against one and they beat the crap out of him before security were able to stop them.'

'Go on.'

'The three men were laughing as security took them out. One of them lashed out at the security guard and cut his face with a ring or something that he was wearing. The poor guard ended up with three slashes on his face, like Bruce Lee, you know?'

Trevor perked up at this, remembering what Kendra had told him about the vicious knuckle duster. If the gang member had lashed out wildly, that was exactly the sort of damage it would do.

'So how did you know they were with the ELC?'

'The guy that lashed out was a nasty piece of work. He shouted at the security and told them they would be hearing from the East London Consortium again very soon. He was evil, you could sense it.'

'Did you hear anything else?'

'The man they beat up had to go to hospital. My friend knew him and later found out that they had beaten him up because he'd tried to chat up one of the girls the group were there with, a girl called Rhianna. We know where she works.'

'Thank you, Zoe, that is good to know. Anyone else hear anything?' There was nothing more from the group.

'Okay, please remember, these guys are animals and won't

think twice about cutting you, or worse. Keep your ears to the ground and let me know if you hear anything else, okay? I want to know if they are closing in on our patch here.'

'Okay, back to work!' shouted Mo to his group, and the youngsters went back to their places. Trevor waved Zoe and Charmaine over. That had been very valuable information and he wanted more.

'Zoe, that was brave of you to come forward like that, thank you. What can you tell me about Rhianna, where does she work?'

Zoe looked to Charmaine, who nodded. 'She works at the spa in Barking, the one in Cambridge Road. I think she's a receptionist or something like that.'

'Do you know anything else that might help?'

'Not really. Seeing how they beat that poor guy up scared me, they didn't give a shit who was there or what might happen to them. I hope there's not more of them because they will cause problems here too, which is why it was easy to speak up.'

'Again, that's very brave of you and I am very thankful. Charmaine, you have a great fighter here, great job.'

'Happy to help, boss,' Charmaine said, winking.

'Let me know if you hear anything else, okay? The more we know, the better we can prepare in case they come our way.' They both nodded and turned to go back to their session.

It wasn't much, but it was better than nothing.

Let's hope Kendra has a plan, he thought, making his way out of the ring and then outside, to make the call.

'THANKS, Dad, it's better than a kick in the teeth. I'll have a look tomorrow at work and see if anything comes up. It's a shame Andy isn't here, he would know who she was, where she was born and what she'd had for breakfast by now!'

'Yeah, well, he isn't here, so let's do the best we can until he comes back. I'll investigate the spa and keep you posted. If you get anything at work, let me know, and we'll catch up again tomorrow, okay?'

'Don't worry, Dad, I will. Jeez, you're starting to sound like one of the bosses upstairs!'

'There's no need for insults, young lady,' Trevor replied, 'now get back to work before I give you more paperwork to do.'

Kendra laughed as she ended the call. Her enthusiasm and drive had increased significantly these past few months. The helplessness she had felt when she'd realised most criminals were getting away with it had been replaced with the exhilaration of knowing she was doing something about it. She wanted to hold on to that euphoria for as long as possible. Breaking the law to serve justice was just fine with her.

She looked at her phone for the umpteenth time in the past hour, hoping for a message from Andy. She was missing him more than she'd expected and was both concerned and content at the same time.

'Sod this,' she suddenly exclaimed and typed out a message.

'*Hope all is well, how are you getting on? K x.*'

It had only been a few days and she had hoped to hold out as long as possible, hoping he might message first. She had caved.

She stared at the phone, willing for it to respond. Nothing. 'Bastard,' she whispered.

The phone pinged.

'I take it back,' she said out loud, smiling.

'*A bit sore but the op went well. Feels weird, keep wanting to scratch the sole of my foot and it isn't there anymore! Will try and call tomorrow when the drugs wear off a bit. Hope you are ok. A xx*'

'*Get some rest, we can chat tomorrow. K x.*'

As his confidence had come back, Andy had the air of a dashing pirate or an ace fighter pilot from the books she had read as a child. She looked forward to his return, not least because they would need his help with this new gang. But she had other reasons, too.

She looked through the copies of the crime reports she had made at work, reading them over and over to see if she could establish any pattern to the attacks or the locations. There were none, and that was a big red flag.

'This lot know exactly what they're doing,' she murmured.

It made for an unknown challenge ahead. Yes, the Qupi gang were ruthless and vicious, but there was information about them, and they'd been relatively easy to research. Trying to put an operation together was impossible without knowing who the subjects were or where they lived.

'Come back soon, Andy, this one is gonna be tricky.'

4

THE ELC

As he walked along Cambridge Road in Barking, towards the spa he was looking to scout, Trevor couldn't help but admire the progress that had taken place in the area since he was last here. It was no longer run-down and sinister but developed in a way that made it look modern, safe and appealing to visitors.

He nodded in appreciation as he looked up at the futuristic tower blocks that overlooked the relatively modern building that housed the spa. Some were still behind hoardings as the finishing touches were made to release them to their new occupants. It was inspiring and gave him hope that one day he would see more of the same throughout East London.

There was a steady trickle of people going in and out of the building, which hosted several assorted businesses along with the spa. It seemed the modern-day way of doing things, minimising the risk, and spreading the costs between many tenants rather than just one or two. It seemed to be working very well.

He crossed the road and entered the tall glass-fronted building, which opened into an airy open-plan foyer. There were a number of small desks and chairs scattered around, allowing people to work or make calls while they waited for appointments. Trevor made his way to reception, where a smartly dressed middle-aged woman stood behind a brushed-steel counter. It was clean and minimalist, seemingly the theme for the area.

'Hi there,' Trevor said.

'Good morning, sir, how can I help you?' The receptionist's smile was genuine and welcoming.

'I was hoping you could give me some information about the spa.'

'I can direct you to them where you can ask in person, if that works for you?' she replied.

'Thank you, yes.'

The receptionist pointed to the stairs. 'Go up to the first floor and you'll see the signs pointing to the left. Just follow the corridor and it will take you right there.'

'That's very kind, thank you,' replied Trevor as he set off towards the stairs. When he entered, he couldn't help but exclaim, 'Whoa!'

The spa's reception area was like Santa's grotto. There were thousands of fairy lights hanging from the ceiling, covering it all, giving the room a welcoming golden glow. There were several well-maintained plants strategically placed, and the tan and cream décor looked classy and modern at the same time, complemented by the polished parquet flooring and the leather chairs meant for the waiting clients. It had a familiar Japanese feel that was designed to keep people as relaxed and comfortable as possible. They had done a great job.

'Welcome to the spa, sir, how can I help you today?'

Trevor hadn't seen the receptionist step out from behind a discreetly placed screen that he could now see led to a small office to one side. She was now standing behind the counter, smiling, welcoming a potential new client. She was a tall Caribbean beauty in her early twenties and dressed in a simple white blouse and black trousers, her curly, well-groomed hair tied in a tight ponytail that showed off her exceptional cheekbones.

Trevor clocked the rectangular name badge that was fastened to her blouse.

'Hello ...Rhianna. I was hoping you could give me some information about the spa.'

'I can do better than that, sir, I can talk you through exactly what services we currently offer, if you have a couple of minutes to spare?'

Trevor smiled. 'That works for me, thanks!'

'Well, as you can see, we like all things Japanese, so we have tailored our services to reflect that. We offer organic facials, massage therapies, holistic programmes, bespoke yoga services and more. It all depends on what you require. Is it for yourself, sir?'

Trevor paused before replying. 'It's for someone special. Do you have a brochure I can take with me?'

'Sure.' The receptionist leaned down and grabbed a glossy brochure from the shelf under the counter. 'Everything you need is there; if you want to call and make a booking, just ask for me.'

'So, I just ask for Miss ...'

'Rhianna usually does the trick, or if my manager answers the phone, you can be more formal and ask for Miss Dyer, whatever works best for you.'

'That's very kind of you, Miss Dyer, I shall do just that. Thanks again for your help.'

'You're very welcome, sir, we hope to see you again soon.'

Trevor was soon walking back along Cambridge Road towards Station Parade, past the new tower blocks and towards the car he had parked in a small hotel car park. He now knew what Rhianna looked like, and her surname. He understood why someone would want to try and chat to her in a club but was surprised she would want to be what in essence was a gangster's moll.

'Well, what do I know?' he muttered as he reached the car.

───────

KENDRA WAS at work in the Intel Unit when she received the call with the information. At the earliest opportunity, she was able to search the records and find an address where Rhianna was registered as a voter, in Dunbar Road, Forest Gate, which was a short, twenty-minute drive to the spa. She was also able to find mention of Rhianna in a crime report from the previous year, where she had been named as a non-cooperative witness at the scene of an assault against her father. Three young men had attacked him in her front garden. Rhianna had witnessed the attack from an upstairs window and had come to her father's aid when she had heard his cries.

By the time the police had arrived, the attackers had fled, her father was on the floor unconscious and she was holding a pack of frozen peas to the black eye she had received for her trouble.

When questioned about the attack, she had initially said

that she'd recognised one of the attackers but had quickly changed her story and told the reporting officer that she did not know any of them. The seasoned officer had been studious enough to make detailed notes despite her changing the story, proving she had initially named one of the attackers as Denny Brathwaite. Brathwaite was well-known to police for a range of petty crimes and minor assaults in the Stratford and Forest Gate areas, but there was nothing to link him to the ELC, so this was potentially a significant breakthrough.

Kendra downloaded as much information as she could for later reading, including known associates and crime reports related to Brathwaite and anyone linked to him. She was pleased to see there were a good five or six of his acquaintances that fit the bill for the ELC – all of them vicious in one form or another. It was a good place to start.

LATER THAT EVENING, as she relaxed in her flat, Kendra spent several hours going through the intel she had gathered that day. In the main, it was typical of the area: plenty of threats, assaults, criminal damage, the usual that comes with the younger generations. As she weeded through the reports, she made notes of the suspects involved and started to see a pattern forming. It wasn't concrete, but it was enough for her to start with, and more than her overworked and underpaid colleagues had achieved to date.

Eventually she had a list of four names that were potentially connected to the ELC via Denny Brathwaite, if indeed he was a member. It was his tenuous but evident connection to Rhianna that was the thread Kendra was now unravelling.

'You are a nasty piece of work, Mr Brathwaite,' she murmured. 'What to do next, indeed.'

She was missing Andy; they brainstormed well together and would have been halfway through a devious but effective plan by now. Even with Trevor, they would have started to formulate something.

Kendra looked at the picture of the suspect. 'I know you now, Brathwaite, and I'm coming for you.'

She knew exactly what was needed.

'YOU WANT ME TO DO WHAT?' Trevor said, in a high-pitched voice.

'Not you personally, silly,' Kendra replied, giggling.

'Well, you should have made that perfectly clear, young lady!'

'It can't be anyone from around here, Dad, because it would lead to trouble. It has to be someone from another area, someone that won't be recognised or known. That's why I asked you, because you know a lot of people from all over.'

'Thank God for that, because I'm not comfortable about being bait in a lover's quarrel! Tell me again?'

'So, my plan is to have someone go to the spa and get friendly with Rhianna. That's part of it, anyway. The other part is for us to spread word that someone is sniffing around Denny Brathwaite's girl. Then we wait for the reaction and for the scum to come out of their hidey- holes.'

Trevor's face looked like a surprised emoji.

'You are way too devious to be my daughter.' Trevor laughed. 'Kendra, the only thing that concerns me is that

Rhianna might get hurt from this and she doesn't deserve that just because she's with an evil shit like Brathwaite.'

'We will be keeping a close eye on her, don't worry. As well as bringing in a gigolo, I was going to ask you to bring in a handful of friends that can help if there is any aggro, again from outside the area.'

'Don't worry about that, I have connections at boxing clubs all over the country, I know where I can get some help.'

'Great, I'll leave that to you. Hopefully, Andy will be back soon and he can help with the surveillance and any live feeds we may need.'

'When do you think he'll be back?' asked Trevor.

'I'm due to speak with him tonight, hopefully in a week or two, all being well.'

'That's good, give him my regards. Now pass the wine, I've had a bit of a shock, you know!'

***

ANDY CAUGHT up with Kendra via Facetime later that night.

'I still have the occasional urge to scratch my foot, which is weird, because even before it was taken off, I hadn't felt anything for months due to the injury.'

'Apart from that, is there much pain?' Kendra asked. 'You don't look like you're suffering too much, Mr Smiley Face.'

'A fair amount, especially the first few days, but it's manageable. They removed it just above the ankle. It's a little gory to explain, but what they've done is taken the end of the bone off and cemented in a metal pin that can accept a prosthetic foot. Wanna see?' He moved his phone towards his leg as if to show her.

'Don't you dare, Pike!' she shouted. 'Very funny. Wait, so

you'll have a removable foot? So, you can have different types? That sounds pretty cool!'

'Yeah, it means I can use a blade as well as a realistic-looking one, depending on who I want to impress.'

'Well, get yourself fit and well, we're missing you back here, there's a lot to catch you up on.'

'I'll probably be at least another week; I have to get used to it and there's a fair bit of physio that they insist on. Don't worry, though, I'm keeping track of everything and keeping busy on the laptop when I'm resting up in bed.'

'You've been buying stuff on eBay again, haven't you?'

'I get bored easily, Kendra, you know that. Besides, I can afford it now, can't I? I'll catch you up with my bargains when I get back.'

'Listen, I have no interest in Batman toys or X-Men comics, so don't worry about it!'

'I may surprise you, Miss March. Now get yourself off the phone so that I can get back to my browsing. I'll speak to you soon.'

'Bye, Andy, good to see your smiling face again,' she said.

'Nighty-night, Miss March,' he replied, blowing a kiss.

Kendra smiled and went over the call in her mind. She was realising that her calls with him, and indeed his very presence, were becoming increasingly important to her. She hoped he would come back soon so they could talk about it. It felt like an unspoken pact between them, and that it was time it became a spoken one.

That should make for an interesting icebreaker, she thought.

Still, that did not mean she would care a jot about toys and comic books. No chance.

5

WALSALL CONTINGENT

Three days later, Trevor convened a gathering at the factory, where he would brief the team he had assembled. Only a select few were privy to what was behind the scenes there, and it was important to Trevor that they kept it that way.

'Thanks for coming, guys, especially our friends here from sunny Walsall, I appreciate it.' He waved at a small group and nodded his thanks.

The six men were all in their early twenties, tall and athletic and with a confidence about them that was obvious to all in the room. One of them raised his hand in acknowledgement.

'Please thank Frazer again, tell him I owe him one,' Trevor said.

'So, what's this all about, Trev?' asked Mo, intrigued by the gathering and the strangers alike.

'You've heard me asking about the East London Consortium these past few weeks; well, we've decided that we must try and do something about them before they cause any more harm. Before I go on, if you don't feel this is a good fit for you then you are free to leave and nobody will think any less of you.' He paused for a few seconds to see if anyone took him up on his offer of backing out.

'Nobody? Good. Okay, our friends here from Walsall have come a long way to help us with our little plan, as it must be carried out by someone that isn't known in the area.'

Before Trevor could continue, Amir shouted out, 'Walsall? Is that a real place? I thought it was in a cartoon or something!'

There were lots of laughs, including from the visitors and it helped break the ice.

'Sorry about Amir here, lads,' Trevor said, shaking his head, 'he's a bit of a smart arse, thinks he's funny. Amir, you're not funny!'

More laughter.

'Right then, let me continue. The ELC have been causing a lot of problems in this part of London and have hurt a lot of people, including the elderly and the vulnerable. They are growing in confidence and the police have no clue who they are or what to do about them, which is where we come in.'

'We have to protect ourselves, otherwise they'll overrun the place in months,' added Mo.

Trevor continued. 'We managed to find out where a girlfriend of one of the main men is working and from that, we now believe we know who he is and who some of his nasty friends are. Thanks to our associates here, we're going to put together a little sting operation to try and draw them out of their holes, as we still don't know where they are living.'

'How do we fit in, boss?' asked one of the Walsall guests.

'What's your name, brother?'

'It's Darren, and these are my mates from the gym – Rory,

Izzy, Clive, Martin, and Jimmy. Frazer told us we'd be guaranteed an adventure,' he said, looking at his colleagues and laughing.

'Well, Frazer knows me all too well. I'm sure it will be an adventure, but you guys need to know that it will be a dangerous one, okay?'

'Understood, boss,' Darren replied.

'That's good, because I'm going to need you to volunteer the ladies' man of your group for a little job that needs doing.'

The Walsall contingent, apart from one, immediately turned to look at one of their colleagues.

Darren gave him a little nudge from behind and said, 'This is Jimmy, and he is a proper ladies' man.'

Jimmy raised his hand, embarrassed. 'Thanks, mate,' he said.

Trevor laughed at his discomfort and continued. 'Jimmy, don't worry, mate, she's a lovely girl. We need you to sweep her off her feet and show her how a real man should look after his lady, but we also need you to treat her nicely, okay? She isn't who we're after, so no harm must come to her in any way, I can't stress that enough.'

Jimmy nodded. 'Don't worry, boss, I only do nice. I will look after her.'

'The name of the game is to draw out the scum from the ELC when they find out someone – you, Jimmy – is checking his woman out. We'll be watching your back, so you won't have to worry about being hurt,' said Kendra.

'What about the rest of us?' Darren asked.

'Darren, you guys are important to this plan,' said Trevor. 'Nobody from this part of the world knows who you are, so there will be no repercussions to anyone local or their families. We don't want people getting hurt. That's why you'll be acting as the muscle when things kick off – which I am sure they will. That way, they won't have a clue who to go after.'

Darren smiled and looked around at his crew.

'Yeah, we can manage that, no problem.'

'Good. In the meantime, we need to set up surveillance to make sure the spa is covered from all approaches. Then we'll make sure to place you nice and close so that you can get to Jimmy before his pretty face gets slapped around.'

There were a few laughs as Jimmy pretended to be offended.

'Jimmy here might be a pretty boy,' said Darren, 'but he is also the meanest, nastiest fighter of us all, so don't worry about him – he can look after himself until back-up arrives. Right?'

'Yeah!' the Walsall crew shouted in unison. They were a well-trained team; Frazer had done a great job.

'Mo, Amir, grab some of the mini cameras you used before and take them to Barking. I want you to place them so that we have the door covered, and the junction with George Street, so that we can see which direction they go in, or where they arrive from. Also, cover the corner by the new flats that they're building. That way, all routes in or out are covered.'

'Consider it done, Trev,' said Mo as he and his twin brother made to leave the gathering.

'Send me the link and password when you're done so we can monitor them from here, okay?' Kendra added.

'Oh, and those of you that haven't taken one yet, the GPS tags are in this box. Put them somewhere on your person that is hard to find, in the hems of trousers or shorts or something like that. Also, make sure the van is ready, we may need to bring the nasties back here. We'll prep the rooms in the back just in case.'

Trevor was referring to the newly refurbished detention cells at the back of the factory, which had been fully equipped as a business premises, thanks to Qupi's financial contribution. The cells were far enough away and properly insulated so that no visitor to the premises would inadvertently hear them. Trevor had also cleared the rear yard, allowing for full vehicular access to the enclosed loading ramp leading to the cells. Once inside, the 'guests' would have no idea where they were. It would be an effective holding camp until it was decided what to do with them next.

Trevor unfurled a map on a table.

'Where do you want us then, boss?' asked Darren.

'If you look here, around the corner to the spa, there are a number of building sites. If they come in that direction then they have to go to the end of the road, where there is a T-junction.

There is a hotel there, where two of you can park around the back out of sight. When we get the go-ahead that they have been spotted, that will give you enough time to move closer and continue on foot. That way you'll be nice and close when it kicks off.'

'What about the other three?'

Trevor pointed to a car park next to a college at the junction near the spa. 'This is a multi- storey car park. Try and park close to the exit so you can get out quickly, otherwise move to this side road a little further away.'

'Sounds like a plan. I'm guessing we'll have plenty of notice, right?'

'Yes, we'll have eyes on the front door, and I'll make sure to give a running commentary from the time Jimmy goes in,'

Kendra said. 'It may take a day or two before they react, but we'll be spreading the rumours from the time Jimmy walks in.'

'How many of them do you think will turn up?'

'That's a good question, Darren,' said Trevor, 'but one I can't answer just yet. I would guess, based on the previous behaviour that we heard about, that it will be four, maybe five of them. We have some intelligence on the likely scumbags that will turn up.'

He pulled out some photos Kendra had copied for him.

'This is the main man, Denny Brathwaite. He is a nasty piece of work and is known to be extremely violent and merciless. We believe he is the one that young Rhianna is connected to.'

'That is unfortunate,' said Rory, 'she seems like a nice girl.'

'Well, until Jimmy is able to tell us otherwise, we have to treat her with caution. She may be a nice girl but if she is genuinely involved with this bastard then she could turn on anyone without a thought,' said Trevor.

'Agreed and understood,' was the reply, with several others nodding in agreement.

'These other three chaps are his close associates that we know of, who have previously come to the attention of the police. They may or may not be with him; until we get them on camera it will be hard to say. They are Travis Mulligan, Gerry Tate, and Ricky Ali. Again, all violent and don't give a shit about anyone, so be careful, okay?'

'Like I said, don't worry about us, we'll handle this lot – no problem,' said Darren.

'What can you tell me about the girl?' asked Jimmy.

'She is gorgeous, you can't miss her. Also, she'll be

wearing her name badge, her name is Rhianna, Rhianna Dyer,' said Trevor. 'Take this, and if you have to join as a member then just pay for a month's membership or something,' he added, handing Jimmy a hundred pounds.

'Cheers.'

'I'll be close by in the van with Charlie, so if it kicks off and we have to take people away we can bring it to you. When you finally meet the scum, try and do it away from any cameras or witnesses, otherwise it could cause us problems with the police. Kendra will be monitoring everything from here, as she said. Any questions?'

They all shook their heads, happy with the briefing.

'Great, just remember to keep safe and stay away from prying eyes, we need this to be nice and quick, okay?'

This time it was nods all round.

'Right then, show us our cars and we'll make a move. We'll stop off for some sarnies on the way,' said Darren.

'Here,' said Kendra, giving Darren two hundred pounds, 'that should cover you all for a few days. Jimmy shouldn't be the only one having fun, right? If you need more just give me a shout, okay?'

'That's very generous, thank you,' he said, before they all turned and left.

Trevor turned to Kendra. 'Well, let's hope we haven't forgotten anything. Did they all take the GPS tags?'

'Yes, Dad, don't worry, once the cameras are in, then we'll be up and running, everyone will be in place within an hour. Then we can start the gossip!'

THE 'GOSSIP' Kendra had referred to had been started by the girls at the boxing club who knew of Rhianna. The plan was to spread the word verbally, not through social media, to ensure anonymity as much as possible. The girls would all be given some spending money and then go off to known local clubs where they would undoubtedly bump into friends old and new alike, where the conversations would quickly turn to gossip.

'*I was surprised to hear Rhianna was seeing someone new ...*'

Or '*Rhianna didn't take long to start seeing this new man ...*'

Or 'She's a brave girl, that one, after what happened last time ...'

And so on.

It wouldn't take long for the rumours to spread far enough to reach the ELC and the intended targets.

All being well, by the time the rumours had started, Jimmy would have become friendly with Rhianna. He didn't need to do anything more than that, just make sure that no harm came to her. The rest would take care of itself. Once the ELC had turned up at the scene, the Walsall contingent would help grab Brathwaite and get him to the factory.

Or so it was hoped. Trevor always factored in that something could go wrong and spent much of his planning time accounting for this.

Kendra rang her father to let him know the plan was underway, and the girls were briefed and knew what to do. The seeds would soon be being planted, just as they had planned.

JIMMY LOOKED up at the building that housed the spa. He had taken some time to prepare for his role, changing into his favourite – and most expensive —Boss tracksuit, a rich navy-blue with light-blue hints on the sleeves and collar. A bright-white Ralph Lauren t-shirt hosted a heavy gold chain, and a new pair of Nike VaporMax trainers completed the look, one that screamed confidence and success.

He smoothed back his hair as he crossed the road, smiling confidently as he strode towards the entrance. As he walked into the lobby, he briefly scanned his surroundings to familiarise himself with the layout, before walking to reception and asking for the spa. Following her directions, he was soon at the upstairs entrance. Trevor had given him a brief description of what to expect inside, having been surprised himself. It didn't stop him from exclaiming loudly when he entered to the spectacular light show on the ceiling.

'Wow, didn't expect this!' He stood there staring up at the lights, all thoughts of staying cool, calm, and collected completely out of his head.

'Can I help you?'

Jimmy quickly turned towards the voice, embarrassed to be caught off-guard.

'Sorry, I ... whoa,' was all he could say as he stared at the receptionist who had uttered the welcome.

Rhianna smiled at the young man's reactions. She knew she was a looker, and at times it was fun to be acknowledged as such, but Rhianna was also frustrated with the lack of respect that followed when her intelligence surfaced – and which typically brought the opposite reaction. In this instance she was pleasantly surprised by the way the man stared at her, but strangely it didn't feel as though he was being misogynistic or even disrespectful.

'I'm sorry if I startled you, sir,' she said.

'I...I am...what?'

'Sir? Are you ok?'

'I...I'm sorry, can we start again?' Jimmy replied, shaking his head and slapping his cheek in mock disgust.

'Start what again?' she asked innocently.

Jimmy held up one finger, as if to tell her he'd be back, and promptly walked out. Rhianna stared at the door in confusion.

Seconds later the door to the spa opened again, followed by a smiling Jimmy, who confidently walked to the counter and said, 'Hi, can you please tell me about your facilities here? I'm interested in joining.'

He rested one hand on the counter, the other on his hip, as he stood tall and proud in an exaggerated pose.

Rhianna laughed and said, 'Good afternoon, sir. Why, yes, I can. In fact, I can do better than that, and show you if you have the time?'

'Why thank you, Miss ...'

Rhianna pointed to the badge on her lapel. 'Rhianna, sir, please call me Rhianna.'

'Yes, ma'am, I can do that. I mean, yes, Rhianna, I can do that!'

Jimmy shook his head in mock horror, again exaggerating his body language to elicit a humorous reaction.

It worked. Rhianna laughed again, and said, 'You're funny, sir, I'll give you that.'

Jimmy smiled, returning to his usual, confident persona that had worked so well for him in the past. The secret to his success was putting women completely at ease before befriending them. What happened after that was always led by the woman and how she reacted to his charms. He never pushed or persuaded, and things often evolved organically as a result.

'Please, call me Jimmy,' he said. 'I'm far too young to be called sir, that's what I used to call my teachers!'

'Well, we are a professional outfit here, Jimmy, so we always treat our clients with respect. And I'll only call you that because you asked so nicely.'

'If you can't ask nicely then you shouldn't ask at all, right?'

Rhianna smiled. 'Absolutely. Now, if you follow me, I will give you the tour.'

'Why thank you, Miss Rhianna,' he replied, bowing, and offered his arm. She took it without thinking; it seemed so natural.

'Shall we?' he said.

She laughed again, and this time it was her turn to shake her head in mock horror as she led him through the doors into the treatment areas.

6

MEET MARGE!

'Thanks, Darren, I appreciate the update. Give Jimmy a pat on the back from us and we'll catch up again tomorrow with the follow-up.' Trevor ended the call. He picked up his bottle of beer and sat down next to Kendra on her sofa. It had been an interesting day and they had much to discuss.

'Go on then, how did he get on?' she asked.

'Well, Jimmy was true to his word. He managed to get a tour of the place from Rhianna, and then a coffee as they discussed potential membership. That conversation went well, and it turns out she is responding to his flirting quite nicely. He's going back tomorrow for a treatment and more coffee. The lad knows what he's doing, that's for sure.'

'I do feel bad using her like that, but needs must,' she said. 'So, what about you, how did the girls get on today?'

'I've had plenty of messages saying that the seeds have been planted in half a dozen places, so it won't take long for things to filter back to Brathwaite and his cronies.'

'Good, good. So, what's next?' Trevor asked.

'Let's assume he takes the bait and visits Rhianna. It may be that he goes to her home address, which is bad news for us as we don't have that covered. Hopefully, he'll want to catch the bloke that's messing with his girl red-handed at the spa. So tomorrow we make sure we have it well covered and can get to Jimmy quickly if anything happens.'

'Shouldn't be a problem, we can—'

Trevor was interrupted mid-sentence by a loud honking noise from outside.

'What the hell was that?' he asked, moving over to the window. Kendra joined him.

The flat, with its delightful views of the river Roding, overlooked the well-lit rear car park. They watched as a run-down Iveco camper van trundled into view, stopping in the middle of the car park as if to show itself off. It was a long-wheelbase version which accentuated how neglected it had been. There was one small window on the nearside towards the back, along with a sliding door for entry. It was not an attractive-looking vehicle in any sense of the word.

'What an old jalopy that is,' Trevor remarked, 'why would they want to draw attention to themselves?'

They continued watching as the driver's door opened and a man stepped out, gingerly, taking his time to step down to the ground with care. He was carrying a cane in one hand. He looked up towards the flats and waved.

'Wait,' said Kendra, 'is that ...?'

'No, he wouldn't, would he?' said Trevor, perplexed, before realisation set in. 'Yep, he would. That right there is your idiot boyfriend!'

Kendra stood open-mouthed, waving back slowly, not sure how else to react.

'What have you done now, Pike?' she muttered.

She got up to leave the flat, giving her dad a playful punch on the arm on her way out. 'He's not my boyfriend, Dad!' She was neither convincing, nor convinced.

Smiling, Trevor followed behind, eager to hear what Andy had to say.

ANDY WAS WAITING by the passenger door, his arms wide, as he introduced the camper van with a flourish, as if he were introducing a magic act.

'Well? What do you think? Isn't she amazing?'

Kendra didn't look at the van but instead looked him up and down, checking him over carefully.

'Are you okay? We weren't expecting to see you for another week. What happened?'

'It's nice to see you too, Kendra. And you, Trevor,' Andy replied as her dad joined them.

'What the hell have you gone and bought, man? This looks like a hunk of junk!'

'Doesn't it? I think it's brilliant, if I may say so myself,' came the reply.

'What's brilliant about it? Is it even legal to drive?' asked Kendra.

'Absolutely, she was tested a couple of days ago and came through with flying colours. Do not be deceived by her looks, that is intentional, because Marge has many interesting and exciting secrets.' Andy patted the side of the van lovingly.

'Marge?' said Kendra, 'as in the Simpsons?'

'A gold star for you, young lady. Yes, like Marge Simpson, she is full of surprises and utterly dependable.'

Kendra rolled her eyes and joined Trevor. They walked slowly around the van, shaking their heads in unison at the dents and the rust that they came across.

'Not sure how she can make up for this,' Trevor muttered, pointing to the damage.

'What surprises are you talking about, Andy?' asked Kendra.

'Before I show you, aren't you going to ask?'

'Ask what?'

'Ask me how I'm able to drive, and walk a little differently, you know?'

Kendra was mortified. 'I'm so sorry, Andy, I completely forgot! This bloody van thing has stumped me. How is your foot? What did they end up doing?'

She looked down at his feet, quickly realising that there didn't seem to be anything different about him.

Andy smiled and tapped his cane against his left foot, the one that had been permanently damaged by the knife. The noise the cane made was a dull solid note, as if hitting a piece of plastic or a lump of wood wrapped in something. He lifted his trouser leg and showed off his new prosthetic foot. What Kendra could see was a trainer with a carbon fibre joint coming out of it, connected to a rounded cup-like socket that covered what must have been the end of Andy's leg.

'Wow, that actually looks cool. How do you feel?' she asked.

'I feel great. I mean, it hurts like crazy sometimes, but I am much more mobile now, which is why I wanted to do it.'

'Good for you, man,' added Trevor, nodding in appreciation. 'That's a nice bit of kit, that.'

'Thanks, Trev. I hope you both don't mind me popping

over like this, I was champing at the bit to show you what I've been up to!'

'Why the van, though, Andy?' Kendra asked.

'Kendra, this is no ordinary van. Don't forget, this is Marge, and she is my current favourite thing.'

'Honestly, stop beating around the bush and show us, will you?' Trevor said, losing patience.

'Fine, step this way,' Andy said, reverting to the exaggerated arm movements as if on stage.

Kendra rolled her eyes - again.

Andy opened the side door with a flourish, showing off the interior. Kendra could see he had been busy. On the side of the van with the sliding door were three monitors fixed about twelve inches off the working surface, each with a computer tucked neatly underneath, with their respective keyboards fixed onto the narrow work surface. There was a comfortable- looking bench for the user or users to sit on.

Along the other, longer side, was another bench, running almost the full length of the rear compartment. Above and below the bench, and along that side of the van, was an array of shelves and drawers that could hold a large amount of equipment, including cameras, GPS tracking units, taser guns, and much more. There were two more monitors, one above the other, in a narrow space created between the shelving, along with one more computer and peripherals. At the back of the van was a narrow bunk bed, with two narrow beds made up and ready for use. It was a fully equipped mobile operations room, and it was ready for use.

'Bloody hell, mate, when did you find the time to do this?' asked Trevor.

'Believe it or not, I bought everything you see here,

including the van, online. I paid someone to drive it to the hospital, where they allowed for it to be parked out of sight around the back. A carpenter mate of mine did the shelving and the other woodwork.'

'And the rest of it? I mean, it isn't exactly a small job, is it?'

'Easier than you think. The electrical gear was also off the internet, and also delivered to the hospital. It didn't take long to fit it all in; they let me have a few hours here and there providing I didn't overdo it, which I didn't. The only thing I haven't done yet is get some kit from home and the factory, and it's ready to go.' Andy seemed very pleased with himself.

'Wow,' was all Kendra could say. 'And you did this because ...?'

Andy's demeanour became more serious.

'Kendra, you know me, and you know I can't sit still for too long. I just need to vary what I do, you know? I don't want to be sat in front of a computer all day while you lot are out having lots of fun.'

'You think that was fun?' said Trevor. 'I got shot, dude!'

'You know what I mean. I'm not trying to make light of it, I know it's serious, but I also know that I can contribute more, that's all.'

'Well, if you think you're gonna be going out and fighting gangsters any time soon, you can think again,' said Kendra. She wasn't entirely happy, but she could understand his point.

'I know, I know, I must be patient. But look at what more we can do now, with Marge. Surely you can see the benefits?'

'Well, she looks like crap, but she is well equipped, I'll give you that,' said Trevor.

'That's the whole point, Trev, nobody will take her seriously if what they see is a hunk of junk, they won't give her a second look. But I've had her fully refurbished underneath, she has a great engine, and everything is like new under this rough exterior. Trust me, she will do well for us.'

'Okay, well, we can chat out here all day, but it won't do any good. Park her up and come in for some pizza, we can catch up inside,' Kendra added.

'Pizza? Yay!' Andy exclaimed as he jumped into the driver's seat and started the engine.

'He's right,' Trevor said, as he walked back to the flat with his daughter, 'she looks like shit, but she sounds great. That hunk of junk may prove useful after all.'

'We'll see,' Kendra said. She might not have approved of the camper van, but she was happy to see Andy again, and in such great spirits. The bonus was that he felt great, too, and was more mobile than he had been for months.

They sat up late into the night going over the past few days, mixed in with Andy's experiences at the private hospital and how he had fitted Marge out.

'One thing we need to keep between just the three of us, Andy, is the existence of the operations room in your cellar. That must not go further than us, in case anything goes pear-shaped, okay? It must remain our insurance and our safe haven.'

'Agreed. I'll keep it updated and ready for use, but I want to do more from the factory and now from Marge,' Andy replied.

'Fair enough, but I'm actually keen to keep the van and our full capabilities at the factory as a secret, too, or as secret as we can. The fewer people that know about it, the better. You can shadow us from behind the scenes, and make the occasional appearance at the factory, but we really should try

and keep your devious skills as secret as possible,' added
Kendra.

'Understood. I guess things will not always go to plan,
right?'

'Yep,' added Trevor, 'and these youngsters are great at the
moment, but who's to say they won't turn on us later on? As
much as I trust the majority of them, as we grow, we may let a
few bad apples through, and we'll have trouble to deal with.'

'Let's not go into that now,' Kendra said, 'let's just focus on
the job at hand. These scumbags are likely to turn up tomorrow, so I want to be sure we are ready for them, okay?'

'Yes, ma'am,' replied Andy, smiling. He was glad to be back.

THE FOLLOWING DAY, by mid-morning, the team had
reassembled and were all in position covering the spa. They
had been joined by Charlie, Trevor's assistant from one of the
gyms, who had helped with the Albanians and who was now
driving a van for transport, if required later. He had parked
the van close to their camper, for convenience. Andy had
stocked up on a few items of kit that might prove useful later,
such as zip ties, tasers, GPS tags and cameras, along with
some body armour and masks. He had left the van further
away in a local caravan park, blending in nicely with the
other mobile homes that were parked there.

'Don't make me regret agreeing to this,' said Trevor, now
on one of the benches monitoring the camera feeds. He
hadn't intended to sit in the van, but Andy had been persua-
sive and keen to show him the benefits.

'There's nothing to regret, Trev. It's comfortable, nobody

will notice you, we can take turns checking the cameras, and we're literally just a minute or two away. It's great!'

Kendra, sitting alongside her dad on the bench, was not so enthusiastic.

'It's very cosy in here for three of us, Andy, please tell me you have good ventilation?'

Andy laughed. 'Of course, it's nice and fresh in here, don't worry.'

'Easy for you to say,' she muttered, 'I'm not a fan of enclosed spaces, remember?'

'That's why this van is ideal, it's long and tall, it's like being in a small room and you'll get used to it. Fancy a sandwich and some crisps?' He picked up a cool bag from under one of the benches and showed them a selection of sandwiches and drinks. The crisps and other snacks were in a plastic bag.

'I stopped off at the supermarket on the way; it never hurts to be prepared, right?'

Nodding in agreement, Trevor fished out a tuna-and-sweetcorn sandwich and a bottle of water, his reservations quickly forgotten.

'I'm good, thanks, maybe later,' Kendra said, turning back to the monitor that covered the front entrance to the spa. 'What time did you say Jimmy was going in?'

Trevor looked at his watch. 'In about two minutes.'

'Right then, let's make sure everyone is ready,' Kendra said, and started messaging the drivers of the two cars nearest to the spa.

Within seconds, two separate thumbs-up emojis pinged on her phone, along with a message confirming that Jimmy was on the way.

'Here we go, gents, Jimmy is en route. Let's see how long it takes them to show up, eh?'

Trevor's phone rang. 'It's Darren. How's it going, mate?'

Kendra could sense that something was up, as her father's brow was deeply furrowed in concentration.

Trevor responded to Darren. 'That's a good spot, mate. Make sure the others know and keep an eye out for more of them, they're probably close by. Cheers.'

He ended the call and turned to the others. 'Darren has seen what looks like a possible hostile spotter, opposite the spa and looking at the entrance. He thinks it may be one of the baddies keeping an eye out. Let's check all the camera feeds and keep them posted.'

Kendra and Andy both turned to their respective monitors to give as much notice as possible to the Walsall contingent. Andy picked up the phone and called Darren back.

'Darren,' said Andy, 'tell Jimmy to invite Rhianna for a coffee on her lunch break. Let's see if he can get her to join him outside, where our potential friend can see them together.' He paused for a few seconds, nodding as he listened, and then replied, 'Thanks, mate, and watch your back out there, okay?'

'There's Jimmy now, just approaching the entrance,' said Kendra.

She watched as Jimmy went inside, waiting to see if the hostile did anything further. There was no movement and Kendra couldn't see him from the angle that she had.

'I'll keep an eye out on the junction, that seems the most likely place for him to go, or meet with someone,' said Andy, shifting to the other bench and workstation.

They continued to watch the monitors diligently, with

nothing of interest happening for the best part of an hour. It was around lunch time that they finally saw movement.

'There's Jimmy, and Rhianna is with him!' exclaimed Kendra, excited to see Jimmy had been successful. 'Get ready, gents.'

The pair came out, smiling and talking as they turned left towards the sharp bend that led to Station Parade and the coffee shop.

'Bingo!' shouted Andy, as the hostile spotter finally came into view. He was now talking on his phone as he followed covertly behind the couple.

Trevor picked up his phone. 'Darren, they're walking towards Station Parade, I think they'll probably go to Costa. Move yourselves closer, in case anything happens. I doubt this man will do anything himself and will probably wait for his cronies to turn up. Thanks, mate,' he said, ending the call.

'We're still good here, no need to move,' Kendra said. 'We're about to lose our live feed, is there anything you can do with the council CCTV cameras, Andy?'

'I'm sure I can, K,' he replied, flexing his fingers and then typing at a faster rate than anyone else Kendra knew. 'Thank God for Cyclops, eh?'

Cyclops was the programme Andy had bought on the dark web, which gave access to CCTV systems that weren't as secure as they should be, which in this council's case was not very.

'Okay, that was easy, their firewalls must be ten years' old, dreadful,' Andy said after what seemed like only a minute. 'And here we go.'

Kendra leaned over and saw that Andy had the two monitors both covering Station Parade, busy mainly with commuters using the railway station there. Opposite the station was a Costa coffee shop. It was ideally placed, as his colleagues could blend in with the commuters and use the station and the other shops for cover.

'There's our friend, still on the phone.' Trevor pointed and relayed the information to Darren that the hostile following Jimmy was about fifty yards behind on the opposite side of the road.

As Jimmy and Rhianna turned into Station Parade, the hostile lost sight of them for a few seconds and picked up his pace to catch up. Jimmy and Rhianna were crossing the road to the opposite side when he turned the corner and he immediately slowed down again once he had them in sight.

'That's right, my little fish, take the bait and reel yourself in,' Andy muttered as his fingers continued to type and move around the keyboard.

'You're loving this, aren't you?' Kendra said, enjoying his enthusiasm.

'What's not to love? I'm doing what I always wanted to do, only now, I am also able to break the law to do it better. It's bloody fantastic, if you ask me!'

'Well, don't get too excited, they're about to go into Costa.'

Sure enough, a few seconds later, they could see Jimmy opening the door for Rhianna, bowing with a flourish as he did so. She gave him a playful slap on the arm, and the CCTV quality – although not the best – was good enough to show that she was smiling. They looked like a regular happy couple enjoying each other's company.

'Let's see what our friend does now,' Andy said, zooming in.

The hostile stayed on the opposite side of the road and sat at a bus stop opposite the coffee shop, still on his phone. It was very busy with pedestrians so he would be hard to spot. Costa was bustling with customers, too.

'And now we wait,' said Trevor.

Kendra and Trevor kept an eye on the coffee shop and Andy monitored the surrounding area. He had seen a couple of the Walsall contingent blending in nicely. If anything were to happen now, they would be able to assist within seconds.

They didn't have long to wait.

'Hang on,' said Trevor, 'that's Jimmy and Rhianna leaving, what's going on?'

'They probably didn't have any tables free and ordered take-out, Dad. Shouldn't be a problem. Better that they're outside than in, should anything happen.'

They continued to watch as Jimmy and Rhianna walked back towards Cambridge Road and headed for the spa. Trevor immediately called Darren to keep him informed. They could see that the hostile was just as surprised by the pair leaving so soon and was now talking animatedly on his phone as he got up and walked after them.

The couple were just around the corner from the spa.

'Hang on, I see something,' Andy said urgently, pointing to one of the two monitors. Three men were getting out of a black car that had pulled up beside the man who was following Jimmy and Rhianna. He joined them and pointed towards the bend the couple were about to reach.

Trevor quickly checked the map of the area and called Darren to advise him that there were now four hostiles.

'Darren, tell Jimmy to walk past the spa and into the church gardens on the corner, where they can sit at a bench. They won't be seen by anyone from the street, so when the scumbags join them, you can take them out without any issues. Get yourselves there as quick as you can, okay? And be careful, mate.'

Kendra could see Jimmy using his phone and nodding as he continued to walk with Rhianna. He turned to her and then pointed to the churchyard on the corner, which she acknowledged with a nod. The hostiles had cleared the sharp bend and were now fast approaching. As the couple entered the churchyard, they were only fifty or so yards behind.

'Look,' Andy said, pointing to the shadowy figures that were now taking up position in the churchyard. Trees and bushes gave them good cover, out of sight of Jimmy and his friend, as they lay in wait.

Seconds later, the four hostiles entered the churchyard and approached Jimmy and Rhianna as they sat at a bench enjoying the coffees and chatting casually. Rhianna turned abruptly, no doubt responding to her name being shouted by one of the gang.

'This is where it could all go very badly wrong,' muttered Trevor.

JIMMY AND RHIANNA'S casual conversation had been disturbed by Denny Brathwaite himself, when he had shouted out her name upon entering the yard.

Rhianna had turned towards the voice, shocked by his presence. 'Shit,' she said. 'Not him, of all people.'

'What's going on, Rhianna? Who are these guys?'

Jimmy had reacted immediately, standing and placing himself in front of her as the gangsters approached. The four young men looked angry, as he had anticipated, so he was ready.

Brathwaite pulled out a knife. 'Boy, you're gonna wish you'd never been born.'

Jimmy feigned surprise. 'What do you want, money? I've got like twenty quid, mate. You can have that if you want, I don't want no trouble.'

'You think I want your pennies, boy? You're messing with my woman, and you think I give a shit about a few quid?'

'I'm not your woman, Denny, I just had a few drinks with you, that's all. That doesn't make me your woman.'

'It makes you whatever I want, girl, so just shut up while I play with your new friend here for a bit.'

As his cronies stood back and watched, smirking, Denny moved forward, waving the six-inch blade in front of Jimmy.

He didn't expect the whip-like jab that hit him flush on the nose as he got within range. Denny staggered back, stunned by the blow. He looked up and stared incredulously at Jimmy when he found that the punch had drawn blood from his nose. He looked at his three companions.

'Slice him up, boys.'

The three cronies each took out a knife and headed straight for Jimmy, who was edging slowly backwards, keeping Rhianna behind him. He could see Brathwaite staring at her, full of evil intent. Jimmy was confident, though, even more so now that he could see his Walsall colleagues emerge from their hiding places and approach the gangsters stealthily from behind.

Denny saw the expression on Jimmy's face change from serious to smiling and turned to see what he was looking at behind them.

Darren, Rory, Izzy, Clive and Martin were all experienced boxers. Knowing in advance that their adversaries would be armed with knives, they had come prepared with wooden batons, which they had made from brooms. Under normal circumstances, taking a broom handle to a knife fight would only do so well for so long, but in the hands of skilled fighters, they could do a lot of damage.

They rushed Brathwaite's men as Jimmy steered Rhianna safely away from the melee and walked her towards the exit. The adversaries clashed as wooden poles struck arms and heads loudly and painfully. Two of Brathwaite's men, who were facing Rory and Clive, soon lost their knives to blows on the wrist by the boxers, followed by raps to their heads, stunning them and allowing for Rory and Clive to pick up their blades.

Martin challenged Denny as Darren and Izzy battled with the remaining gangster. Martin was able to get a few strikes in on Denny's body but was unable to dislodge the knife from his hand.

Denny, a ferocious fighter, attacked Martin with kicks and swift knife-slashes that struck his side, drawing blood from shallow cuts. Martin continued to fight back, using his feet well to avoid more serious injury as he moved out of range. He could only do so for so long, though, and Denny had soon gained the upper hand against the smaller fighter. His attacking momentum took them both away from the other fighters as they started to spread out in the yard.

Darren and Izzy quickly overpowered their opponent, knocking him out with head-strikes. Once his knife had been taken, they soon had him under control with zip ties. Darren looked up to see that Brathwaite had the edge over Martin, and said to Izzy, 'Look after this piece of shit, will ya? I'm going to help Martin.'

'No probs, go!' came the reply. Izzy turned his defeated opponent onto his stomach and searched him for weapons.

Darren ran over and joined Martin against Denny, striking the gangster quickly with a baton to the left knee, causing a wobble. It was a reprieve for Martin, who was tiring, and losing the fight, so Darren's intervention was a godsend. Darren then pressed his attack and turned the tables on Denny, who was also now tiring and hurting from his badly bruised knee. He had no answer to the rapid baton strikes.

Martin then re-joined the fight and they both attacked Denny with strikes to the body, before Darren was able to knock him down with a ferocious blow to the head. Denny fell to his knees, stunned. Before he could recover, Martin, smarting from his injuries, kicked him in the side of the head, knocking him immediately unconscious.

Darren turned to Martin. 'Really? A kick to the head? Haven't we talked about this before?'

'Sorry, Darren,' Martin said, 'I just lost it for a second, it won't happen again.'

Darren looked him up and down, noticing his injuries, and said, 'Well, if you're going to do something like that, do it properly, so good job. Now put some zip ties on this arsehole and let's get out of here.'

Patting Martin on the back, he turned to see if his colleagues needed any further help. He saw that the other three baddies were all lying on the ground with their wrists zip-tied, completely under control. His friends had some bruising to their faces, and he noticed a few slashes in their clothing, but other than that they were fine, no major injuries. He took out his phone.

'Trevor, we have four scumbags that need taking away from here, can you send the van? Cheers, mate.'

He sent Izzy and Clive to check on the entrance and exit

to make sure there were no issues from the public, in case they had been seen. Fortunately, they had not; the enclosed yard was well screened and the church itself was closed. A minute or so later, the van, driven by Charlie, was parked in the yard and the gangsters manhandled into the back of it.

'Fucking feds, I thought so. That bitch is gonna suffer for this,' screamed Denny, conscious again, mistaking the Walsall team for police officers. That suited them all just fine. Martin slapped him hard on the side of the face, causing him to hit his head on the side of the van.

'Sorry, lost it again.' He shrugged. Darren shook his head in mock annoyance.

Martin and Izzy stayed with their captives in the back of the van, while Rory and Darren returned to pick up their vehicles and join their colleagues at the factory, where the gangsters were being taken. Clive took Brathwaite's car keys and went to retrieve their car from where it had been hastily abandoned.

Izzy dressed Martin's injuries from the first-aid kit that Charlie had given him, to stop any blood loss until they could check him over more thoroughly later.

Darren had collected all their belongings, including their weapons, phones – which he had switched off as instructed – a small quantity of drugs, and wallets that would help identify them. He looked over the vicious knuckle duster that he had taken from Denny's prone body and whistled. 'This is one nasty piece of work.'

JIMMY HAD WALKED Rhianna back to the spa and assured her that everything was fine and that he'd look after her.

'He's not my boyfriend, you know,' she said quietly. 'He wants to be, and he thinks he is, but he isn't. I hate people like him, nothing but badness in them.'

'That's good to hear,' replied Jimmy, smiling. He was starting to enjoy her company more and more.

'I prefer people like you,' she suddenly added. 'You look the part, and you act the part, but you have a good soul. I like that.'

Jimmy wasn't sure how to reply. He felt guilty that he had used her, but as he had gotten to know her, his intentions had changed. Knowing that she wasn't Brathwaite's girlfriend was very promising indeed.

'I'm glad, and I like that you like that!'

Rhianna laughed and said, 'Can we go for a coffee again later? Maybe something to eat?'

'I don't think I can do anything later as I have some work to do, but if you give me your number, I'll call you soon, okay?'

'Okay,' she replied.

They exchanged numbers and then Jimmy made to leave. Before he got to the door he suddenly turned back and gave her a gentle kiss on the cheek. 'I really do hope to see you again soon, Miss Dyer.'

After the shock of seeing Brathwaite again, Rhianna was now smiling broadly and hoping that Jimmy would indeed follow up and call her soon.

By the time Charlie had picked up his cargo, Andy, Kendra and Trevor were already on the move, making their way back to the factory by Tilbury Docks, a twenty-five-minute drive.

'That went surprisingly well,' said Kendra, now sitting in the front, with Andy driving. Trevor sat in the back, the hatch between the rear and driver's compartments open so that he could engage with them.

'You say that, but one of the boys had some nasty cuts that'll need seeing to. And a couple of the others have some nasty bruises. So, not brilliant.'

'Dad, you can't expect us to get away with everything without some cost, surely? We talked about this, people are going to get hurt, we just have to try and limit it, that's all we can do.'

'I know, I know, but it doesn't mean I have to like it,' came the disgruntled reply.

'On the bright side,' said Andy, 'how good was Marge, eh? I told you, she is going to be a great asset.'

'I must admit, it was handy being so close,' said Kendra.

'Let's not tell too many about her, the more secrets we have, the more effective we're likely to be,' added Trevor.

'You like your secrets, don't you?' Andy said. 'But I agree, the less that people know, the better for us.'

'So, what's the plan when we get back?' asked Kendra.

'We split them up and let them stew for a bit. They'll talk, I'm sure, none of these shitbags are likely to sacrifice themselves for another shitbag, I can assure you,' said Trevor.

'Get me their phone, first chance you get, so that I can have a look. Get the boys to unlock them so that there aren't any issues with access,' Andy added.

'Shouldn't be a problem,' Trevor said, 'I'll speak to Darren.'

'Isn't this fun?' Andy suddenly exclaimed. 'I've missed this excitement, haven't you?'

Kendra rolled her eyes. 'Here we go again.'

'Oh, come on, say it, you're having fun,' he replied. 'Go on, say it, say it!'

'Shut up!' Kendra and Trevor shouted in unison. They laughed, equally happy to have him back and amusingly annoyed by his antics.

'There you go, I knew you loved me, really.' He smirked.

7

LOCKED UP

The factory, as it was affectionately called by the team, was a converted warehouse close to the river Thames, next to Tilbury Docks, away from the hubbub of the docks but close enough to benefit from its facilities. They had access to a secure mooring, which they had successfully used in their recent venture to 'export' the human-trafficking gang to a mine in deepest Africa where they would serve their punishment in servitude, breaking rocks deep underground so that they would be fed. It was a fitting punishment for a group of uncaring individuals, who had been responsible for the deaths of many and the suffering of even more. The factory had been refurbished in recent months to accommodate similarly nasty individuals as investigations continued. It had also been transformed into a plausible business venue for accidental visitors, with a reception area, a conference room, offices, and a small canteen. A brand-new modern sign was affixed proudly above the entrance – *Sherwood Solutions*, the registered business name of a new security company.

It was part of Trevor's plan to induct many of the youngsters who had assisted recently, and many more from the boxing clubs, into the security industry, where they could train and learn a business that could ultimately give them a secure and rewarding future. He fully intended to spend some time growing the business into something viable and successful, such was his forward thinking.

At the rear of the conversion were two dozen secure rooms, previously storerooms, over two floors, that served as holding rooms for their 'guests'. There was plenty of space, and facilities for the team to rest, to store their equipment, and to monitor their activities from a state-of-the-art operations room that Andy had convinced them to install.

The best thing about the impressive facility was that it had been paid for in full and then converted, at no small cost, thanks to the funds the team had 'obtained' from the criminals they had previously guarded there. The trio frequently laughed at the irony of the criminals paying for their own summary justice. Now that it had been vastly improved and ready for action, Kendra was keen to see how it fared against a different type of guest. A rowdy, vicious one that was well-known and well-connected in the East End of London.

One of the changes made was to ensure that when arriving at the facility, the van or vehicles attending would drive around the back, out of sight from any motorists or passers-by, and then drive into a loading bay where the shutters could be closed before their cargo was unloaded. That way, nobody got to see what or who went in, and the guests would have no idea where they were being kept.

Trevor had also installed a small gym for his team to work out in, which was located next to the loading bay, so whenever there was a delivery, it was likely that there would be help at hand to take control of the captives.

He had called ahead to get everyone ready for the van, making sure that they wore masks so as not to be recognised.

'We should keep our people away from them as much as possible, do you think the Walsall boys can stay and help with their detention, too?' asked Kendra as they arrived.

'I'm sure they won't mind, it's like a holiday for them,' replied Trevor.

Andy parked Marge out of sight and they went inside to make sure everything was set.

'Mo, Amir, how's it going? Is everything ready for our guests?' Trevor asked, as the twins approached. They were in the loading bay and had opened the shutters in advance of the van's arrival.

'All good, Trev, as soon as they get here, we'll split them up into different rooms and make sure they're properly searched and spoken to,' said Mo.

'Good man. I sent Clive, one of Darren's boys, to Stav with a car belonging to one of our guests. Can you get someone to go and pick him up, please?'

'No problem. Just so you know, I've told our guys to make sure they keep contact with this mob to a minimum and to always wear masks. I don't want them talking to them either, just in case.'

'That's good. Hopefully, they won't be here long.' Trevor was delighted with the twins, they had taken their responsibilities seriously and relished their new roles within the wider team. Trevor had called ahead and asked Stav to scrap Brathwaite's car, to make sure there remained no trace of it, and to sell whatever parts were untraceable. They had a good relationship and had also profited greatly from the Albanian gang's cars in recent months, so Stav was happy to oblige. Brathwaite's two-year-old BMW M3 would make him a tidy profit and he was happy to assist Trevor in their venture. In return, he would loan Trevor cars whenever they were needed, and frequently rotate them to avoid any connections to – or recognition of – the team.

'Right then, we'll go to the ops room and leave you all to it,' Kendra said as she and Andy walked off.

'See you later,' said Trevor. 'Give me a shout if you find anything useful on the phones.'

They didn't have long to wait for the van, as it appeared in the rear yard. Trevor had worn a snood in advance of its arrival and had pulled it up over his mouth and nose, making him unrecognisable. The van reversed into the loading bay and the shutters quickly closed. Four of Trevor's team met the van by the back doors, waiting to assist as they were opened from within.

Darren was first out, turning and dragging Brathwaite with him.

'What the hell is this? This ain't no police station! What are you, fifth columnists? You're gonna pay for this, boy, you don't know who you're messing with!'

He thrashed around, trying to free himself from Darren's firm grip, but without success. One of Trevor's masked team went to assist and led them to the waiting room. Darren handed Trevor the Faraday bags containing the gangsters' phones, along with their other belongings in a carrier bag.

'He's a nice chap, isn't he?' Amir said from behind his mask, indicating towards Brathwaite.

'Yep, a nasty piece of work, he is. We'll have to think long and hard about what we're going to do with him,' said Trevor.

The next man out was the 'phone dude' who had

followed Jimmy and Rhianna and called Brathwaite to update him. He didn't say anything but also tried desperately to free himself from Izzy's grip, again prompting one of Trevor's team to intervene and lead him away.

The other two were similar, quiet compared to Brathwaite, but they did not want to make it easy on their captors. They were also dragged unceremoniously away from the loading dock to their guest quarters. Within a couple of minutes, they had been secured in their respective rooms, searched, handcuffed, and told in no uncertain terms that any shouts for help or any attempts to injure their hosts or escape, would be met by a well-aimed jolt from a taser. Brathwaite needed such a prompt and shook violently, like a caught fish, before he stopped his angry whining.

'Good work, guys,' Trevor said to the Walsall contingent, once they had returned.

'That was fun,' Darren said, shaking Trevor's outstretched hand. 'They put up a bit of a fight but they're nothing but bullies, nasty evil bullies. They need a good slap, to be honest, and then thrown down a hole somewhere they won't ever be found.'

'Yeah,' said Trevor, 'we're wondering what to do with them once we have the information we need, it's a tough one.'

'Whatever you do, make sure they can't carry on with what they've been doing, 'cos someone is going to die soon, I tell you.'

'Darren, are you and your guys up for staying a little longer, maybe another week or so? I'm worried that my lot might give themselves away, so I was hoping you could take on the role of jailers until we move them on. Are you able to assist?'

Darren looked at his team who were nodding, happy to assist further. Martin, in particular, looked very pleased.

'Look at his happy little face, Trevor. Martin, please man, you ain't gonna hurt him again, okay? Enough already!' Darren laughed as he spoke, turning back to Trevor and shaking his hand.

'Happy to stay and help, mate, I like what you're doing here.'

'That's great, I really appreciate it. Now, let's go and have some grub, I'm starving.'

ANDY HAD PLACED the Faraday bags inside a large mesh Faraday cage, which allowed them to deal with the appropriated phones without the risk of detection. Once inside, Andy switched them all on and waited for them to boot up, before attaching cables and hooking them up to his computer.

Each phone had been unlocked by Darren's colleagues and then the passwords changed to 1234 so that all were now accessible to him as he worked to find out more about their owners.

'Right, let's see what these hoodlums can give us, Miss K,' he said, once again flexing his fingers before turning them loose on the keyboard.

'It'd be good to find out how many of them are working together, I can imagine it's more than four as we've had reports of five and six beating up on victims,' Kendra said.

'Well, none of them have many friends, there's only about twenty or thirty numbers on each phone. The phones are all identical, too, so it looks like they are more skilled in the art of evasion than we thought.'

'Which one is Brathwaite's?' she asked, hoping that Andy could tell the difference.

'This one here, with his photo on it as taken by Darren,' he replied, giggling, showing her the photo of the unconscious Brathwaite.

'Good old Darren, he knew it would help, and it has!'

'He has about a dozen more contacts than the others. I can imagine that all the contacts in these phones are linked in some way, just give me a sec while I try and match them up,' he said, his fingers moving faster than Kendra had ever seen. He was certainly in his element.

Just a few minutes later he turned to her and said, 'What we have here, on these phones, are thirteen contacts that all four of them have in common. From that, we can assume the gang is likely fourteen-strong, making them quite the threat.'

'Are they saved in their real names?'

'Sadly, no, in their nicknames, so it will be hard to track them down. We're going to have to get clever with this one, for sure.'

'Okay, anything else of interest?'

'Yes. Brathwaite has a number on here that he calls twice a day, religiously, once at eleven in the morning and the other at ten o'clock at night. The number is saved as three *pound* signs, which is bizarre.'

'Maybe it's someone he owes money to? Or who owes him?'

'Or maybe it's the man who pays him, as in his boss?'

'Well, whoever it is,' said Kendra, 'I guess it's time to work your magic and find out more about these people. I'll leave you to it.'

She patted him on the shoulder, a friendly gesture that felt a little awkward to her even as she did it. She rolled her eyes as she walked off, not seeing Andy staring at her as she left. It was a face of confusion, his brow furrowed. Well, that was weird, he thought.

———

TREVOR WAITED until the guests had been given water and snacks before deciding to speak to Brathwaite. Unbeknownst to him and his acquaintances, they had been given crushed sleeping tablets with their water, to make them more pliable. It served a double purpose, the main one being that it kept them quieter and made it less likely that they would kick off, and the other being that it made it easier to speak to them. It wasn't a fool proof method, as Trevor found out when he went into Brathwaite's room.

'What do you want, batty man?' Brathwaite slurred, trying his best to maintain the angry, hostile persona. He was hand-cuffed to a metal post next to the bunk he had been lying on.

Trevor laughed, not wanting to give him any satisfaction that he had been insulted.

'It's cool, man, I just wanted to see that you're okay, you know?' he told the surly occupant.

'What do you care, bitch? Why have you put me in here? What the fuck is going on?'

'Just want to ask you something, big man. I know how tough you are, I hear the stories. I just want to know why you are doing it, you know?'

'Doing what? What are you talking about?'

'You know, the nasty robberies and burglaries where you slash people's faces and leave them scarred for life with this little toy of yours.' Trevor brought the knuckle duster out from his pocket.

Brathwaite's demeanour changed immediately. 'I want that back, you hear?'

'Why? So you can carry on using it on elderly people? You're nothing but scum, you know that?' Trevor stared the man down.

Brathwaite looked away. It was easy to do those things when you were with your crew, your mates, when you don't care about anything or anyone. He knew, though, that anyone outside his circle would see things differently, and consider it cowardly of them.

'What do you know, man?' Braithwaite said, and lay back on his bunk, looking away.

'What's wrong, big man, are you embarrassed that I know these things about you? You don't think I'm going to tell everyone that you mug old women for a living? Must make you feel big and powerful, eh?'

'Just fuck off and leave me alone,' Brathwaite said, but the anger and hostility was gone, replaced by humiliation. He kept his back to Trevor in the hope that it would end the conversation.

'I ain't going anywhere, bro, I'm gonna stay here and find out why, if it means staying up with you all night. You hear me?' Trevor purposely sounded jolly to both rile him and frustrate him with his presence, hoping it would loosen his tongue a little more. He started to whistle.

'Go away, man,' Braithwaite shouted, the frustration clearly showing.

'Tell me and I'll go,' came the swift reply.

'Just fuck off, will you?' he shouted back.

'Nope.'

Brathwaite struggled meekly against his handcuffs, his frustration reaching boiling point, the feeling of helplessness only adding to it. Trevor could sense what he was fighting and leaned in, menacingly.

'Tell you what, Denny boy. How about I give you a taste of your own medicine and slice your face open with this?'

Trevor placed the knuckle duster slowly on his hand, so that Brathwaite was transfixed.

'You think I'm scared, man? Go ahead, do your worst.' Brathwaite glared at his captor.

Trevor lashed out at speed, striking him on the forehead before he could react. Luckily for him, it was not the hand with the knuckle duster, but it came as a shock, nevertheless.

'Oops, sorry,' Trevor said, smirking, 'you still brave, Denny? Where will the next one come from, I wonder?' he added, blowing on the knuckle duster and polishing it on his shirt.

Brathwaite shook his head, stunned by the blow. The fear was back; it was exactly what Trevor needed to see. Brathwaite needed to be scared before he was ever going to give up any useful information.

'Now, let's try again, shall we?'

Brathwaite's body language changed as he effectively conceded defeat. He sat up and looked up at the masked man before him.

'If I say anything I'll be a dead man before the morning,' he whispered.

'Nobody will get to you here, Denny, so don't give me that shit. Tell me what you know, and I'll make sure nobody touches you but me.'

'So, what, you gonna do me in, then? Is that what you're saying now? I'm telling you, these people would kill their own kids if it meant they got what they wanted.'

Trevor knew it wouldn't be easy, and he also knew that he

had to be brutal to get what he needed, it was the only language Brathwaite would understand. Before replying to him, he lashed out again, this time with the knuckle duster, striking his captive in the abdomen. The knuckle duster sliced through Brathwaite's Boss polo shirt, leaving the distinctive three slashes and drawing blood. He doubled up in pain.

'Shiiit!'

'That's my last warning, Denny. Tell me what you know or the next one will be aimed at your face.'

Brathwaite raised his hand up in defeat.

'Alright, alright, just give me a second,' he said through gritted teeth.

'Time's up, boy, I ain't waiting no more,' Trevor said, pulling his arm back ready to throw another punch.

'I don't know his name, ok? The boss man, I don't know who he is. We speak every day, and he tells me where to go and what to do. He sends money twice a week. That's all I know.'

He looked up at Trevor, relieved to see that the arm had come back to a resting position.

'Tell me everything. Times, places, money, all of it. Don't try to hide anything because I will know. Don't play games with me, because I will hurt you good and proper. You got me?'

'Yes, man, I got you,' Brathwaite said, his arm raised in defence and defeat.

'Good, now start from the beginning.'

8

INVESTIGATION

'Well, look who's finally graced us with her presence,' joked Detective Sergeant Rick Watts when Kendra walked into the office the following morning.

'How's it going, Kendra, have you been on holiday again?'

'Sarge, you use the same line every time I walk in, it's getting kinda stale. You haven't got anything against part-timers, have you? Isn't there an HR issue there somewhere?'

'I'm just kidding with you, it's going to take me some time to get used to working with a part-timer, it's weird, is what it is.'

'You're weird, Sarge, I made my choice, and you should've gotten used to it by now. Don't make me tell everyone that you're a dinosaur who can't accept change, ok?'

'Guilty as charged, I'm old-school and proud of it. Anyway, enough banter, you're here now, let's sort out a quick update for everyone, say ten minutes?'

'I'll take care of it,' Kendra said, walking back out to gather everyone together.

Ten minutes later the Serious Crime Unit were assembled in their large open-plan main office, some seated and others standing. They were joined by Detective Inspector Damian Dunne, who was typically happy to let the team get on with things without too much intervention. It was unusual for him to be giving an update, so the team knew something was up.

'This shouldn't take long,' Dunne said when the hubbub had died down. 'As you know, we've been working on the mysterious disappearance of the Qupi gang. Trying to trace their current whereabouts has turned up absolutely nothing, zero, which has mystified everyone upstairs.'

'I would have thought they'd be delighted, Guv, not to have to deal with them again. They were a nasty group of individuals, a lot of good people died because of them,' Rick Watts added.

'Yes, but you know what they're like upstairs, they don't like loose ends. They're considering escalating the investigation and bringing in other teams to assist.'

'What? Why? We've tried every avenue, and nothing has worked, what makes them think that outside help is going to change that?' asked Watts.

'Well, one of the bright sparks upstairs thinks it's very convenient that we can't find anything and has assumed that something is amiss with our investigation. He is clearly after the next rank and wants to ruffle some feathers.'

'So he thinks we're crooked?' asked Jillian Petrou. 'Seriously?'

'Don't take it personally, Detective, like I said, there's always someone chasing the next rank and they think pissing someone else off is the way to do it,' replied the DI.

'Guv,' said Watts, 'with respect, are you saying that we are going to be investigated for not investigating properly?'

'It seems that way, yes,' came the reply.

The room went quiet as everyone considered this development. Kendra was concerned that she hadn't covered her tracks as well as she thought and tried to think of any issues that were likely to be picked up on. She couldn't think of anything, but the development still made her very nervous.

'Guv, can I take a month off, please?' asked Nick McGuinness, hoping to ease the tension.

'Yeah, me too, Guv,' added Wilf Baker.

'And me,' came several other voices.

'Alright, alright, that's enough, people,' Watts said, standing and waving them all to sit down, 'let the Guv'nor finish.'

'Thanks, Rick. Just to be clear, I'm not happy about this and have made my feelings very clear. They've given us another couple of weeks to get a result, otherwise they'll bring in the Department of Professional Standards, and we all know how much the DPS are loved, don't we?' continued the DI.

'So, we have a couple of weeks, that's it?' said Pablo Rothwell. 'We've been at this a lot longer, and honestly, we can't find a thing, Guv. Granted, it seems very odd, but there are a lot of smart people on this unit; if anyone can find them it was always going to be us.'

'Yes, I know that, Pablo, but like I said, this is a decision from the almighty in the ivory tower. What they say goes, however much we dislike it. I suggest you start again, afresh, and see if you've missed anything at all, however small. Now, are there any questions?'

'You mentioned other units being brought in to help, sir?' said Kendra.

'Yes, they are considering bringing back our friends from

the NCA, who I know one or two of you have already had the pleasure of meeting.'

'Oh no, you mean the douchebag? I thought we'd seen the last of him,' she replied.

'Yes, that's the one, the infamous Eddie Duckmore and his hand-holding partner Dave Critchley. I thought I'd seen the last of him, too, Detective. Sadly, the bosses upstairs thought they may be able to help sift through the evidence and pick up on anything we may have missed.'

'Well, I'm telling you now, that will not go very well at all,' Kendra said, 'Duckmore is a nasty man who will purposely rub anyone up the wrong way just to get a rise, he is as toxic as they come.'

'Yes, well, we'll just have to try not to give him the satisfaction, okay? Now, if there is anyone else with a question?'

There were none, the room was silent, and there wasn't anyone in it that was pleased.

'Thanks, Guv,' Watts said. 'I'll take it from here.'

'I'll be in my office if you need anything,' the DI said, leaving the office.

'Well, that was a crock of shit, wasn't it?' Norm Clark said. 'They're basically accusing us of being bent, Sarge. I ain't having that.'

'Well, you're going to have to swallow your pride and accept it, Clark, because if the DPS start investigating us, things are going to get very uncomfortable around here for some time.'

I just pray they don't find anything here, was all he could think.

'HOW DOES THAT AFFECT US?' asked Andy, as Kendra relayed the update.

'It means the DPS will scrutinise everything and everyone involved in the Qupi case to make sure we all did our jobs correctly,' she replied. 'And trust me, they will be thorough.'

'We took all the correct measures, Kendra, so don't worry too much, I'm sure we'll be fine,' Trevor added.

'Regardless, it's a small kick up the arse to make sure we keep on top of things, the last thing we need now is to get caught,' Kendra added.

'Don't worry, between us we can keep a tight ship,' said Andy. 'Thanks. So, what's the latest? Any more luck with the phones?'

'Well, thanks to young Trevor here, our guest Mr Brathwaite spilled the beans and outed his boss – although all we have is a phone number, as they've never met in person. As I expected, it is a burner phone, so it's not registered, but I can still trace it to a rough location.'

'Anywhere we know?' asked Trevor.

'Well, It's a fair trek from the factory, maybe a fifty-minute drive. The phone is currently somewhere in the Dalston area, that's all we can narrow it down to at the moment.'

'So, what do we need to do to find the exact location and person?' asked Kendra.

'It's not going to be easy,' said Andy. 'You should also know that if he's getting calls twice a day then it won't be long before his boss realises he's in trouble and gets rid of the burner phone. You'll need to act quickly.'

'We might need to get a little sneaky, K, what do you think?'

'Reckon you can pull off an angry young gangster voice?' she asked.

'Oh, I see where you're going with this, Detective March,' and I like it! If you can keep the person on the other end of the line I can trace the phone more accurately.'

Trevor shook his head. 'I don't suppose I get a say in this, do I?'

'Nope, but it may be worth having another quiet word with our guests to see how the whole phone call thing works with his so-called boss,' Kendra added.

'We haven't much time, so I'll get over there and have a word now. Andy, is Marge kitted out for the trace?'

'You better believe it!' was the enthusiastic response.

'Well, then, let's go while we have time.'

Andy clapped his hands animatedly. 'Good old Marge, I told you she'd make a great team member, and the bonus is that I get to go out on the job yet again.'

'Don't get too excited, GI Joe, you'll be sat in the van doing your thing with the phone, not playing secret agent,' Trevor said.

'Killjoy,' Andy replied.

Trevor shook his head once more.

MARGE PULLED into the rear yard of the factory just thirty minutes later. Trevor had a quick chat with the men looking after the guests, including Darren and his contingent who were working out in the gym. Kendra and Andy stayed in the back, readying Marge's state-of-the-art equipment for what they hoped would be a successful trace.

'I've cloned Brathwaite's phone so that I can plug it into the computer and link it to the original while Trevor is talking. When he gets back, we should be ready to go.'

'Great, hopefully Brathwaite has stopped being a dick for long enough to be useful,' Kendra said.

Ten minutes later, Trevor returned from speaking with Brathwaite. He was smirking when he closed the door behind him, before sitting on the bench opposite Andy and Kendra.

'What's funny, Dad?'

'Our guest tried to get funny with Darren again, so he was tasered a couple of times. He's in a right state and was actually pleased to see me. These Walsall boys are great, aren't they?'

'Did he say anything of interest?'

'Not really, only that he gets a call twice a day, like he said earlier. I asked him how he responds to the call, and he told me.'

'Go on.'

'He answered like this, if I can get the accent right – *boss man, what you have for us tonight?*'

Trevor's impression wasn't bad at all.

'And then?' she pressed.

'And then his boss tells him the area they will be targeting the following night. They don't do it every night, apparently, so for example, on the call this morning, he was told to wait until tonight.'

'So, when he gets a call tonight it will be for tomorrow?'

'It appears so.'

'Ok, we have fifteen minutes before the man should call, so how do you want to play this?' asked Kendra.

'What we need is to find out where this guy lives and who he is. The call may allow us to trace his current location,' Andy said. 'But it depends on how the call goes, so keep him on the phone for as long as possible.'

'That may be a problem,' said Trevor, 'because the calls last for thirty seconds or less, according to shitbag over there.'

'Well, then we go to plan B,' Andy added, 'which I assumed would be the better option. The cloned phone is ready to go, I have uploaded a virus to it that will allow me to do a couple of things to his phone remotely.'

'Like what?' asked Trevor.

'For example, I can turn his camera on, so we can see the person talking, or if it is a smart phone, then I may be able to turn his locator app on, so that we know where he is at all times, that sort of thing.'

'Bloody hell, you can do all that shit?' Trevor asked.

'Things have changed, old man, best get used to it.'

'Less of the "old man," boy, I can still kick your arse, remember?' Andy nodded in agreement, smiling broadly.

'I remember, Trevor, I do. In my defence, I am one-legged and one-eyed, and you wouldn't want to smack a disabled person, would you?'

'Don't play that card with me, boy, I'll still kick your arse however many eyes or legs you have.'

'Enough already, the pair of you,' Kendra said, laughing, enjoying the banter but sensing that they were close to receiving the call.

'Let's be sure everything is ready, we will only get one shot at this.'

'HERE WE GO,' Trevor said, picking up the phone. The ringtone was an old-fashioned ringer sound that reverberated inside the camper van.

'Boss man, what you have for us tonight?' Trevor answered.

There was a short pause before the mystery man responded. 'Victoria Park, tomorrow, get your people ready, and make sure to leave your mark.'

'Yes, boss man, I hear you,' Trevor replied. 'What time of day you want us there?'

'I'll let you know in the morning, be ready,' came the reply, before the call was ended.

'Well, that was short and sweet, wasn't it?' Kendra said. 'Did anything work, Andy?'

Andy looked up from his computer station. 'Why, yes, Miss March, it did.'

'Excellent, what did you do?'

'The virus has been delivered, so now we wait until it works its magic so that we can track the phone.'

'Bloody hell, that seemed easy, Andy, does it happen a lot?' asked Trevor.

'Not as much as you fear. It's a trick that government agencies and high-level hackers use for espionage purposes, mainly. It is highly illegal, just so you know.'

'How did you learn this stuff?' Trevor asked.

'I was a detective, remember? In my past postings, I've been lucky enough to work with the same government agencies that use these techniques, especially when keeping track of terrorists. I learned a lot of it then, and afterwards kept up with new methods in the groups that I am a member of on the dark web. It's very restricted and only a handful of people exchange codes and methods on there.'

'Lucky us, then, right?' Kendra remarked.

'Well, I'm not just a pretty face, you know. I may come

across as a dashing, funny, interesting guy, but behind the scenes I am so much more.' Andy smiled innocently.

It was a few seconds before Kendra replied. 'Sorry, I was lost for words for a sec, trying to take that all in. We are mightily grateful for your extreme skills, Mr Pike.' She bowed theatrically, prompting a laugh from Trevor.

'You just won't learn, will you, Andy? It takes a lot more than that to impress my daughter, and don't you forget it,' Trevor added, proud of his daughter.

Andy blushed as the smile disappeared from his face, bringing a laugh from Kendra.

'Now,' she said, 'is that special virus of yours ready yet?'

'I'm hugely offended,' Andy replied, exaggerating his response dramatically as he turned and started to type again. 'Nobody appreciates my genius anymore, maybe I should volunteer my services to other, more grateful law-breaking ex-colleagues.'

Trevor and Kendra shook their heads and exchanged a smile.

'He can be such a knob sometimes,' Trevor remarked.

'Well, this genius may be a knob, but he's just tracked the location of your boss man,' Andy exclaimed in triumph.

'Really, that quickly?'

'Yes, sir! The phone is currently located in this area here,' Andy explained, indicating to a map on the second monitor.

'Where is that?' asked Kendra.

'That is a map of Hackney, Dalston to be precise. The phone is currently within this radius of fifty metres,' he added, pointing to the flashing cursor close to Dalston Kingsland overground station. 'I'll be able to track it from now on and will know whether this is where the owner lives or if it's just a temporary stop.'

Andy switched to satellite view to show the most recent satellite images of the area. As he zoomed in, they could see the outline of an unusual circular building, which looked more like a football stadium with a fully enclosed roof.

'What is that?' Kendra asked.

'Let me try something else,' Andy said. He then switched to street view and followed the road around to the large structure. It was not a football stadium.

'Here you go. This is a recent development, a fifteen-storey tower block called *Fifty-Seven East*. And as you can see, the cursor is pretty much on top of it. Because of its size and the space around it, the tracker has narrowed it down to someone in that tower block.'

'Wow,' Trevor said, 'this is like watching one of those CSE series on TV, it's all true!'

Kendra laughed. 'Dad, it's CSI, and that is very much exaggerated.'

'It's an impressive looking building, very futuristic,' Trevor said as he inspected the images. 'So how do we narrow down who the phone belongs to?'

'That's the hard part,' said Andy, 'because it doesn't tell you which floor or anything like that, it isn't pinpoint-accurate either. Hopefully when we can access his camera, we may get some clues.'

'When will you be able to do that?' asked Trevor.

'We need to be careful, because if we activate the camera and the person is close by, they may realise something is up. I think we should wait until the morning phone call and switch it on then, while he is on the phone to our guest. I'm pretty sure I can turn it on so that it only works one-way, so that he won't see anyone on the screen.'

'Fair enough. Let's call it a night, then, and pop back

tomorrow,' Kendra said, stretching, after what had turned out
to be a long day.

'Tomorrow it is!' Andy remarked, dramatically pointing to
the sky. There was more headshaking as they left him in
the van.

9

THE LEADER

The following morning, as Kendra was not due in work, she was at the factory by ten o'clock, well in advance of the next important call from Brathwaite's mystery boss. She was surprised to see Andy and her dad already in the operations room, poring over a computer screen, murmuring to each other.

'Am I interrupting something?' she said, startling the two men. 'I didn't expect you both to be here so early, what's going on?'

'Morning, darling, nice to see you so bright and early,' Trevor said, 'I thought I'd beat you both in this morning, but then I saw that ugly van parked around the back.'

'Well, you know what they say about the early birds,' Andy said, 'always get the juiciest worms.'

'And, pray tell, what worm is it that you managed to hook, Mr Pike?' asked Kendra, impressed by them both. 'What am I looking at?'

'I've basically tracked the movement of the phone since the call last night. As you can see from the red lines, it has hardly moved at all. That pretty much confirms that whoever owns the phone is currently residing in that tower block.'

'That's great, so we just need to find out which of the eighty-odd flats he lives in, right?' 'Talk about buzz kill,' Andy said. 'This is progress, Detective March, don't you remember the importance of baby steps?'

'I do remember, smart arse, and it's pigeon steps,' she replied, crossing her arms defiantly.

Trevor remarked, 'let's not forget why we're here, okay? We have the call in about forty minutes, so let's make sure we're ready and on the ball. I'm going to go and speak with Brathwaite again, to make sure there's no code words or anything else we might need to know.'

'I'll go and make us some coffee, you want one, K?' Andy said.

'Sure, thank you.'

Alone in the room, Kendra tried to think ahead. What if the call spooks the man? What will we do when we locate the flat? And so on. She was an excellent planner, especially proficient in emergency back-up plans, so she scoured the map and the area around the tower block to try to anticipate potential problems, and to determine whether there were any weaknesses to the security there.

'It's not going to be an easy one, that's for sure,' she muttered to herself.

'BRATHWAITE WAS HIS USUAL HELPFUL SELF,' Trevor said as they met up with five minutes to go until the call came in.

'That's good, right?' asked Andy.

'He is really not cut out for prison life, I think he may

even be a little claustrophobic, so the tasering he received, along with the sleeping pills we've been giving him, means he is being very compliant at the moment.'

'Oh, that's unlucky, poor thing. I know, let's put him in a smaller room, just to make sure,' Andy added.

'Stop it,' Kendra said, punching him playfully on the arm. 'Are you ready to go?'

'Yes, ma'am. And ouch!' Andy rubbed his arm.

'What did he have to say, Dad?'

'Not much more, to be honest. There are no code phrases, you'll be happy to hear. He did mention that he normally asks about payment in the morning. So, I guess that's what I'll do when he gives me instructions.'

'As soon as you answer I will activate the camera on his phone, so the longer he is on it, the better chance we have of getting clues to his location.'

'I'll do my best,' said Trevor.

The phone rang at exactly eleven o'clock, just as Brathwaite had said it would.

'Morning to ya, boss man, what you have for us?'

'Change of plans. I want you to go to Victoria Park during daylight hours and target several people in front of witnesses. I want them all marked. Do not get caught,' said the mystery man.

Trevor wasn't expecting that, but his response showed that he was up for the challenge.

'Boss man, you sure about that? Gonna cause us problems, you know?'

'Do as you're told and I'll double your fee if you don't get caught. Send a message and photos when you are done.' The call was abruptly ended.

'Damn,' said Trevor, 'I didn't even get a chance to ask him

about the money, this man is always in a hurry to get off the bloody phone.'

'That's a bit ominous, asking them to rob people in broad daylight, don't you think?' asked Kendra.

'That is a worrying development, for sure,' Andy said, 'and it's weird they're being told what to do and where to do it. It's like a futuristic Fagin running a bunch of nasty robbers instead of petty thieves.'

'That's a good analogy, Andy, I'm pleased to hear you have read books,' Trevor said.

'Not very nice, but I'll take it as a sort of compliment.'

'Tell me you got something, Andy,' Kendra said, 'anything that gives us a clue would be great.'

'Well, it isn't much, but let's see what it looks like when I slow it right down.'

He played the recorded feed on the monitor. The resolution was pretty good, considering. The footage that had been recorded was mainly black, with some dark shades of grey and faint, light skin tones changing as the phone moved slightly against the caller's ear.

'Well, it's safe to say that the boss man is a white dude,' Trevor said.

There was a sudden flash of pale blue and white, before the phone went dead. It was as if the caller was moving the phone towards a pocket as he was switching it off, which happened in a split second.

'What was that?' asked Kendra. 'Can you go back?'

'Sure.'

Andy slowed the footage down to a stop as it came to the blue and white.

'Is that what I think it is?' asked Trevor.

'Yes, sir, I believe that we are looking at the bright blue sky and clouds of Dalston.'

'And that looked like a flash of blond hair,' added Kendra. 'So, the boss of the vicious robber gang is a rich, blond, white man who lives in a fancy tower block. That is mystifying, don't you think?'

'Also, I think he lives on the top floor, or one of the flats with access to the roof terrace,' Andy said.

'Why do you say that?'

'If it was a normal flat and he was on a balcony, it would be shaded, wouldn't it? Look at the images of the tower block. The balcony is completely covered, so you wouldn't be able to see the sky as clearly. Unless he was hanging over the side of the balcony, which is highly unlikely. That can only mean he was on the roof.' Andy started typing furiously.

'Take a look at this,' he continued, shifting back to the monitor. He pointed to a screenshot of the tower block and zoomed in.

Kendra had to squint but she could see two men standing on the roof of the tower block.

'What are they doing? Are they holding bows and arrows?'

'Actually, they are crossbows, and they're aiming at a target up against the wall there.'

The roof was divided into three terraces. The larger of the three took up half the terrace, while the other two were a quarter each. The two crossbowmen were in the larger of the three terraces.

'That is an odd thing to do on top of a tower block, isn't it?' she asked.

'It certainly is, can you imagine if one of those bolts missed and flew over the parapet into the street below? That is some pretty dangerous shit they're doing, for sure,' Andy said.

'You think our man lives on the top floor?'

'I guess I do, yes. That is a penthouse flat, so only someone with a ton of money will live there, I can assure you.'

'Can we find out who owns that particular flat?' asked Trevor.

'Yes, sir, I believe we can. Let me just check the voter's register and start there,' he continued, typing like a madman.

'Nope, he hasn't registered to vote, naughty man. Let me see if there is any record of anything in that block on open source. Nope, nothing there, either.'

'I'll have a look tomorrow,' said Kendra. 'I'm due back in the office and can check all systems while I'm there.'

'Okay, we've made some good progress here, good job,' Trevor said. 'We can start looking at this block of flats and come up with a plan of action.'

'I suggest you go and take a look tomorrow, Dad, have a look all around and see what security we have to contend with.'

'I can do that, no problem,' came the reply.

'Can I go with you?' asked Andy meekly, 'it would be a great opportunity to test Marge out in the field again.'

'I don't see why not,' Trevor said, 'it's only a recce, what harm can you do?'

KENDRA WAS BACK at her desk in the SCU the following morning, waiting to see what the day was going to bring. The announcement that they were to be investigated had dulled the atmosphere on the team.

The DPS were known to be sticklers for standard operating procedures, and they usually found something to use against officers, however small and unconnected. This is what generally made people wary of them and therefore gave the DPS a bad reputation.

'Let's hope they decide not to call them in, eh?' Jillian Petrou said, sitting next to Kendra.

'I wouldn't put anything past the suits upstairs, Jillian, they have not exactly covered themselves in glory recently, so they'll always look for a scapegoat – in this case, it's us.'

'Well, let's hope we can find something that keeps the dogs away, as they say.'

'We will certainly try; I just hope they don't bring the NCA in too soon as that will cause more issues than you can imagine.'

'Wow, you must have had a really tough time with them back then, are they really that bad?'

'That Eddie Duckmore is a bloody nightmare, he's a misogynistic, overbearing, swollen- headed bully who likes nothing more than to order people around like a dictator. The man is a complete arsehole, or douchebag as we all called him.'

'Well, don't bother mincing your words, Detective.' Jillian laughed. 'Tell it how it really is!'

'It comes with the territory, I suppose, him being like that,' Kendra said.

'What do you mean?'

'You know, he's like that because he's got a teeny tiny penis,' came the reply. They both laughed loudly, prompting a visit from Rick Watts.

'Good to see you keeping your spirits up, ladies,' he said, crossing his arms and waiting for them to stop.

'Sorry, Sarge,' said Jillian, 'we were just discussing the benefits of having the NCA around us.'

'And you found some? Good for you, maybe you can share them with the rest of us,' he replied.

'To be fair, it isn't the NCA that it's aimed at, Sarge, just one of their finest,' Kendra added.

'Oh, you mean that tosser, Duckmore? Yeah, I know all about him, my mate at Border Force had a run in with him too, so I've heard everything about him. Sadly, he and his sidekick are joining us from tomorrow, so I'll just enjoy the laughter while I can, because we probably won't hear any more for a while.'

'Right,' said Kendra. 'I'm going to get cracking with the searches again, Sarge, I'm going over all the logs to see if we've missed anything. If it's alright with you, I'll pop down to my desk in the Intel Unit and see if I can get some help from my team.'

'No problem, the more help we can get, the better. We'll have a catch-up later, hopefully someone will find something soon.' Watts left the room.

'Okay, that's my cue to foxtrot oscar out of here and get cracking on the evidence lists. See you later,' Jillian said as she left to return to her desk.

'See ya, Jillian, I'll give you a shout at lunch if you're up for it.'

Kendra looked around the spacious open-plan office and saw that the team were all busy in one way or another, searching for the clues that would get the investigators off their backs. It was likely to be like this for the next couple of weeks: intense, uncomfortable and counterproductive, with other crimes and investigations left unattended.

'Right, let's go and have a look then, shall we?'

She left SCU and went downstairs to the second floor where she had spent the last few months. It was here, in the Intelligence Unit, that she had realised the futility of police work in so many cases that had been left unsolved, or where the criminals had used legal loopholes to escape justice. She had spent her time there wisely and was glad to be back, if only to visit her Intel Unit colleagues.

'Hello, stranger,' Paul Salmon said as soon as she walked in. 'How's it going up in the marble halls of the SCU?'

'Very well, thanks, but I missed you guys so I thought I'd work here for the day, so we can catch up.'

'How's it going, Kendra?' asked Sam Razey. 'Good to see you.'

'All good, thanks, Sam. It's super busy upstairs so I thought I'd pop down where it's nice and peaceful.' She waved to Imran and Geraldine who were both on phone calls.

'Anything we can assist with?' asked Paul.

'Actually, maybe you can. They're talking about bringing the DPS in to investigate us regarding the Qupi gang.'

'Damn, we all love the DPS, don't we?' said Sam, feigning looking around for spy cameras.

'You know they've disappeared, so Rick figures if we can find any trace of them then it will get them off our backs. We've tried searching everywhere but have had no luck. Any ideas you have would be greatly appreciated.'

'Hmm,' said Sam, 'let me have a think about that, I've helped with a few missing persons cases and have a few tricks that may help.'

'I'll have a sniff around too, you never know what our informants might come up with,' Paul added.

'Great, thanks, guys. I'll be over there if you come up with anything.'

Kendra sat down at her desk, turned the computer on, and waited for it to boot up. Sam had just given her a good idea; using informants was how they'd been able to covertly pass intelligence about Qupi's shipments without giving anyone away. Perhaps they could use the same trick to lay a trail for the investigators to follow. That way, they might be able to put the investigation to bed early.

She signed onto the system and started some generic searches within the case files, making sure there was a trail, if anyone were to check her workload later. Her real intention for being in the second-floor office was so that she could dig around and try to identify the rich blond man who had been organising the robberies. She could only do that when some of her colleagues were at lunch, and she could log in using their credentials.

Lunch was a good three hours away, so she used the time to continue searching for Qupi evidence, which was strange for her, already knowing their whereabouts.

I hope they are suffering in hell, she thought.

'BLIMEY, it's busy around here, isn't it?' Trevor said as they drove along Kingsland High Street towards the Fifty-Seven East tower block.

The road was chock-a-block with traffic, and pedestrians who were crossing between vehicles, trying to get to Dalston

Kingsland station on one side or the infamous Ridley Road Street market on the other.

'On a positive note, it means we won't have any trouble blending in,' said Andy, excited to be on the recce with Trevor. He had missed the excitement of field work.

'I'm more worried about where we're going to leave this monster, there doesn't appear to be much parking around here,' said Trevor.

'Don't worry,' Andy said, 'I have it all under control.'

He whipped out a light-blue disabled parking badge that allowed vehicles to park anywhere.

'We'll park around the back, where the service entrances are, in Boleyn Road. Parking is restricted everywhere around here, but this beauty will allow us to park anywhere we want.'

'How did you get one of those?' asked Trevor.

'Believe it or not, it is legitimate. I could have bought one on the dark web, but I'd already applied for this months ago when I knew I'd be driving again. Good, eh?'

'Man, you think of everything, don't you?' Trevor nodded in appreciation.

'Well, detectives are supposed to be well organised, right? I tend not to leave things for later and do them when I think of them, it's what has helped me my whole life.'

'That's great, Andy, it's a good quality to have. I see why my daughter likes you, now.'

'What? She likes me? What?' Andy spluttered.

Trevor laughed. 'Not so organised now, are you? Don't get your knickers in a twist, boy, I mean she likes you as a person.'

He had slipped up there and quickly managed to row out of it. 'Phew, ha ha ha, I knew that, phew, you almost had me.'

Trevor smiled at his obvious discomfort. 'There's Boleyn Road, turn right there.'

It was much quieter off the main road, and although still busy with parked traffic, it wasn't long before Andy had found a spot, close to the rear service entrance for Marks and Spencer.

'Okay, let's go for a walk, shall we?' said Trevor.

THEY STARTED at the rear where it was quieter. M&S had a large store on the main road, so they had to cross the tower block's courtyard to get to the rear of the store. Having the service entrance and storage area at the back like this was the only solution for them.

'This looks like a way into the block,' Andy said, looking at a set of security doors next to the shutters.

'And there's another one further down,' Trevor added.

They continued along Boleyn Road and back onto the main road, Kingsland High Street, where the pedestrian traffic was thick and fast. As they approached M&S, Andy nodded and said, 'Here's the main entrance to the tower block, number fifty-seven.'

It was adjacent to M&S and newly constructed, so the door was locked, as it should be.

'What do you think?' asked Trevor. 'How are we going to get in?'

'We wait until someone comes along and then we blag it, simple,' Andy replied confidently.

They stood around the entrance for twenty minutes, trying not to look out of place, before someone approached and opened the door and went inside. Before the door could slam shut,

Trevor put his foot in the way, keeping the entrance open.

It was stark and almost hospital-like in the hallway, but it wasn't long before they had walked through the building and were back outside, in the open courtyard of the impressive tower block. It looked like something out of a science-fiction movie, an unusual, slightly oval shape which was bizarrely narrower at the bottom few floors before tapering outwards, with lots of modern construction touches in its impressive façade. It had only recently been built. The courtyard was well-designed and land-scaped, with large, hexagonal planter beds filled with a variety of plants. It was clean, modern, attractive, and unusually quiet considering how close the bustling main road was.

'Well, this is very nice indeed,' Andy said, craning his neck for a better view of the imposing tower block.

'It certainly is,' agreed Trevor, admiring the gardens.

'Strange thing, though,' Andy said, as they walked around the tower, 'I didn't see a car park, did you? Where do they keep their cars?'

'I have no idea. Living next door to the station and on such a busy main road probably suggests that not many of them will need a car.'

'I'm pretty sure our wealthy friend will, though, so where does he keep it? Interesting.' They went to the main entrance where they were welcomed by a concierge, a smartly dressed elderly man who greeted them with a smile.

'Gentlemen, my name is Harvey, how can I help you this fine morning?'

'Hello, Harvey,' said Trevor, looking around and nodding in appreciation. 'This is a lovely place, a friend of mine told me that I should pop over and have a look as I'm in the market for a flat.'

'Well, sir, I'm not sure there is one available at the moment. I know one sold last week, but they do come up for sale often, so I may be mistaken.'

'That's alright, I noticed there are no parking facilities here, is that right?'

'That's correct, sir, most of the people living here work in the city so they don't really have use for a car.'

'That's understandable,' Trevor said. 'Is it a good place to live, in your opinion? And please be honest, Harvey.'

The concierge looked around before answering. 'Well, I shouldn't be saying this, but it's more for younger people, if you know what I mean. Lots of loud music and that kind of thing, you know, parties and that. If you like that sort of thing, then it will be heaven for you.'

'Yeah, I bet it's great, especially in the penthouses. I hear they're great,' Andy said.

'They are wonderful, sir, floor-to-ceiling glass, enormous rooms, wonderful roof terraces with incredible views, and they have their own lifts, too. They're pretty pricey, though, the last one sold for a million-and-a-half, and that was one of the smaller ones.'

Andy whistled and said, 'Well, that takes care of that. Maybe we should look further out, uncle?' he said, turning to Trevor.

'Yes, I think you're right ... nephew. Thank you for your time, Harvey, we appreciate it.'

As they went back outside, Andy couldn't help but snigger. 'Sorry, I couldn't resist it,' he said.

'I should kick your arse for that, you little shit,' Trevor replied, 'but we should get out of here, we've seen enough.'

'Yes ... uncle.'

Trevor's kick was well-aimed and elicited a grunt of pain.

———

KENDRA'S PATIENCE was rewarded when her colleagues in the Intel Unit went to lunch. She told them that she wanted to catch up with work and would eat at her desk, so she had the room to herself. Without showing any change in her body language, in case the CCTV footage was ever checked, she swiftly logged out and then back in as Geraldine Marley. She typed in the address of the tower block to see if anything came up in the crime reports. She wasn't surprised that there weren't many entries; the block had only recently been built. There was less than a handful of neighbour- or domestic-disputes, with one report of criminal damage. There was one other report that did intrigue her – reports of a loud party on the roof, where screams were heard.

This report, from around two months earlier, indicated that local police had attended and been allowed entry. Their report noted that the party guests were mainly scantily-clad young women, about twenty of them, and that only four men were in attendance. The reporting officer spoke to the owner of the house, who gave his name as Michael Eastwood, aged 32, described as five-foot-three with short blond hair, wearing a dressing gown. The other three men were of a similar age but larger in stature, and although they were engaging with the female guests, they were still dressed relatively modestly; one was shirtless, and the other two wore shirts that were unbuttoned. All three, though, still had their trousers and shoes on.

The officers had presumed that the party was primarily

for Michael Eastwood's benefit and that his three male guests were employees. When questioned about the screams and the loud music, Eastwood had laughed it off and told the officer that they had played a trick on a young lady by wrapping a snake around her neck when she wasn't expecting it. The snake was seen, back in its vivarium, midway through the act of swallowing a rodent.

The police had left with no further action taken, other than to ask for the music to be turned down. Because of the scream and the assumed threat to life, the report had been logged.

Kendra searched for Michael Eastwood and came up blank; there was nothing about him at all on any crime database. The only thing she was able to find was a driver's license from 2012, and a recently issued passport, which replaced an earlier one from 2012. That was it.

She cleared the last few search items from the browser history and logged out of Geraldine's account and back into her own, continuing as normal for the benefit of anyone watching later. Although she was disappointed that she hadn't found much, she had now uncovered the correct address and name of the occupant. Good intelligence, indeed.

———

'HIS NAME IS MICHAEL EASTWOOD, and the address is Penthouse One, Fifty-Seven East,' Kendra relayed to Andy. 'I'll send you his passport and driver's license information by messenger, when I get back inside,' she added, as she stretched her legs in the back yard.

'That's a good start,' Andy said, 'what else was there?'

'Well, that's the strange thing,' she replied, 'there is absolutely nothing else. It's uncanny and very unusual that there is nothing else. Can you have a dig around on your systems?'

'Of course, leave it with me. Uncle Trevor sends his love, by the—OW!'

Kendra heard the loud slap and laughed, assuming correctly that her dad was with Andy. 'He doesn't like being referred to as old, which you essentially just did, so you had that coming,' she said.

'Very funny. Now, get yourself back to work and we'll see you later. Right, unc...'

The call ended, with some sort of violence against Andy. Kendra laughed out loud as she made her way back to the office, stopping off to grab a coffee from the canteen.

'How's it going, Kendra?' asked Imran as she sat with her colleagues.

'I can't complain, thanks. This investigation is causing a lot of stress upstairs, I can tell you. My old team are not happy at all.'

'I can't imagine anyone would be, would you?' said Sam Razey. 'They're a nasty bunch, and although someone has to do that job, they do rub people the wrong way.'

'They do, and there will be some anger when that happens, can you imagine?'

'Hopefully, it will all be done with soon,' said Paul Salmon, 'but I hear you have Detective Sergeant Douchebag starting here tomorrow to help. We all remember what a charming man he was.'

'No he wasn't, he was a dick,' Kendra said. 'And I imagine he still is a dick.'

'You'll be fine, Kendra,' Paul said, 'he's just all mouth and no action, trying to impress everyone that he engages with to show how superior he is. He's after promotion, probably, which sounds about right because we need more wankers like him in senior positions.'

They all laughed, everyone more at ease as a result.

'You know, you're quite astute for someone with so many years in the job. Why didn't you go for promotion?' asked Kendra.

'Well, I'd like to think it's because I'm not a wanker, but that would be a disservice to all the good guvnors out there, wouldn't it?'

More laughter.

'I'll be sure to mention it to Mister Dunne, who worked so hard to get his pips,' she replied.

'You know what he means, Kendra,' Imran added, 'there are plenty of great bosses in the job but it's arseholes like him that give the senior officers a bad reputation, which isn't fair.'

'No, I get that, don't you worry,' she replied, 'but they need to bring in some new measures to stop the arseholes from getting promotion, otherwise it's only gonna get worse.'

'You'll get no arguments from us here,' Paul said.

'Won't happen in my lifetime,' added Imran.

'So, on that happy note, let's just leave it that the douchebag is going to come here and try to make our lives miserable, shall we? But we won't let him get away with it, how's that?' Kendra added.

'Sounds like a plan,' Paul replied.

'I'm taking my coffee up as I have too much shit to sort out before I leave today. See you all later,' Kendra said, as she readied to return to the office.

Tomorrow was another day and there was likely to be a lot less laughter.

10

THE RUSSIAN CONNECTION

'Well, that is interesting indeed,' Andy said. 'Who are you really, Michael?'

Andy had searched for any further intelligence on the mysterious Eastwood. He had researched all the main databases he had at his disposal and also all open-source sites. There was nothing to be found in addition to that which Kendra had already sourced.

'Looks like I'll be diving into the dark web again,' he said, flexing his fingers and switching computers. He was back in his basement operations room at home, smaller, cosier and safer than the others, where he could do anything he wanted without worry. Including wearing his favourite red silk dressing gown, his Star Wars boxer shorts, and his enormous furry Hobbit slippers. It was safe to say that he only dressed like this when he was alone and not expecting company. His reputation meant a great deal to him, and sci-fi underwear was not going to help that at all.

'Okay, Mr Eastwood, let's see what we can find.'

He searched high and low, called in favours – and failed.

After an hour or so of searching, he decided to change tack and focus on the address instead.

'Now this is more like it,' he said, digging up some interesting information about the tower block. He finally had something to smile about, without thinking of the gigantic furry slippers.

He picked up his phone and called Kendra and Trevor.

LATER THAT EVENING, they all convened at Andy's house, where he had pre-ordered pizza and beer. Trevor and Kendra updated him further about their dealings during the day, going into more detail than their usual phone conversations. It was something they did routinely, as even the smallest piece of information could make a difference.

'Is it my turn? Marvellous!' Andy said with a dramatic flourish.

'Oh, for Pete's sake, will you just get on with it? Or do I need to slap your head again?'

'Sensitive, are we?' Andy said. 'Don't worry, it'll be worth the drama.'

'Come on then, Mr Smarty-pants, what have you got?'

'Well, Detective, I found a couple of little nuggets about that weird tower block our boss man lives in, which were rather surprising, to say the least.' He paused for dramatic effect but moved on quickly when they both started moving towards him threateningly.

'Anyway, I checked the land registry records on the building, and it turns out that the land was bought and then developed by a Russian company, MVC, which is headquartered in Moscow.'

'Really? I know that a lot of Russians have bought property in London over the years, but I've never heard of anything outside of Central London,' remarked Kendra.

'Well, if you think that snippet was interesting, you'll like this even more. MVC was owned by a gentleman called Mikhail Vordorovsky, who, at one time, was one of the top ten richest men in Russian, a billionaire oligarch.'

'What's so interesting about that?'

'Well, I'm glad you asked, because in 2005, Mr Vordorovsky was exiled from Russia after serving five years in prison for calling the Russian President a tyrant. He came to the UK and his company was taken over by the Russian government and renamed. He lost most of his fortune but had the foresight to have accounts around the world that were safe from Russia's grasp.'

'Where are you going with this, Andy? I'm still confused,' Trevor said.

'Ok, so, the land wasn't bought until 2015 and the building finished in 2020, some fifteen years after he lost the company.'

'So, he kept the name of the company going, what's the big deal in that?' asked Kendra.

'It turns out that he registered the company in the UK as soon as he arrived here but kept the Moscow address as headquarters, in order to make his loan application look good—the loan he took out to pay for everything. It all looked great, legitimate, and a potential gold mine for all involved. He put a ton of money into the development hoping to make a killing on the property market, but it hasn't worked at all. It was wildly over-budget, too expensive for the locals to afford, and so most of the flats have been rented out or sold on the cheap to show some turnover and pay some of the loan back. Ultimately the project failed miserably, losing him millions of pounds. He died a couple of years later.'

'How does this impact what we're doing?' asked Kendra.

'So, I did a little more digging on Mr Vordorovsky and his folly here, and guess what I found in the company accounts?'

'That he lost a fortune?' Trevor said.

'Yes, it goes without saying. But what I found was another little nugget. One of the directors listed in 2009 is a Mr Mikhail Aleksei Vordorovsky the second. It's quite common in Russia for successful men to name their sons after themselves. It appears that his son is a director in the company. And that's not all. That name no longer features from 2012, and guess which name seems to have replaced it?'

'It's not Michael Eastwood, is it? Surely not?' asked Kendra.

'I think that's exactly it, K. There's nothing further back about him because that persona didn't exist until then. He changed his name, not through the legal channels, but because he wanted to blend in more easily without his heritage being an issue. That's when he applied for a driver's license and passport, in 2012. That's when he made the big change, when he was, according to records, twenty-two years old.'

'That's pretty ambitious and impressive by someone that young, to make such big changes,' Trevor said. 'So he pretty much owns the building, doesn't he?'

'You'd like to think so, but like I said, it lost a ton of money. So as a director, he has some responsibility relating to the company losses. He may not have as much control of the building as a result, albeit that he lives in the biggest, plushest flat in the tower.'

'It begs the question then,' said Trevor, 'and it's something we haven't touched on yet, why the hell is he involved with a bunch of nasty robbers, what is his game here?'

'Could it have anything to do with devaluing property in the area?' asked Kendra.

'No idea, I can check and see how the prices have been affected in recent months, but I can't see that being the reason.'

'Could it be a drugs thing?' Trevor asked. 'Is he trying to make it a no-go area so that he can control the drugs scene?'

'Doubtful. I can't find any debt registered in his name, so there must still be a pile of cash in his accounts. His dad is a clever man, and they would have covered all bases, I'm sure.'

'Well, then, I'm stumped,' Kendra said, falling back onto the sofa in frustration.

'Another weird thing, probably unconnected, is that Eastwood has been on social media regularly, mocking the Russian president, calling him some very offensive names and adding photoshopped images of him doing weird things with animals and other men. It's pretty obscene stuff.'

'I guess he's upset that the bad man took all his daddy's money,' Trevor added.

'Maybe, but if the Russians find out who he really is, there could be some repercussions, not just affecting any family he has left in Russia but also here. I wouldn't put it past them to send a squad over and sort him out.'

'Well, they've certainly done that before, quite a few times,' said Kendra, 'which may explain the change of name and the lack of any intelligence anywhere.'

'True,' Andy said, 'but it's worth noting for the future, isn't it?' They sat in silence for a minute, gathering their thoughts.

'I guess that just leaves one thing to do, then.' Trevor stood up and clapped his hands together.

'What's that then, Dad?'

'We do some more digging around, there must be something we can find that will give us a clue. But we have a small problem: what to do with our guests in the meantime.'

'Ooh, I have an idea,' Andy said, raising his hand.

'Go on then, spit it out,' Kendra said.

TWO MINUTES LATER, Trevor put his arm on Andy's shoulder and said, 'That, my friend, is a cracking idea. But it doesn't mean I won't keep slapping you if you're acting like an idiot.'

'Why, thank you, oh wise one,' Andy replied, ducking quickly as another slap headed his way.

KENDRA WAS BACK at the police station the next day. Almost as soon as she walked into the third floor SCU office she was summoned by Rick Watts. As she entered his office, she saw the smiling faces of Detective Sergeant Eddie "the Douchebag" Duckmore and his minion sidekick, Detective Sergeant Dave Critchley.

'Morning, March, I believe you know these gentlemen; they have been assigned to assist with the Qupi investigation, which we are all familiar with.'

'How are you doing, princess?' Duckmore said, smirking. Kendra stared at him in disbelief.

'Really?' she said, 'do you really think that is appropriate?'

'Gents, if we're going to work together on this, then I'm going to insist on some decency and respect, okay?' Rick Watts said, 'otherwise it will be a long, awkward, and uncomfortable relationship – and that's just with me. Do we understand each other?'

Duckmore bowed his head. 'Apologies, Rick, no offence was meant, I thought – incorrectly – that we had a decent rapport going here, but I was wrong. Sorry, Detective March.'

Kendra nodded, but Duckmore's insincerity was written all over his face.

'Okay, now that we understand each other, let's get cracking, shall we?' Rick continued.

'Kendra, show the gentlemen the workstations we've set aside for them and liaise with them should they require anything else, okay?'

'Yes, Sarge,' she replied, straight-faced. 'Follow me, please.'

She was not happy about this duty but understood that she was the natural choice. She led them to the newly installed desks, butting up so the two men would sit opposite each other. Computers had been plumbed in and user accounts allocated to them both.

'Here you go. There's tea, coffee, and biscuits in the kitchenette next to Rick's office, if you fancy anything.'

'You mean Detective Sergeant Watts, don't you?' Duckmore replied, glaring.

She kept his gaze and replied, 'Yes, Detective Sergeant Duckmore, that is correct. Now, if you don't mind, I have work to do.'

As Kendra walked off, Duckmore turned to Dave Critchley and said, 'She's a lively one, I'll give her that.'

'Be careful, Ed, that woman looks like she knows how to take care of herself.'

'Yeah, well they all think that, don't they? Now, let's go get a coffee and biscuit, shall we?'

TREVOR HAD RETURNED to the factory, where he spoke with Darren and his colleagues and checked up on the guests, who had been there for a while now.

'We've been doing everything you said,' Darren explained, 'making a note of all the calls that have been made to them. It's always the same numbers, like you said it would be.'

'What about the boss man, did he call again?'

'Yes, he did, and when there was no answer, it hung up pretty quickly.'

'Okay, get me the phone, I'll take care of it.'

A few minutes later Brathwaite's phone was handed to Trevor. He dialled the number for the boss man and waited.

'Where the fuck have you been?' Eastwood said.

'Boss, we got arrested yesterday and only just got out, I'm sorry,' Trevor said in his improving Brathwaite accent. 'The pigs kept us almost twenty-four hours, you know? We just got unlucky, and they caught us with blades in our car. It won't happen again.'

There was a long pause as Eastwood considered his options. Had the plan been affected? He thought not.

'Listen very carefully. Tomorrow, you will go to Victoria Park, like I said, and you will cause chaos. Do you understand me? Women, children, old people, the lot. If I see that you have done as I ask, then I will send twice the usual amount. If you fail me then I will send people to beat the shit out of you, do you understand?'

'Yes, boss, it will be done, no worries.'

Eastwood ended the call.

'Dude, that was intense,' Darren said, his eyebrows arched.

'That may be, but we now have a problem. We either do as he asked, or we are left with just twenty-four hours to sort this whole mess out.'

'What do you have in mind?' asked Darren. 'We're happy to help, as you know.'

'I appreciate it, Darren, I need to think on this. I'll call you later, okay?'

Trevor was concerned and needed to speak with Kendra and Andy urgently.

'WHAT ARE WE GOING TO DO?' Kendra asked. 'There's no way we can go to Victoria Park and start hurting people, that's for sure.'

'I know that, love, so we must come up with another plan, and we must do it quickly. Let me speak with Andy and I'll let you know. I have an inkling of what we can do to get around it. I'll call you back once I've spoken with him.'

'Speak later, Dad, it looks like I'll be here most of the day but I'll try and join up with you guys later,' Kendra said, and he hung up. It was an intense situation, very different to those they had previously dealt with. She hoped her dad would come up with something very quickly.

'SO THAT'S where we are, Andy, we need to do something quickly otherwise Eastwood will know something is up.'

'That's a tough one, Trev, you have anything in mind?'

'Kind of, but I'll need you to work your magic online. We need to buy a couple of days at least, so that we can sort the gang out and find a way to neutralise Eastwood's operation. Problem is, we don't know what that is, so we have a double conundrum situation, don't we?'

'You can leave Eastwood to me, I have an idea how to find out what he's up to. It'll give me a chance to try out a new toy of mine,' he added.

'Okay. I think we need to find a legitimate way to keep Brathwaite and his gang from being able to attend Victoria Park tomorrow, and the only thing I can think of is an anonymous tip that there is a dead body buried there, where they have to close the whole park off. If we give a name of a missing person and a vague description, will that do the trick? What do you think?' 'That's pretty good but you might be overthinking it. I think a simple call to New Scotland Yard that a bomb will be detonated tomorrow midday will do just as good a job. They'll have to bring in all sorts of squads to investigate, it's a big park so it'll take them hours, and they'll need a uniform presence at each entrance to keep people out.'

'Will they believe the tip-off? They must get hundreds of those,' asked Trevor.

'I know what to say and how to make the call untraceable. I'll mask my voice and use some terrorist terminology, but the call will be like a whistleblowing call, from a terrorist with a conscience. It'll confuse them enough, I think.'

'Is there such a thing?' Trevor asked, 'a terrorist with a conscience?'

'Oh, hell no, they're all egotistical maniacs, but I'm pretty sure they'll do the minimum, which will be to close off the park and start a thorough search.'

'Okay, I'll leave that to you, and then tomorrow I'll make the call from the park itself. I'll go down with a couple of the lads and take some pics.'

'Good idea. In the meantime, what are you going to do with the guests?'

'Ah, yes, Our guests. I think it's time we rounded up a few more of the gang, don't you?' Trevor said. 'They must be getting a little tetchy by now, not having seen their leader for a few days. Send me the info and we'll start tonight.'

'Ooh, I like! Can I come with you? Please? Pretty please?'

'If you promise to stay in the van then you can come, it'll be useful to track their movements if we need CCTV feeds.'

'Great! I'll prepare everything we need, meet you at the factory?'

'Yes,' Trevor said, 'see you there at seven. Bring those night vision goggles too, they'll be very useful.'

'Will do, see ya!'

Trevor smiled as the call ended. He enjoyed the banter with Andy, especially when it came to affectionately slapping him around the head when he was out of line.

He was sure there would be plenty more of that to come, and he was looking forward to the games ahead, it brightened up some dark moments.

11

BOMB THREAT

At the factory later in the evening, Trevor gathered the Walsall contingent and laid out his plans for the night. He had given instructions for his local trainees to take over caring for the guests, with strict instructions to maintain minimum interaction, to wear face coverings and not to speak. He drilled into them that there would be consequences for them and their families if this gang were to get even the slightest whiff of who they were.

'Darren, it looks like you may be getting some action after all,' Trevor said to them.

'That's good to hear, boss, we feel like we're getting a little stale here looking after these cockroaches.'

'Well, tonight, we're going to try and round up another cluster of these cockroaches, and you guys are best suited for the job, if that works for you?'

'I told you, Frazer promised us a lively time down here, so we want to go back with some good memories, you know?'

'I know. But I must stress that these guys are as nasty as they come. You saw what they were like in the park, expect much of the same again. Only this time, you'd go better prepared, okay?'

'We hear you. What do you have for us?' asked Darren.

'Well, first off, if you want to avoid bare-knuckle fighting like you encountered before, as much as you seemed to enjoy it, then we have some items that will help. For a start, we have taser guns that will knock an elephant out. We also have some fine night-vision goggles that may come in useful, especially where we are heading, and some body armour which I insist you wear, as they will most likely be carrying knives, if not worse.'

Darren looked around to his friends, who all nodded in agreement.

'Take the zip ties with you as well, they will be very useful as this lot like to kick off. We'll have a few hours to play with, so we can pick them off a couple at a time and the van can bring them back for processing quickly, before returning for more. How's that sound?'

'Sounds good, man, so what do you have on these...cockroaches?'

'Okay, here's their info and pictures, all pretty recent, that we managed to get hold of.' He led them to the table and showed them the ten profiles he had laid out.

'So, there's only ten of them?' asked Izzy.

'That we have traced, yes, but we may be wrong, it may be slightly less or slightly more, these are the ones that we have intel on, so they'll have to do.'

All ten were seasoned criminals, some with prison history, all in their mid to late twenties. They were a step up from the regular street gangs and robbers that most police had to deal with, these were vicious individuals specially chosen for that evil streak Eastwood seemed to look for. From the phone logs, it was likely that there were two to four more in the gang, but they were more likely to be younger members on the periphery rather than the violent, seasoned robbers or burglars like this lot.

'Take your time looking through all this while I go and check on current whereabouts and progress. I'll be back with updates shortly.'

They waved him off as he went off to meet with Andy.

Andy had prepared the order in which he was going to message the targets from Brathwaite's phone. He had a map on a desk that pinpointed some of the current known addresses, and that was important so as to group the attacks.

'Are we ready to go?' asked Andy as Trevor entered the operations room.

'Yes, who have we got first?'

'First off, we have Travis Mulligan, aka Tre, and Gerry Tate, aka Sugs, who live in the same estate in Amhurst Road, Hackney, the Evelyn Court Estate. It's an old estate opposite Hackney Downs Park, so maybe consider that as an option to catch up with them? These two are the furthest away so you should probably go after them first.'

'Okay, let me send them a text and see what we can do,' said Trevor. He unlocked Brathwaite's phone and said, 'Speak of the devil, young Mr Sugs has sent a couple of messages today – *where you at, bro?* and *seriously, wass goin on?*'

'My, my, they're missing him,' Andy replied. 'What are you going to say?'

Trevor read his text out loud as he was typing it.

'*Meet in park by pavilion in one hour, can't talk now.*'

'*cool cool,*' came the reply. Trevor could sense the relief. He typed again. '*Bring Sugs.*'

'*He here, will do,*' came the swift reply.

'Okay, let's get the van down there pronto, tell Charlie to meet the guys in the loading bay and I'll go and talk to them now,' he said, 'and I'll be back for us to prep the next lot.'

'Great, see you in a bit,' Andy said, getting back to his preparations.

Less than a minute later, Trevor handed the files of the two targets to Darren and said, 'Charlie is waiting for you in the loading bay. You have a forty-five-minute drive to Hackney Downs Park, where you will sit up near the pavilion and wait for these two scrotes, who will be there in one hour. As soon as you have them, call me and we'll sort out the next, okay?'

'Will do, speak soon,' Darren said, picking up the photos.

'Charlie knows the area so he will talk you through where the best place to wait will be.'

'Woo hoo!' shouted Jimmy, as the five men ran off towards the loading bay.

'Stay safe, guys!' Trevor shouted as they left.

He returned to the briefing room where Andy had laid out the next targets.

'Meet Joseph Campbell, aka Jeps, and Ricky Ali, aka Rails. They live relatively close to each other in Bow, which is thirty-five minutes from here. Campbell lives in Winchester House, which is in Merchant Street, and Ali lives in Spanby Road, which is the other side of Tower Hamlets Cemetery. There's a small car park near a couple of the entrances in Cantrell Road, the van can sit up there quite easily, and the road there isn't overlooked by anyone. See this maze here? That would be a good place to meet them.'

He pointed to a sandy maze-like shape that had been cut in the grass, which appeared to have been put there for kids to ride their bikes around.

'Good spot, we can do that. I want to wait until the guys get back from the first outing, though, just in case.'

'Not a problem, we can plan the others in the meantime.'

They spent the next forty minutes looking over the remaining files, addresses, and likely spots where they could deal with the remaining six gang members. Their planning was meticulous, and they looked for all possible escape routes, quieter meeting places, and any potential hazards.

Trevor's phone beeped and he saw that it was a message from Darren. It said, simply, '*in position*'.

'Okay, here we go, rock and roll,' he replied, and showed Andy the message.

'*be safe,*' he responded. The thumbs-up emoji was comforting.

CHARLIE WAS able to park right by the sports pavilion, next to two council vehicles that had been left there by park staff for the night. The pavilion itself was closed, as it had been for some time. It was almost exactly centrally located in the park and had eight paths from all directions leading to it. Fortunately, several of those paths were suitable for – and used by – vehicles, so it would not be unusual to see a van driving on one of them.

As the Evelyn Court Estate was on the west side of the park, the Walsall contingent left the van and took their places on the east side of the sports pavilion, so that they would not be seen by the approaching gangsters. The park was in dark-ness now and completely empty of pedestrians; it was not a place that warranted a visit in the dark.

Almost exactly on the hour, Darren, from his vantage

point on a bench under a tree, barely visible, spotted the two gangsters walking briskly towards the red-brick building. He looked over to where Izzy was seated, similarly obscured, and Rory, also nearby, and gave them a wave. He knew where Jimmy and Clive were and relied on the others to give them the nod.

Mulligan and Tate both wore dark clothing and walked in that arrogant way wannabe gangsters did, despite the fact that there was nobody there to impress or scare. They slowed down as they went past the building, towards the circular seating in the centre. They looked around for their leader and proceeded to sit down on separate benches while they waited. It was then that Mulligan spotted Darren get up from his bench and walk towards them. It was hard to see who it was, but he was sure it wasn't Brathwaite. He hissed a warning to Tate and they both stood, wary of the approaching man.

They both slowly reached behind their lower backs, the serrated hunting knives that were placed there giving them a small degree of comfort.

'Who you, boy? You a batty man?' Tate shouted at Darren, who was now less than ten feet away. Darren raised his hands to show that he was unarmed, before stopping a safe distance from them both.

'I'm not here for a fight, gents, so hear me out, okay?'

'What you want?' Mulligan said. 'You better come out with it, or I'll cut you bad.'

He removed the bowie knife and waved it from side to side, trying to intimidate the newcomer.

'Seriously? That's all you got?' said Darren. His plan had always been to distract the men while his friends approached silently from behind. They did a fine job and were right there, undetected, just as planned.

Mulligan's confidence got the better of him as he laughed and said, 'You think you can take us both? With no weapon? Is you stupid, boy? You got a death wish?'

'No, I'm not stupid, and I didn't say I didn't have a weapon, did I?' Darren smiled as he pulled out a taser gun from his inside jacket pocket. 'Oh, and I didn't come alone, either.'

He tilted his head in acknowledgement towards his friends, making both men turn around momentarily.

'Shit, what's goin' on here? Who the fuck are you?' shouted Tate.

They were back-to-back now, moving around slowly, defending themselves as best they could against five men they'd never seen before.

'Never you mind,' said Jimmy, also holding a bright yellow taser gun.

He fired directly at Tate, aiming for the chest. He missed, hitting the right forearm, the arm he was holding the knife with. Mulligan, seeing this and anticipating the same treatment from the others, ducked behind Tate and made a run for it into the darkness. Izzy and Clive gave chase, leaving Darren, Rory and Martin to stay with Jimmy. They watched out for Jimmy but left him to deal with Tate alone, confident of the outcome.

The taser did not have the same effect as it would have had in the chest, but it was still painful, and Tate shuddered from the sudden shock. He was quick-thinking, though, and managed to yank the barbs out with his other hand, pulling at them to drag Jimmy towards him. His right arm was numb from the shock and the pain. Jimmy was unprepared for this and was met with a crashing left-hook from Tate, who was starting to gain some mobility with his right arm. Jimmy, stunned by the blow, reeled backwards out of harm's way. What Tate didn't know was that Jimmy was a champion boxer and recovered far quicker than he did. As mobility in his arm continued to improve, he wielded his knife more freely, from left to right, and moved towards Jimmy, his confidence growing. Jimmy was expecting this and ducked under the attack, grabbing Tate's knife arm with one hand and his face with the other, shoving him down towards the ground.

Tate screamed in pain as his contorted body was rammed to the ground, his legs splayed behind him. Jimmy's move had been so fast that he didn't have time to shift his feet, leaving them anchored to the floor and making Jimmy's move all the more effective.

His back and leg muscles were strained to breaking point, and the pain only eased when Jimmy turned him to his side, having removed the knife from his right hand. Tate whimpered as Jimmy quickly secured his wrists with zip ties.

'There you go, all sorted,' he said. 'Good punch, though, mate,' he added, rubbing his jaw. He turned to see his friends clapping and laughing.

'What are you laughing at?'

'That was a good punch you took there, mate, I can't remember the last time you let someone in that close,' said Rory.

'Yeah, well, learn from that, because it's what happens when you're too confident.' Jimmy pulled Tate to his feet.

'Let's go and see how Clive and Izzy are getting on,' said Darren, turning towards the direction they had given chase.

Fifty yards away, in the gloom, they could make out some figures struggling with each other.

Darren arrived just as Mulligan was removing his knife from Izzy's side, which wasn't protected by the vest he was wearing. Izzy dropped to the floor, the taser gun dropping from his numb hand. At the same time, Mulligan received a savage punch to the temple from Clive, knocking him out instantly. Clive went to the aid of his friend.

'Izzy!' he shouted.

Darren arrived with the others, Martin and Rory securing the still-unconscious Mulligan while he helped Clive to stem the flow of blood from his stomach.

'Rory, go and get Charlie to drive the van as close as he can. Let's get these bastards in the back asap. Clive, let me check the wound,' he said, moving Clive's hand away from it.

Izzy moaned from the pain, barely conscious. Darren lifted his t-shirt and saw the wound, which was still pulsing blood. It seemed such an innocuous cut, barely an inch and a half, but it was deep. Fortunately for Izzy, it was his side and not his stomach, and Darren hoped it had missed his internal organs.

'We need to apply pressure to the wound, like Frazer taught us. Martin, cut this bastard's hoodie off with his knife so I can use it to stop the flow. Clive, hold it here until we get the van, Charlie may have some kit with him. I need to call Trevor and let him know what's going on.'

His friends quietly but efficiently carried out their instructions, and within thirty seconds Clive was stanching the blood with Mulligan's hoodie.

Darren called Trevor to let him know that they'd be making a hospital stop on the way back with the van, and that they would be delayed and two men down, as someone needed to stay with Izzy.

'They'll probably call the police, so whoever stays with

him will be there for a while, okay?' Trevor said.

'I understand, but we can't leave Izzy on his own, we'll just have to manage without him.'

'Don't worry about that; Darren, get your boy safely to hospital and bring those bastards to the factory.'

Charlie arrived with the van as the phone call ended. Trevor's right-hand man quickly alighted from the vehicle with a first-aid kit and ran to attend to Izzy.

'Make some room here, guys, let me have a look,' he said, opening the kit.

Clive removed the hoodie. The wound was clean, and the blood had slowed down.

'That's good, I think he's a lucky boy and it hasn't damaged his intestines. I'll patch him up here, but we need to get him to a doctor now.'

They gently helped Izzy into the front of the van, with Clive next to him on the double seat. Mulligan and Tate were secured in the back, and had their legs tied to avoid any thrashing around.

'I should kill that bastard,' said Clive.

'Don't worry, mate, there is a worse fate in store for him when Trevor gets hold of him.'

The van pulled away slowly, with Charlie waiting until he was on one of the paths before picking up speed.

'I know a doctor who may be able to help,' he told Darren. 'And it's not too far out of the way. We can try there first, and if he recommends medical attention then we can go from there. You cool with that? If our friend here has got internal injuries then only a hospital will do, but Doc will be able to check whether that is the case.'

'Sounds good, Charlie, thank you.'

'No need, my friend, no need.'

12

ANDY SAVES THE DAY

'Is he going to be okay?' asked Andy, after Trevor had told him of the incident.

'They think so, it's a deep wound but Charlie has dressed it and is taking him to a doctor pal to check for internal injuries. If he doesn't have any, he may not need to go to hospital, so we'll have to wait and see.'

'So, what happens now? We're two men down, will we make it in time?'

'It's going to be really tight, I'm not sure. There is only one way I can think of to take all six out,' Trevor said, immediately regretting his words.

Andy beamed in anticipation. 'You mean us, don't you? The dream team on the road facing danger at every turn. It's us, right?'

Trevor shook his head, not to dampen Andy's enthusiasm, but to denote regret. Andy could tell and raised his arm in the air in triumph.

'Yes! Come on!' he yelled.

'Seriously, don't make me change my mind. Is Marge ready to go?'

'Marge is always ready!'

'Right, so Darren and whoever he is left with will be dropping Izzy and Clive off, before coming here to drop those scumbags off. They will then go and take on Joseph Campbell and Ricky Ali. That leaves us with the other two shits, Maurice Young, aka Mo, and Luka Novak, aka Ivan. They're the closest to the factory in Forest Gate, so we need to find somewhere we can lure them to.'

They both examined the map on the computer.

'Young lives in Kitchener Road and Novak in Forest Street, so how about here,' Andy said, pointing to the northern part of West Ham Park.

'There is a cricket club there, so it wouldn't be out of place to see someone driving around to deliver or pick something up,' Andy continued. 'If we get them to meet us by the changing rooms, we'll be hidden from the housing in Ham Park Road and so should be able to take them out there. What do you think?'

'I'm not happy with taking the camper van down there, no. How about you park it here,' he said, pointing to Reginald Road, around a hundred yards away and out of sight. 'It's less than a minute away, and then when we take them out you can drive in and pick us all up.'

'Wait, what do you mean? Who's we? I thought I was doing this with you!'

'Mate, you are lucky to be involved at all, this lot are as nasty as I've ever seen, and they've just badly wounded an experienced fighter. You were never going to be involved in any confrontation.'

'So, who are you taking?' Andy asked.

'I'll take Kendra and the twins. I'll make sure that we're all masked and kitted up. The four of us should be enough.'

Andy paused for a moment, trying to think of a reason to be upset. He could not fault Trevor's decision but it didn't sit right with him that he wasn't able to contribute physically, or that he couldn't protect Kendra as he was previously able to.

'Fine, but at some point, I will be getting more involved, okay? I'm not a desk jockey and I deserve to be out there again.'

'I hear you, Andy, but until your surgery heals completely there is no way I want to risk you. You are way too valuable to this operation to put yourself in danger for scumbags like that.'

Andy nodded. 'Okay, I get it. I'll get ready myself and will meet you in the van. And to be clear, surgery was successful, and the pain isn't bad at all, so it is going much better than planned, okay?'

Trevor nodded and picked up his phone to call Kendra. 'How are you doing, love?'

'Good, I should be with you in about five minutes. Everything okay?'

'We've had a bit of an incident, but I'll explain when you get here, on the way to Forest Gate.'

'Wait, what? Incident? Forest Gate? What the hell have I missed?'

'Speak soon, K.' He ended the call and went over in his head what was required, making sure all bases were covered. He went downstairs and spoke to Mo and Amir, who were delighted to be involved and quickly went off to don their kit.

He then spoke with the guys that were guarding Brathwaite and his other friends and informed them of the incoming van so that they could be prepared for those and the others due later in the evening.

'Go get 'em, boss,' one of them said as he walked off. Trevor waved in response and went out to the yard.

'I'm too old for this shit,' he said out loud, 'but I wouldn't swap it for anything.'

Despite the setback with Izzy, he was still able to smile, enjoying the thrill of it all. Now I know why Kendra loves her job so much. Who knew, eh?

THE FIVE MET in the rear yard where Marge had been parked. They were all now fully prepared with their protective vests and other accessories. As Andy drove them away from the factory, Trevor explained what had happened to Izzy and the others.

'And that's why we're doing this, to make sure we take these arseholes off the streets before they kill anyone.'

He showed them the photographs of Young and Novak and explained the plan.

'When we're parked up, I'm going to send a message from Brathwaite asking for them to meet him by the cricket changing rooms. Andy will be parked nearby, and we will go on foot and cover the meeting point here and here,' he said, pointing to the places mentioned on the map displayed on one of the monitors.

'Andy will come and pick us all up when we have got them under control. It'll be a tight squeeze back here, but we should manage. Remember to keep your masks on in their presence and don't speak unless you have to, okay?'

They all nodded in understanding as the photos and

intelligence were passed between them as they approached the park.

'I'll drop you off here, there's nobody around so you won't attract too much attention,' Andy said, pulling over just short of the entrance. 'I'll be close by, so call if you need anything.'

'Thanks, Andy, see you soon,' said Trevor, as they all alighted and moved off towards the park entrance, before taking their places.

Trevor and Amir stayed near the changing rooms, sitting on a bench by the poorly lit path. Kendra and Mo were close by, at another bench. From both positions they were able to watch for anyone approaching from the two closest entrances, as the gates to the park were still open, which also made it easy for Andy to drive in when needed.

'Okay, let's rock and roll,' Trevor said as he typed out his message to Young.

'*Mo, need to see you now. Meet by changing rooms in west ham park. Big job coming.*'

There was no response initially and Trevor thought his plan had failed, before the phone beeped in response, much to his relief.

'*where you been, man? we been callin ages now. wass going on?*'

'*get here now and I'll tell you. Callin Ivan too, need u both,*' Trevor replied.

'*I hear u.*'

Trevor then repeated the message to Novak, who also acknowledged and said he'd be five minutes.

'Okay, get ready, they'll both be here soon, so keep an eye out.'

It wasn't long before Kendra noticed a car pulling up to the entrance that she and Mo were covering. She heard the engine switch off and one door being closed, indicating a lone occupant.

'Here we go, Mo, get ready,' she said. They both pulled their masks up.

They sat on the bench in the shadows and watched the silhouette of a tall man walk into the park and continue on the path towards the changing rooms. His pace was swift and confident, and he made progress with a swagger. As he got close to the building, he shouted, 'Yo, where you at, bro?'

Kendra recognised him as Maurice Young.

When there was no reply to his call, Young changed course, aiming for the closest bench. It was as he sat down that he noticed the two people coming towards him from the trees, at pace. It was then he realised they were wearing masks and stood hurriedly, looking around for more potential threats. He immediately pulled a long slim-bladed knife from behind his back and waved it slowly in front of him.

'You better turn back and piss off out of here, now,' he threatened. Kendra and Mo stopped just ten feet away from him. They separated so that they could cover the knifeman better, keeping their eyes on him.

'Put that down, Mo,' Kendra said, hoping to surprise the man. 'We don't want to hurt you, okay?'

Kendra was right, he was surprised.

'What, are you pigs? What ya want wiv me?'

He continued to wave the knife, but there was uncertainty in his voice.

'I told you, we don't want to hurt you, so don't make me use this,' she said, pulling out the taser gun from her jacket pocket.

Young laughed nervously, and said, 'What you gonna do with that, bitch?'

'Why don't I show you?' Kendra replied, firing the taser and taking him by surprise. It hit him square in the chest. His t-shirt presented no obstacle to the vicious barbs that were embedded in his skin and sending thirty thousand volts into his unprotected body. He fell to the ground, face-forward, as if he were a plank of wood, and started thrashing around uncontrollably from the shock. It lasted just five seconds but seemed like five minutes to him. The lethal knife dropped from his hand and was collected by the smiling Mo.

Within a few seconds of the convulsions ending, his wrists were zip tied and he had been searched and all his possessions taken from him, including his phone and car keys. They were all placed in the bag that Mo had been carrying in his pocket, which was preventing his phone from being tracked.

'Let's move him to the bench until Andy comes to get us,' Kendra said, as they dragged him unceremoniously to the nearest one. In no position to resist, Young moaned as he recovered from the shock.

Kendra took her phone out and called her dad to see if there had been any sighting of Novak.

'Hang on, love, I think that's him just turning up,' Trevor said, quickly hanging up.

He was right, it was Novak that was approaching them from the other entrance. From what he could tell, Novak was on the phone, but he couldn't hear him speaking. As Novak approached them, he called out, 'Yo, Mo, you here, man? Denny ain't answering again, bruv.'

It was then he saw Trevor and Amir, both masked, approaching quickly from the side. 'Shit,' he said, and pulled out his weapon from his waistband.

Luckily for Trevor and Amir, Novak had panicked and

was running on adrenaline when he pulled out his Beretta 9000. The 9mm self-loading pistol was a favourite with London gangs. He aimed towards Trevor and Amir, who were closing in fast, and pulled the trigger twice. The adrenaline had affected his already poor aim and his shots were well wide of the mark. Trevor and Amir both ducked instinctively.

Novak took the opportunity and bolted back in the other direction. They both gave chase but were soon fifty yards behind, and he was fast. The adrenaline may have affected his aim, but it was aiding his getaway. He soon reached the fencing that ran around the park and quickly vaulted over, running towards Warwick Road. Trevor stopped and called Andy immediately.

'Andy, Novak is getting away! He's just entered Warwick Road, so keep an eye out!'

'Roger!' Andy replied, and Trevor resumed his running.

Novak was familiar with the streets and wanted to weave his way through them to avoid detection. He turned and saw the two men behind him, some hundred yards behind. As he turned into Reginald Road, he saw an opportunity to gain some distance and aimed to turn immediately left into Stork Road. He crossed the road, still running at full pace, and went to run alongside a large white van on foreign plates, before making the turn into Stork Road. As he reached the van, which was facing towards him, the passenger door unexpectedly opened. He had nowhere to go and hurtled straight into it at full speed, dropping like a log. He was dazed as he lay on the ground but still very much conscious and stood up quickly, picking up his gun. Looking around, he couldn't yet see his pursuers.

As he was about to resume his running, he was met by a strange-looking man who wore an eye patch and leaned on a cane. 'I should kill you, fool,' he said, raising the Beretta at Andy.

Andy's move was slightly quicker, as he smashed the lead-weighted cane into Novak's gun hand. The Beretta once again fell to the ground as Novak briefly grabbed his throbbing wrist before reaching for the gun again. Andy quickly reversed his cane and struck him on the head, dropping him to the ground instantly. It was at that moment that Trevor and Mo arrived, both out of breath, to see Andy breathing on his cane and polishing it melodramatically. They watched, open-mouthed.

'One of my toys,' Andy said nonchalantly, before pulling a slim rapier-type sword out of it.

'I never got to use the sword though, shame.'

'Quickly, let's move this bastard into the van before anyone sees us,' Trevor said, quickly zip-tying Novak's wrists. Seconds later, the assailant was safely secure in the back of the van, where his feet were also bound. The gun and his other belongings were safely secured. He could see some curtains twitching and hoped that nobody had had the sense to take Marge's number plate, although Andy had changed the real plates to German ones.

'Let's go get the others,' Trevor told Andy, who was now back in the driver's seat.

'No problem, heading there now,' Andy replied, as if nothing had happened.

'Good job, man, good job,' Trevor said, patting him on the shoulder. 'That was turning into a very bad situation.'

'It's nothing, Trev, it's what I'm here for, right?'

They quickly reached Kendra and Mo, who both looked relived to see them.

'What the hell happened? We heard the shots and then nothing. Are you okay, Dad?' she asked.

'We're fine, love, it's all under control, thanks to this young man here,' Trevor said, his thumb aimed at a smiling Andy.

'I got to use my cane! Life is good!'

'Let's get the hell out of here before we're spotted,' Kendra said, shaking her head. Within a minute they were back on the road to the factory.

Trevor, who was sat in the front with Andy, called Darren for an update.

'Thanks, Darren, great job tonight, honestly, I can't thank you enough. Frazer is gonna want a bloody big drink out of this, I tell you!'

As he ended the call he turned to speak with Kendra and the twins in the back.

'Good news, guys. Izzy is gonna be just fine. It's a nasty cut but the doctor sewed him up, he'll be as good as new in a few weeks, and up and walking around in a couple of days.'

'That's fantastic, Dad,' said Kendra. 'How did they get on with the other two?'

'After they took Izzy and Clive off to the doctor's, they dropped Mulligan and Tate off at the factory and then went straight back out to get Campbell and Ali. The three of them managed it just fine, with Charlie's help, and they're also now back at the factory. So, despite a setback or two, tonight has been a success. We can now move on to tomorrow and how we're going to deal with Eastwood.'

'We have time, boss, don't worry,' Mo said, 'now that the soldiers are out of action, the army has nowhere to go, right?'

'I wish it were that easy,' Trevor said. 'Remember, that son of a bitch lives in a bloody fortress, and it's not going to be easy to get him out of there.'

'Don't worry, Dad, we'll find a way. Right, Andy?'

'Right, K, and it will also give me a chance to use my other new toy. It's going to get very interesting.'

'He loves his new toys, doesn't he?' said Kendra, secretly delighted with Andy.

'Well, if the new one is anything like the cane he surprised us all with, then it should be a real good 'un,' said Trevor.

THE DRIVE to the factory didn't take long, but it gave time for Young and Novak, who had recovered from their ordeal, to shout obscenities and threats to their masked captors.

'You gonna die, bitches, you don't know who you're messin' wiv,' shouted Young.

'You heard good, there's a world of pain comin' your way, you hear?' added Novak.

They both shut up quickly when Kendra pulled out the taser gun and aimed it at their faces.

'Carry on and I'll use my friend again, okay?'

They arrived at the factory and both captors were removed and placed into custody.

'Remember to explain to them what happens if they step out of line,' Trevor said as they were led away.

'We'll go and help with that, boss,' Mo said, leaving with Amir. 'We don't want these youngsters to mess up now, do we?' They both laughed as they left.

'Right, let's go and have a chat, to see how we are going to take care of young Mr Eastwood, eh?' said Trevor, leading them towards the operations room.

───────

'THE ONLY REALISTIC way of grabbing the bastard is on the street, we have no chance of getting to him up in his flat,' said Andy.

'Let's not be too hasty,' Kendra added, 'we need to research the tower block and surroundings more, okay? Without having any idea of his usual regular movements, we will fail, so we need to take our time and do this properly.'

'Kendra's right, Andy, we don't know how he gets about, who he is with, or anything like that. He could get picked up by a small army each day, we don't know.'

'Of course, I get it, so we have to put something in place to find out, right?' Andy replied. 'That way we can plan something concrete instead of hoping something goes our way.'

'What are you thinking?' Kendra asked.

'Well, I told you I have a bunch of new toys, didn't I? That includes a couple of drones I purchased while I was away. Two beauties they are, too.'

'What can we do with drones, then?' asked Trevor.

'Well, one of the drones, who I shall call Mabel, can stay in the air for about half an hour and take fantastic 4K images or live video from around four hundred feet. We can programme her to stay in the same place for that time and monitor activity from Marge. All we need is a heads-up that Eastwood is on the move, and I can launch her.'

'Can we use your miniature cameras for that?'

'Absolutely. We put a couple to cover the back exits and one at the front, shouldn't be too difficult.'

'What's the difference between these drones and the one you had before?' asked Trevor.

'These are teeny tiny, so nobody will see them or hear them at all. Mabel fits in the palm of my hand and Tim is even smaller.'

'Tim?'

'Tim is the size of my index finger. He is designed specifically to spy in enclosed areas. You can't hear him at all, even if you're ten feet away. He can get into the smallest of spaces, too; he is going to be very useful.'

'Well, what do I know?' said Trevor. 'Just don't expect me to fly them, is all.'

'Don't worry about that,' Andy said. 'Mabel I can pre-programme and just press a button for her to launch, do her thing, and then land again. Tim is different, I'll have to fly him. I have special goggles for the whole 3D experience.' He was in his element and enjoying every second of it.

'Well, this is all great, Andy, but it doesn't really help us when it comes to taking him out, does it?' Kendra said, stating the obvious.

'If we can find out where they keep their cars, how many people travel with him, if the flat is left unoccupied, all this is very useful intelligence, K. We can plan around that. As for taking him out, we have other means for that.'

'Please enlighten us,' she said, crossing her arms defiantly.

'I will try,' Andy said, smiling at her discomfort. 'Look, we already have some good kit, the masks, body armour, taser guns and so on, right?'

Trevor and Kendra both nodded.

'Well, this Russian dude is bound to have a bunch of

heavies with him, like the report said about the party. So, we find a way to even the odds a bit more in our favour, that's all.'

'Stop beating around the bush and tell us, will you,' Trevor said, a little louder than he had intended.

'Okay, chill out. I was able to procure some CS gas, for one. If we wear the masks, they will protect us from the gas and we can pick him out from his crowd and take him without the heavies even realising.'

'That sounds way too simple,' Kendra said.

'Why should it be difficult? This isn't a movie or anything, the simple stuff is usually the best, isn't it?'

'Yes, but—'

'No buts, we keep it simple. We look at how they operate for a few days, get some patterns, and then we can decide the time and place. Simple.'

Trevor and Kendra exchanged a look, shrugged, and then nodded in agreement.

'Great, now can I go home and sleep? It's not like I'm getting any overtime or anything,' Andy said, yawning.

'Good call, I'm knackered too. Let's pick this up tomorrow,' Trevor said, patting Andy on the back and giving Kendra one of his trademark hugs. 'Great work today, both of you. Shall I drop you off, love?'

'Yes please,' Kendra said. She gave Andy a peck on the cheek and whispered, 'Night night, hero boy.'

His exhaustion vanished and he sat up straight, watching them both leave, wishing he could go with them.

13

CYCLOPS

Kendra was at the office the next day, keeping up appearances in her part-time role. The research to find Eastwood had been very useful, but now she wanted to see what was going on with the investigation into her team.

'Has there been any progress at all?' she asked Gerrardo.

'Nope. Your friendly douchebag was here for hours yesterday, ordering us around like he was the king of the hill. Man, that guy is vile in so many ways.'

'Don't worry about him, he's just here to make up the numbers. They won't find a thing,' she replied confidently.

'I hope so, I just want things to go back to how they were before, you know, nice and peaceful and productive.' He left for his own desk, unsmiling and unhappy. Two qualities that seemed to be common whenever Detective Sergeant Eddie Duckmore was around.

Kendra logged into her system and went through some routine admin, before deciding to speak with Rick Watts and see whether they had made any progress upstairs.

'Sit down, K,' he said, gesturing to the seat in front of his desk. 'How's it going downstairs?'

'It isn't, really. We haven't found anything new, other than to confirm that Duckmore rubs absolutely everyone up the wrong way.'

'Well, he may be a gigantic dick, but he's here to do a job so we just have to accept him being here and get on with ours, okay?'

'Yes, Sarge, I get it. Is there anything new to report?'

'Well, I sent some of the gang out to speak to some neighbours of Qupi's goons, to see if anything was amiss. One neighbour of Altin Kola, one of the lieutenants that lived in Romford, wasn't around when we investigated first time around. She told Jillian that she had been up late one night and heard a noise from the road. When she got to the window, she saw a couple of men load some bags into a van and then drive off. She didn't think anything of it until the next day when another van turned up and took furniture and a bunch more things. She just thought it odd as the people looked in a real hurry to load up and leave.'

'So how does that help?' Kendra asked, slightly nervous about the answer she was about to receive.

'It may not help at all, but I'm going to send someone to the area to see if there's any CCTV footage. You never know, a number plate may lead to something.'

'That may help. Well, let me know if there's anything I can help with, okay? I'll be downstairs in our poky little office,' she said, smiling.

'Your choice, Detective, remember?' Watts said, smiling back, 'now get out of here and let me get on with some work.'

'Yes sir!' she faked a salute and left his office.

She headed straight for the exit to the back yard, where she called Andy with some urgency.

'Andy, listen, they're sending someone to Romford to check on Altin Kola, one of Qupi's goons. A neighbour saw a couple of our vans, so they're hoping to find some footage in the area. Should we be worried?'

'Leave it with me, I'll get Cyclops on the case,' Andy said, and hung up. He had been able to access many CCTV servers with Cyclops, and Kendra was now crossing her fingers that he would be able to do so again with the local council in Romford.

This could get messy, she thought.

As ANDY WAS STILL at home, he quickly went to his basement operations room where he attempted to access the London Borough of Havering's CCTV suite. His fingers flowed over the keyboard as he activated the Cyclops programme and was soon able to enter the servers that the council used. Remembering the days in question, Andy was able to locate the CCTV in the Romford area where Altin Kola lived, and the surrounding area within a half-mile radius. Thankfully, there weren't as many as he had feared, as the council preferred to focus on busy junctions or areas that had been targeted in the past.

Double-checking the dates and locations, he deleted the files for that area, for a one-month period, covering his tracks so as not to make it obvious what he was trying to hide. When it came to it, any operator would see only a bunch of missing files and would be unable to explain, other than there was a glitch in the system and no files were to be found.

As soon as he had completed his task, he relaxed and messaged Kendra with the following,

'Andy saves the day ... again. I want cupcakes!'

Kendra replied with a facepalm emoji.

Andy tried to hide his disappointment at the reply but quickly cheered up again when she sent another message — this time with three simple kisses.

He started preparing his mini drones for the surveillance operation later, pausing to smile — and to hope.

———

'OKAY, HERE GOES,' Trevor said, typing out the message on Brathwaite's phone. *'Boss man, the park is closed. Pigs are everywhere. We can't go in.'*

He waited for several minutes before Eastwood replied. *'Tomorrow,'* was all that he sent. He was clearly disappointed.

'Great, that gives us some breathing space.' Trevor sighed with relief.

———

THE DAY PASSED QUICKLY and without any further incidents or concerns for Kendra, who left the station and drove straight to the factory where she had arranged to meet with the other two. In addition to the surveillance on Eastwood, they had to decide how they were going to 'relocate' their current guests, because the longer they held them, the higher the risk. Trevor had sent some of the youngsters to collect cars that had been left behind by Novak and Young, who had both driven to the park. The cars were sent straight to Stav for the usual stripping and disposal. The gangsters would never see their pride and joys again.

'What are your thoughts on this, Andy?' she asked, as they sat to discuss the evening ahead.

'We'll take Marge and park close to the tower, in line of sight and without any obstructions for the drones. Mabel has been programmed to go up to four hundred feet above the tower and hover there for thirty to forty minutes before returning to her launch pad and landing automatically. I just need to tweak the programme when we get there, in case we need to park somewhere else. Miniature cameras have been installed to cover all three exits to the tower block, and they have all been checked and work just fine. As soon as we get any indication that Eastwood is on the move then I will launch Mabel. I can then check the penthouse for any activity, in case they leave someone behind. If it's all clear, I'll send Tim to have a closer look. Mabel can get a change of batteries and be ready to go up again if there is any other activity. I'll need one of you two to do that, it's pretty easy.'

'When you say easy, do you really mean that?'

'Yes, Detective, I mean that. You basically swap the battery over with a new one, I'll show you when we get there.'

'Okay, then, let's get ready to go,' Trevor said.

'Dad, what about the scumbags, what's the latest on them being moved out?'

'Don't worry, love, I have Bruno on the case, and he'll be popping over tonight to sort that out.' He smiled mischievously, still pleased with their decision. Bruno was the man on the ground at the nearby docks, who had proven himself invaluable when relocating the Qupis back in the day. His services, it seemed, would be required regularly.

'Good enough for me,' Andy said, grabbing a holdall and moving towards the door. 'Let's hustle, people!'

'Andy, that is a terrible American accent, don't do that again,' Kendra said, shaking her head.

———

BRUNO WAS true to his word and arrived at the factory with a lorry carrying the modified container that had been used in the previous operation. He had made sure it had been returned, something that took many weeks, and it didn't take much time to refurbish it for the new guests. As with the Albanians, the container was supplied with plenty of bottled water and food that would last the long journey, likely to take several weeks. The refreshments would all contain something to keep them semi-sedated for most of the trip, so that they didn't cause too many problems on the way.

Bruno smiled when he saw the ten passengers, Trevor having told him what they had done.

As they were brought out, one at a time, still groggy from the crushed sleeping pills they had ingested at the last meal, Bruno took great pleasure in threatening them with their lives if they were to cause any problems on the journey.

'I will skin you alive, you worthless piece of shit,' he said, many times.

On their own, they did not resist in the slightest as they took their places within the container. Brathwaite was the last one brought out. He was wide-eyed as he tried to fight the sedatives.

'Ah, the big man himself,' Bruno said. Brathwaite stood his ground, defiant to the last.

'I have a special word for you, boy, just one word,'

continued Bruno. 'Remember this when you are thinking of causing me trouble along the way — castration.'

Bruno then pulled out a rusty machete that had seen better days, but which looked like it had seen a lot of action. He raised it above his head, glaring into Brathwaite's face.

Brathwaite knew that confrontation would be futile and raised his arms in fear, giving no resistance as he was placed in the container with his cohorts. He whimpered the entire time as he sat down, his head hung low in defeat. He had no words.

'Remember how you feel now, next time you want to act the big men and hurt people. You are nothing but scum, the lowest form of life. And you are cowards that feed on vulnerable people. You deserve a lot worse than you are getting, remember that too.'

Most did not have the courage to look him in the eye.

'One last thing. Where you are going, if you even look at someone the wrong way, or say one word without permission, they will hack pieces from your body until there is nothing left. Do not forget this, if you want to live. Again, it is what you deserve for what you have done.'

There were more whimpers from within the container as realisation dawned upon its occupants.

'Close it up,' Bruno said, smiling at the guards, who were relieved to be rid of the robbers.

The container doors were shut and padlocked. The key was discreetly hidden where it would be retrieved at the destination by Bruno's contact. The container was ready to go.

'Thank you, my friends, tell Trevor to keep them coming.' He waved to Trevor's men and walked to the cabin. He jumped into the driver's seat, started the engine, and then drove slowly out of the loading bay, as he waited for the shutters to be fully opened.

As the lorry drove out of the factory, the guards still had no idea of where the robbers would end up, only that they would not be troubling anyone for a very long time.

'Job well done,' Amir said to his brothers as the shutters closed. 'That is one nasty group of individuals.'

'Yep, let's get some drinks and celebrate, the guys deserve it.'

14

DRONE SURVEILLANCE

Andy parked Marge less than a hundred yards away from the tower block, in the Gillett Street car park at the other side of the railway lines. Far enough away that they wouldn't raise any concerns but close enough to safely launch the larger of the two drones, Mabel, when Eastwood was spotted. He had found a quiet spot in the corner which wouldn't attract any attention to their endeavours, whilst also hiding much of what they would be doing behind Marge.

Andy retrieved a drone landing pad from one of the cupboards and placed it alongside the van. The metre-square orange pad had a large white H stencilled in the middle of a white circle which would be the take-off and landing coordinate programmed into the drone. Once this was done, the drone would take off at the touch of a button and then fly to its predetermined coordinates, where it would hover for thirty to forty minutes, streaming a live feed to Marge in thermal as well as normal view, until the battery was low enough that it had to automatically return to the pad.

'This is all you have to do,' he told them both, depressing two buttons on the sides of the drone that released the battery, before replacing it with a charged one.

'When you hear the click it is ready to go, so just press the button on the controller and it will take off and do the same pre-programmed flight again,' he continued.

'Huh,' said Kendra, 'it actually is easy.'

'And we have four spare batteries, so plenty for what we need to do.'

'So, to be clear, we launch Mabel when we see that he is on the move, right?' asked Trevor. 'I still can't believe some of these names,' he added, shaking his head.

'Yes, the cameras covering the exits are all working fine. As soon as we see him, the drone will launch and be in the air within seconds, and in position in a minute or so.'

'Great, well, I'm gonna have a nap while you two keep an eye out, okay?' Trevor said, lying down on the bench.

'If he farts again, I'm going for a long walk,' Andy said, pinching his nose.

'Yeah, that took me by surprise, too,' Kendra replied. 'Shame on you, Dad.'

Trevor laughed out loud. 'Well, you wanted pizza and beer, this is what happens.'

Andy and Kendra shared a look and both shrugged their shoulders, turning towards the monitors to take up watch.

'Let's hope we don't have long to wait,' she said.

IT WAS early evening when the cameras detected movement at one of the exits in Boleyn Road, at the rear of the tower block.

'Stand by,' Andy said. 'Seems like a couple of heavies coming out and having a good look around, this could be Eastwood's men paving the way.'

Sure enough, one man stayed by the door while two others turned and walked south away from the exit. Trevor was instantly awake, rubbing his eyes as he looked at the monitor.

'Where are they going, then?' Kendra queried. 'Is it worth sending the drone up now?'

'Yeah, I think so,' said Andy, sliding along the bench to the next computer terminal. He pressed a few buttons on the keyboard to activate the drone. They could hear the faint whirring of the propellors just outside the van as it prepared to take off.

'Safe journey, Mabel,' Andy said, as he slid back to the monitor. The guard was still by the door. They could see that he held a walkie-talkie type radio, which he spoke into very briefly every thirty seconds or so.

'They seem to know their stuff, his protectors,' Trevor said, thinking it would make for a difficult takedown.

'Mabel is up and in place,' Andy said, sliding back to the other terminal. The monitor above it came alive but didn't show much due to the gloom and lack of light. 'I'll switch to the thermal camera, maybe that will help,' he said.

As the thermal camera activated, Kendra could see immediately that it was more effective. She saw the bright splodge of the guard by the exit, and several others of pedestrians walking in the vicinity.

'Is that the other two guys?' Trevor asked, pointing to two bright blobs in a neighbouring yard, which looked more like a loading bay. There were also two small but growing spots of light that were very close to the men.

'That may be them in a couple of cars that they've just started,' Andy said. 'We'll find out in a minute if they move.'

The two fainter bright lights grew larger as the engines warmed up, and then they both slowly started to move towards the gated exit.

'Okay, they're on the move; if it's them, we should see movement by the tower block,' Andy said.

'Yep, our guy with the radio just spoke into it and is now holding the door open. Stand by,' Trevor replied.

Seconds later, the two cars turned right and stopped by the first guard, double-parking in the street.

Turning to the other monitor, Kendra could see a fourth heavy, also carrying a radio, come out of the doorway, look around, and then extend an arm in invitation to someone behind him.

'Here we go,' she said.

'And bingo, there's our guy,' Andy said triumphantly. The cameras were small but high- definition, so the picture quality was excellent. They saw Eastwood come out, dressed in a suit, striding confidently towards one of the cars that waited for him. One of the other heavies was there waiting for him, door open, looking around to make sure his boss was safe. As soon as he was in, the guard moved to the front passenger seat and got in. The other guard joined the driver in the car behind. Seconds later the convoy moved away, northbound in Boleyn Road and out of sight of the cameras.

'Couldn't see the number plates but I recognised the vehicles. They were both Range Rovers and are probably protected with bullet-proof glass and the full works,' Andy said.

'Never mind the cars, or the at least four very large guards that Eastwood has with him at all times, this is not going to be an easy one, is it?' Trevor replied.

'When is it ever easy, Trev?' Andy said. 'We just have to play smart here, that's all. Just because they're big and strong doesn't mean we can't beat them, does it?'

'I like your confidence, Andy, but I also like to hear a good plan, so whenever you're ready, let me know it, okay?'

'Well, first off, I'd like to learn more about where the cars were stashed, so we need to investigate that place next door. It's quite a big yard, triangular-shaped, with not a lot else in it other than some sheds up against the far wall. It's likely that he owns it or rents it just for his cars.'

'It's nice to have money like that, isn't it?' Trevor added.

'Trev, we have money too, remember? Qupi was very generous.' Andy grinned.

'Fair enough. So we can take a look there later when it's quieter. What else are you thinking?'

'We get Mabel back here and send Tim up for a closer look. It would be good to know if anyone else is in the flat, more guards, possibly.'

'Let's do it,' Kendra said, eager to see what Eastwood's penthouse flat was like. 'It may give us clues about what the hell he is doing, because I currently have no clue.'

'Let me get Mabel back and I'll get Tim ready,' Andy said, sending the retrieval signal.

Less than a minute later, they heard the faint whirring of her propellers as she landed back on the landing pad, exactly as programmed.

'I'll get her. I mean it. Stupid name anyway,' Trevor said, stepping out of the camper van and into the car park. He picked Mabel up, amazed at the lightness, along with the landing pad, and was back inside in seconds.

'I'll change the battery, in case we need her again later,' Kendra said.

Andy readied his goggles for when Tim was airborne. The controller for the tiny drone was much larger than the drone itself and it was held at his midriff by a strap around his neck. Before releasing the drone, he checked the toggles and switches to make sure everything worked fine, before going outside.

'Okay, fly safe, Tiny Tim,' he said, holding out his hand with Tim nestled like a giant insect in the middle of his palm. It looked like a miniature military helicopter, completely black, with forward-facing miniature cameras. It wasn't fast, at only thirteen miles per hour, and only had a one-mile range, but that was ideal for missions like this; the almost silent rotors made it perfect for covert operations.

The barely audible whir of the spinning rotors was followed by the tiny flying machine lifting out of Andy's hand and rising silently through the air. Within seconds it was invisible to the naked eye, in hover mode fifty feet above his head.

'That's better,' he said, as the night vision camera streamed the high-definition live feed to the inside of his futuristic goggles. As he worked the controls, he looked up instinctively, following Tim's path toward the tower block's roof.

'This is so cool,' Andy said, 'you won't believe how clear the image is on these things. I'll transfer it to the monitor so you can see it there too.'

'Okay, let's go, Dad,' Kendra said, turning to go back into the van.

'Wait up,' Andy said, 'can you guide me back inside, too?

I'll look like an idiot out here if anyone comes by. I can do this from inside.'

Kendra and Trevor grabbed an arm each and gently guided him back into the van. They sat him on the bench and he continued to look up, as if staring into space.

'That just looks weird,' Trevor said, sitting opposite.

'Wow, he's not wrong, Dad, look at this.'

The image on the monitor was crystal clear as Tim made his way up; they could see what people had on their balconies, even see into their rooms where the windows were open or there were no curtains. It was almost as if they were there.

'Bloody hell,' Trevor exclaimed, 'how can something so small give such a good quality picture?'

'Tim is a military drone, Trev, designed by a genius in Norway who saw the potential applications for something so small. They were designed to go into rooms and spy on meetings and things like that, without anyone ever knowing they were there. They are very cool.'

'And I'm guessing very expensive, right?'

'You don't have to worry about that, but yes, very expensive.'

'Thank you, Mr Qupi, I guess,' Trevor said.

It wasn't long before the drone reached Eastwood's rooftop terrace. They could see enough in the moonlight to determine that it was well equipped with expensive garden loungers, tables and chairs, a gas barbeque, a gigantic hot tub, and a number of potted plants.

'How the other half live, eh?' Trevor said.

'Probably all Daddy's money, I doubt the bastard has worked a day in his life,' Andy said.

'I don't see anything of interest on the terrace,' Trevor said.

'Andy, can you get closer, to see if there are any windows or doors open?' asked Kendra.

'I sure can, Detective,' he replied, guiding the tiny machine towards the building.

Kendra squinted at the monitor. 'Is that sliding door open?' There were only a couple of exterior courtesy lights on either side of the doors, so it was difficult to see. 'Can you get closer?'

Andy moved the drone slowly towards the sliding doors. The penthouse flat was in darkness so it was difficult to determine whether the glass doors were open or closed.

'Hang on, I want to check something,' Andy said, his fingers continuing to move deftly over the controller.

'Switching to the thermal camera, let's see if there is anybody inside before we try and get in.'

'Good idea, Batman,' said Trevor, nodding in appreciation.

'I'm not just a great-looking, super-intelligent hunk, you know, Trevor,' Andy said, keeping a straight face.

Trevor and Kendra looked at each other, trying not to laugh. 'Just get on with it, Brad Pitt,' said Kendra.

The image on the monitor changed to a dark grey one, with slight variations in the darker areas inside the flat. Andy carefully moved the drone from side-to-side to cover as much of the interior as possible, but there were no heat signatures from within.

'Looks clear, let's see if these doors are open or not.'

The monitor changed back to normal view as he changed the camera setting back, showing that it was still dark but with just enough ambient light to see from. Suddenly a bright light shone from the front of the drone into the flat, highlighting another useful accessory on the small drone.

'Tiny is not just a pretty face, you know, he can do many things,' Andy said, 'and if the doors were closed, we would have seen the reflection in the glass. Believe it or not, those doors are wide open.'

'Well, let's face it, it's not as if anyone is going to break into it from the roof, are they?' Trevor said, 'I probably would have left it open, too.'

'Never mind that,' said Kendra, 'can you go inside and look around?'

'Sure thing, K, here we go.'

Slowly, he manoeuvred Tiny into the penthouse flat. With the light on, they could see that it was luxuriously furnished, with two separate seating areas in what was a large open-plan lounge, one of them arrayed in front of a huge television that was mounted on the wall. When the drone panned around, they could see the dining area, along with a well-equipped kitchen, both at the far end and far enough away from the television area that any cooking wouldn't disturb the viewers too much.

'Bloody hell, look at the size of that,' Trevor said. 'It's one of those eighty-inch monsters that you see in the showrooms, which nobody can afford.'

'It's typical that you'd notice the huge TV, Dad, but can you focus on why we're here, please,' Kendra said. 'Andy, can you move down the corridor there; are there any rooms we can look into?'

'Sure thing, Miss,' he replied, turning and moving slowly towards the nearest corridor.

The first door on the left was a WC, with a lavish bathroom next door. There were two closed doors on the right side of the corridor that Andy couldn't see into, which were likely to be bedrooms. Luckily, they were the only closed doors.

The drone continued along the corridor and came to an open door, the next room on the left, which they assumed would be another bedroom. As the drone flew past it, turning sideways for the cameras to view the inside, Kendra spotted something.

'Wait, go back please, Andy. Can you go into that room?'

'Yes, ma'am, I believe I can,' he replied in a mock American accent.

Tim wobbled in the air when Kendra gave Andy a gentle nudge in the ribs.

'I told you about that accent, please don't, because you are rubbish at it,' she said. 'Now go inside that room, please.'

'Can't do anything right,' he muttered.

As he moved Tim into the room, the light from the front illuminated a poster on the wall opposite, and a flag pinned alongside it, which had drawn Kendra's attention.

'What is that? Where have I seen that before?' she asked, the hairs on the back of her neck standing on end.

The flag had a white parachute design, with two yellow aircraft either side of it, on a blue and green background. The poster next to it was of a two-headed bird of prey, its wings outstretched, holding a banner with its claws, a single crown above its heads. It sat inside three Russian words in a circular design.

'Russian Imperial Movement,' Andy whispered. 'This is bad news, guys.'

'Who the hell are they?' said Trevor, confused and oblivious, 'and what is that on the table?' He pointed to the table just to the side of the flag.

'Yep, that looks like a couple of vintage handguns, and some unused grenades,' Andy said, alarmed at what they had stumbled upon. 'Guys, this group has been designated as a terror group. They make the National Front look like a couple of kittens playing with a ball of cotton wool. Honestly, they are the worst of the worst.'

The Tokarev TT-33 automatic pistols had been standard Soviet issue in World War 2, prized amongst collectors in Russia and beyond. The pineapple-shaped F-1 grenades, which had been introduced in the same war, still had their pins in place, seemingly making them viable despite their age.

'This guy is a collector of some very bad things,' Andy continued, 'and it's out in the open, so I dread to think what else he has stashed away.'

'Shit,' Kendra said, 'we need to think long and hard about what we do next. I've heard about this lot, and if Eastwood is a part of it then this just became a much bigger challenge.'

'What the hell is going on?' Trevor asked. 'Can you please fill me in, here?"

'Dad, this group trains the worst type of terrorists. They give paramilitary-style training to neo-Nazis and white supremacists and send them out to sow discord in Europe, America, and wherever else they think they can cause problems. Even the Russian government doesn't like them. They kill indiscriminately: women, children, they will target anyone and everyone.'

'Okay, so how does that affect what we want to do? Our plan was to take Eastwood down, wasn't it? Are you saying we can't do that now?'

'No, but ask yourself, why are they using gangsters to rob

and mutilate people? What is their end game? We need to find out, and fast,' she said.

'Okay, I get your point.'

'Look at this,' Andy said. 'Our friend has a computer, with a top-of-the-range camera attached to the monitor. If we can get into it, we can find out a hell of a lot.'

'How can we do that?' Kendra asked.

'If Tim had hands, I'd ask him to stick a dongle in so that I could upload a Trojan virus, but sadly, he only has two tiny little feet.'

'Really? We're about to take on an army of white supremacists and you make jokes about the drone's feet? You're lucky you have those goggles on, boy, I'd slap your face good and hard,' Trevor snapped.

'Come on, Trev, it's how I deal with things, you know? A bit of humour always helps me think clearer. And thanks to you, I know what I have to do. Now, if I can just take a photo of the router and the back of the computer, we'll be game-on.'

'What? What are you talking about?'

'I'm going to join the Russian Imperial Movement,' he said, 'but before I do, I need to get young Tim back home.'

15

INFILTRATION

'What do you mean you're going to join them?' asked Kendra, as Andy pulled the goggles off his head.

'Good job, Tim,' he said, ignoring her and kissing the front of the tiny drone that now nestled in his hand.

'Don't you ignore me, Mister,' Kendra admonished, 'you know that doesn't work with me.'

'I do, but I also know it winds you up a little, so let's call it compromise,' he said, holding her stare and smiling back.

'You can be so infuriating, you know that? Now will you please tell me what you are going to do?'

'Yeah, because we're both confused,' Trevor added.

'I told you. I'm going to go online and join their group. When I have exchanged a few emails with Chancellor Eastwood, I'll send him a nice picture of a strange man holding a gun, which will have a virus embedded in it. That will give me access similar to Cyclops so that I can mess around in his computer. Easy peasy if you know what you're doing.'

They both looked at him, dumbfounded that he could be so casual.

'Look,' he continued, 'we have no clue at all as to why this arsehole is paying vicious bastards like Brathwaite to do what they are doing. He's up to something very bad and we need to get close to him to find out what. Who knows what else he's up to? This is the only safe way to do that, okay?'

'I think he's right, love. If we can find out without having to take them on, I'm good with that,' Trevor said.

'Oh, you'll have to take them on at some point,' Andy added, 'I may be able to find out what we need, but you still have to come up with a plan to take on an army of white supremacists. That should be a bundle of fun.'

'An army? You mean five men, right?' Kendra said.

'It may be more, who knows?' Andy replied. 'That's why we need to get in. I may even be able to access his phone from the computer, if he's registered online. That would be the best intel we could possibly get.'

'Dad, what do you reckon? Can we take them on? His goons seem very well-trained and are all huge bastards, unlike Eastwood.'

'It's the short ones that are the worst,' Andy said. 'Little Man Syndrome, it's called. These teeny tiny men try and compensate for their lack of height by being complete bastards to the rest of the world. This Eastwood looks like a typical example of that, a small, bitter and twisted man with lots of money, it's a recipe for some straight-up evil.'

Trevor thought for a few seconds, trying to pick holes in the plan that was forming in his head.

'I think we'll be okay. Now that our guests have gone, it has freed up the twins. I was going to thank Darren and his mob for their sterling efforts so far, but maybe they'll want to stay on for this, too. With them and our other guys, we should manage, so yeah, we should be okay.'

'Alright then,' Kendra said, looking back and forth between the two men. 'That sounded a little too easy, but I guess the proof is in the pudding, right?'

'First things first,' Andy said, 'before we can do anything else, we need to find out what their movements are, where they go, if there's a pattern, that kind of thing.'

'I know exactly who to speak to about that,' Trevor said, smiling. 'Like I said, they're free now, so this is exactly the sort of thing they thrive on.'

'The twins!' Kendra and Andy said together.

IT WAS late before Eastwood and his men arrived back at the tower block. They double- parked by the entrance again but this time two men accompanied Eastwood into the complex, leaving the drivers to take care of the vehicles. It only took a few minutes to park them in the yard next door and secure the gate before the drivers also entered the block. Andy made a note of the time and picked up his phone.

'Trevor, they're back, and the cars are secure. Send the twins.'

He had dropped Trevor and Kendra off at her flat for them to get some rest before heading home, where he would also try and sleep. He knew that it would only be for a few hours and had set his computer to activate an alarm on his phone when the cameras were triggered. There had been a few false alarms, so his sleep had been broken, but welcome nevertheless. Now that he had confirmed Eastwood's return, he could turn off the alarms and get some decent rest.

'Go get 'em, boys,' he muttered, before falling back into his bed and almost immediately to sleep.

TREVOR HAD BRIEFED the twins and explained the layout to the yard before settling in for the night. Now that he was awake again, and knowing that Eastwood and his men were back, he picked up his phone and called Mo.

'Are we good to go?' Mo asked, immediately upon answering.

'Yes, they're all back.'

'Okay, we're not far away, just getting ourselves a takeaway and then we'll move in when we're done. By that time, they should all be either asleep or drinking themselves silly,' Mo added.

'Remember, these bastards are evil, so don't discount the fact that they may have security in place there, okay? Tell Amir not to do any more of that cowboy shit he loves so much.'

Mo laughed. 'Don't worry about that youngster, he's getting better with age.'

'Dude, he's like five minutes younger than you,' Trevor said.

'And I told you, I'll never let him forget that,' came the reply.

'Alright, well, just take it easy, straight in and out and nobody will be any the wiser.'

'Roger and out.'

Trevor sat and thought over the plan again, hoping that Andy knew what he was doing. He wasn't looking forward to taking on Eastwood's brutes, but it was unavoidable.

'I'm sure they'll be fine,' he said, flopping back into Kendra's spare bed, hoping that the twins would do their thing without incident.

'Seriously, you carry on eating like that, and nobody will be able to tell that we're even related, let alone twins,' Mo said to his younger brother as they left the fried chicken shop.

'Stop moaning, bruv. I'll burn that extra portion off tonight and will look even better than I do now,' Amir said. 'And I'll still be much better looking than you, old man.'

They walked along the deserted Kingsland High Road and turned into Boleyn Road. There was very little traffic around and they hadn't seen a pedestrian for a while. The car they had arrived in was parked close by and the kit they had brought with them was safely tucked into their pockets.

'Okay, here's the yard,' Mo said, looking around. He could not see any cameras or other form of security inside.

'Let's not take any chances,' he said, taking out a rectangular black box with three antennas at the top, twice the size of an average mobile phone. He turned it on its side and switched on a button, activating a red light that blinked several times before the blinking stopped and it turned green, indicating that it was active.

'Man, that Andy knows his stuff, doesn't he? This jammer is bloody brilliant,' Amir said, knowing that the Wi-Fi and Bluetooth jammer would block any signals if there were any security measures in place here.

'Never mind that, go do your thing, Spider-Man. I'll keep watch.' Mo stepped into the shadows of the closest entrance.

Amir nodded and stepped up to the gate. After one last

look around, more from habit than concern, he jumped up deftly and grabbed the vertical bars. Within seconds he had shimmied up and climbed over the ten-foot gates. It was child's play for Amir, whose parkour skills were renowned amongst his peers.

He landed silently in the yard and had a quick look around, again more from habit, to see if there were any cameras or security measures. Satisfied that all was clear, he approached the right-hand side of the yard, which was out of sight from the street and up against the wall that adjoined the pavement. There was a large, corrugated steel car port covering the length of the wall, with four vehicles parked under its overhang.

Amir recognised the two black Range Rovers that Trevor had described earlier. He also saw a new Mercedes S500, also in black, a luxury car most likely used for Eastwood's more formal functions. Finally, there was a silver Aston Martin V12 Vantage S, a gorgeous sports tourer that Eastwood most likely used to impress his female companions. In all, Amir estimated almost half a million pounds' worth of vehicles.

'He knows his cars, that's for sure,' he muttered.

He continued to look around and saw a couple of large metal lockers that most likely held cleaning equipment to keep the cars looking their best. There was nothing else of interest, so he removed the first of the GPS trackers from his pocket and approached one of the Range Rovers. Believing that the guards would be astute enough to casually check for anything abnormal, Amir got underneath and attached it halfway along the car in one of the recesses, which wouldn't easily be spotted. He used double the amount of gaffer tape that he would normally use, just in case. He repeated the process twice more, for the other Range Rover and the

Mercedes. They had brought one spare tracker unit, thinking that there were only the two vehicles.

'Well, if he uses the Aston Martin, I guess we'd be unlucky,' he said, correctly assuming that the car was rarely used.

Once he was happy that all three units were installed, he stuck a miniature camera high up under the covered area so that it overlooked the cars towards the gate, which would help give a heads-up which vehicles were to be used. He made his way towards the gate, whistling softly, waiting for the same response from his brother for the all-clear. The response was immediate and so he once again jumped up and shimmied his way to the top and then over onto the street.

Mo approached and they both walked silently back along Boleyn Road towards Kingsland High Road.

'See, bruv? Easy. And look,' Amir said, lifting his top, 'not an ounce of fat in sight.'

'Fool,' Mo replied. He shook his head and smiled at his brother, always impressed by his ability to make light of potentially stressful situations.

'Takes one to know one, bruv. Now call Trevor and tell him that his best men have done it again.'

'WELL DONE, boys, now get yourselves home and we'll catch up tomorrow. I want to run some ideas past you about how to deal with those monsters,' Trevor said.

'Dibs on the Aston Martin,' Amir said, before his brother could acknowledge.

'Nice try, Amir,' but you know we can't risk anything so

early, okay? Anyway, Stav has perpetual dibs on all the cars that we grab.'

'I hate that Greek, he gets all the nice toys,' said Amir.

'You lie like a hairy egg,' Mo said. 'You love that guy. He always gives you the best cars to use when you ask.'

'I know, just kiddin', bro, chill out.'

'When you two have finished your sparring, get yourselves home like I said, and we'll talk tomorrow. And again, good job.'

'Night, Trev, see ya later,' replied Mo.

He turned to his brother and said, 'I suppose you want a kebab before we go home, don't you?'

'You know me so well, bruv,' replied Amir, 'let's go to that one in Stoke Newington that I like, they give big-boy portions, too.'

'Yep, I know you so well.'

16

TIME TO PLAN

Kendra was back in the office the next day, hoping there were no more issues with Duckmore and the ongoing investigation.

'How's it going, Kendra?' asked Rick Watts as she closed the door behind her.

'All good, thanks, Sarge. I thought I'd check in with you before I start my day. Anything I should know about?'

'Not really. The CCTV for Romford was a bust, there was a glitch or something and they didn't have any records for a couple of months. Typical bad luck, but not surprising with council records, really.'

'So, what's next?' she asked, inwardly pleased by Andy's successful sabotage.

'Your mate Duckmore is following up some leads from the ships that were impounded. Apparently, he might have some addresses worth looking into, brothels most likely, that the sex workers were being sent to.'

'And how will that help?'

'If Qupi has upped and abandoned his operations here in

East London, then there shouldn't be any brothels left, should there? So, if that twat finds any that are still up and running, we'd have to ask ourselves why he would leave those behind.'

'Fair enough,' she said, 'let me know if I can help with anything. I'll be downstairs typing away like a part-timer.'

'Like I said, your choice, so do the time, young lady.' 'Bye, Sarge, catch you later.'

DOWNSTAIRS IN THE INTEL UNIT, Kendra sat with a cup of coffee and considered what Rick Watts had brought up.

Does it affect us in any way? Even if they find a brothel, what does it mean? She pondered on these questions, trying to get into an investigator's head, but she couldn't come up with anything other than it may cause problems for Brodie Dabbs, who had taken over the brothels once Qupi was out of the way.

'I'll let Brodie know that he may have some police sniffing around soon, don't worry about it,' Trevor said, once they had spoken.

'Thanks. I'm sure nothing will come of it but it's best to cover all eventualities just in case.' When the call had ended, she sat on the bench outside and thought about Andy and how he had changed in the past few months. Thinking about him made her smile and she hoped he would pluck up the courage to do something about it. She had decided some time ago that it was Andy who would have to make that call, she had made her intentions clear several times, hinting for more from him.

Maybe I'll give one last hint and see what happens.

Her thoughts were interrupted by a voice that she found distasteful and toxic.

'How's it going, Detective? Having a break already?' sneered Eddie Duckmore as he and Dave Critchley stopped by the bench on their way into the station.

'That's right, Detective Sergeant, it's what we do here, take occasional breaks. You should try it,' she replied quickly, without thinking. Duckmore's expression changed from a sneer to a much frostier one instantaneously.

'You know, if you were in the NCA, you'd be out on your arse for talking to a superior like that.'

'Well, it's just as well that I'm not in the NCA, isn't it, Detective Sergeant. Now, if you'll excuse me, I have work to do now that my break is over.' She stood and walked away from the two men.

'Look at how the Met treat their superiors, Dave, it's no wonder they're going downhill,' Duckmore said, just loud enough for Kendra to hear.

'Wanker,' she muttered.

KENDRA COULDN'T GET out of the station fast enough at the end of her shift. She had stayed clear of Rick Watts in case he'd spoken with Duckmore and had kept herself busy in the Intel Unit. The day passed without incident and she wanted to meet with Andy and Trevor so they could plan their next moves against Eastwood.

They decided to meet at Andy's house, where they went over the day's events.

'I doubt they'll find anything from the brothels that will even remotely link them to us,' Andy said, confident they were safe from the investigation. 'None of the sex workers or goons that were taken away have any idea of what went on, they were expecting to be picked up at a port and taken to their new homes, so there is no connection at all.'

'I'm sure Brodie will deal with it just fine, he'll probably halt operations or move them until the investigators have been and gone,' added Trevor, who had made the call with Brodie Dabbs earlier. 'He sends his regards, by the way. He's done very well since Qupi was removed and he owes us a stiff drink, so we'll always have some people to help if needed.'

'Great,' said Kendra. 'So where are we now with Eastwood? I'm keen to get this bastard as soon as possible.'

'Well,' said Andy, 'the twins did their usual excellent work and planted some GPS trackers on the vehicles. I can activate them remotely when the cameras on the doors give us a heads-up on their movement, and what I was going to do is allow about ten minutes before turning the trackers on.'

'Why's that?' asked Trevor.

'In case they have any detection capabilities; they may go over the cars before driving. It's standard practice with quality security services, so I figured it was worth leaving it until they were mobile.'

'Good thinking, Batman,' said Kendra, winking at Andy. His eye widened in surprise. After a short pause he continued.

'I figure he has his favourite haunts, so it will be good to know where they are, when he visits, and for how long. That will make it easier for you to do your thing, Trevor, right?'

'I suppose,' he replied hesitantly, 'but I will need a bit of help with this one, like I said.

'Have you spoken to them yet?' asked Kendra.

'I spoke with Frazer earlier and he is more than happy for

them to stay a little longer,' Trevor replied. 'I was going to speak with Darren later, once we had caught up. I'm sure that between us and the twins we'll be a match for those monsters.'

'I'd be happy to assist,' Andy said, leaning forward in anticipation.

'No,' Kendra answered quickly, much quicker than she should have.

'Why not? I can still be useful as a backup with Marge, I didn't mean hand-to-hand combat,' Andy replied, surprised again by her reaction.

'I'll leave you to discuss further,' Trevor said, taking his cue to leave. 'I'll go and speak with Darren now.'

'See you later, Dad,' Kendra said, thankful for the opportunity to speak with Andy alone. It was time to hint one last time.

'What's up, Kendra? You seem a little ... off, tonight. Are you okay?'

'I just don't want you to get hurt again, Andy, that's all. It's still too soon and you need time to recover and get your strength back.'

'Come on, we've had this chat plenty of times now, I'm not a kid, and if I want to take the odd risk then I should be able to.'

'But what happens if you get hurt again? We pretty much come to a grinding halt, don't we? Only you know how to do the dark web and hacking stuff, it's what gives us the edge and the ability to do what we do.'

'I'm not going to get hurt, Kendra, I can look after myself better than most, you know. Stop being so dra–'

'I don't want to lose you,' she interrupted.

'What?' he replied, surprised for the third time in one night.

Kendra looked down and repeated, 'I don't want to lose you.' She looked up again and said, 'It scared the shit out of me, what happened last time. I've been feeling guilty ever since but also, I've regretted that we didn't pick up where we left off before we got caught, you know?'

Andy's expression softened as realisation dawned upon him.

'You know, in my entire adult life, I have never been awkward around women – until I met you. I risked everything that night because I wanted you. It cost me an eye and a foot, which wasn't ideal, but – well, I don't want to lose you either, Kendra.'

She laughed and said, 'Maybe losing an eye and a foot was worth it, eh?'

'Well, only time will tell,' he said. He took both her hands in his, lifting her gently out of her chair. He took her face in his hands and leaned down and kissed her tenderly on the lips. Her hands dropped down by her side as she closed her eyes and responded to Andy's tenderness.

She then brought her arms up around his waist and pulled him closer, changing the dynamic and control as her kiss became more passionate and urgent.

Andy suddenly pulled back and out of her embrace, a shocked look upon his face.

'What's wrong?' she asked.

'I'm sorry, K, maybe this is a bad idea just now. There's a lot going on and we really do need to focus on that rather than ourselves.'

'Come on, Andy, we're both grown up now, we can handle all that,' she replied.

'I don't think we should, though, this isn't a game, Kendra, and bad shit happens all the time. I want to be sure that we're all safe, it's too early to have fun while we're still trying to make a go of this.'

'Really? That's what you think?'

'Also, I just had a horrible flashback to the night we got caught and tortured. If that happens every time we have a snog, it isn't going to end well, is it?'

Kendra looked at him and held his hands.

'You're sure it's just about timing and nothing else, right?'

'I'm sure, K. The feelings are there but so are the doubts and the fear of the future. I need to reconcile them before I'm ready to move forward without fear of failure or—worse, hurting you.'

'Okay, I understand,' she said. 'I don't much like it, but I understand.'

'There's one other thing,' he said.

'What's that?'

'Your dad is definitely going to kill me when we do get together, you know that, right?' Kendra laughed, pushing him away gently.

'Only you can be both charming and a knob within the space of a few seconds.'

'WHAT TOOK YOU SO LONG?' asked Trevor.

'Sorry, Dad, I was in the loo, I think I had one too many slices of pizza.'

'And what about that one-eyed pirate mate of yours, was he having stomach problems too?'

'Dad, there's no need for that. No, actually, he was in the

kitchen making some soup and just forgot to take his phone with him.'

'So, it's all innocent and nothing for me to worry about, right?'

'Right. Now will you please tell me why you're calling? I feel like a fourteen-year-old being grilled about my first boyfriend.'

'Ha, you should be so lucky I missed that. Anyway, I spoke with Darren and the guys, and they are all sticking around to help, including Izzy, who can keep Hopalong Cassidy company in the camper van. We brainstormed a couple of ideas that might work, we have to be a little creative.'

'Sounds like you have a cunning plan, Dad,' she replied, noting the excitement in his voice.

'I'll tell you all about it when I see you shortly, I'm on my way back to Andy's to see what the trackers have recorded. Make sure you're both dressed,' he added, ending the call abruptly.

'Well, that went just about as badly as I thought,' she told Andy, who was sitting next to her on the sofa. 'I think you're right; he's going to kill you if we ever get together. And then he's going to bring you back to life and kill you again. You get where I'm going with this.'

'Well, it will be worth it,' he said, leaning over and kissing her on the forehead. 'I'll just get my passport and can be gone in ten minutes.'

She stroked his arm as he got up, disappointed but hopeful. As he walked away she noted the slight discolouration in his prosthetic foot, along with the line that indicated the join where the real leg met the artificial one, otherwise it would be difficult to tell that he had one on.

'I still can't get over how good that robot foot of yours looks.'

'Well, Qupi paid good money for the best I could get, so it should look great. You should see my blade, it's brilliant. I look like one of those Olympic athletes with it on.'

'That's gonna have to wait for another time, because your soon-to-be killer is on his way.' Andy smiled as he turned to face her.

'We'll be okay, you and me, I know we will.'

'Me too,' she replied.

TREVOR ARRIVED a short time later and glared at Andy as he gingerly made his way to his workstation.

'Trev, you can be really scary, you know?' he said, not daring to look him in the eye.

'Yeah? You should see me when I'm angry,' came the curt reply.

Andy cleared his throat. 'Moving on. I've not had any indication that they've moved yet so I won't turn the trackers on. In the meantime, I've created a new profile which I've added to social media platforms, going back a few years.'

'How the hell did you do that?' Kendra asked.

'Well, truth be told, I stole a profile that's been on there for years without being used and changed it all. That way they can conduct their due diligence without us having any problems.'

'Again, this hurts my head, knowing that you can do this so easily,' Trevor added.

'It's actually not easy at all, they've introduced lots of new measures to prevent this sort of thing, so it only really works with dormant or rarely used accounts where the security hasn't been updated. I've actually hijacked about half-a-dozen male and the same number of female accounts for future use.'

'So, what's next?' asked Kendra.

'There's a couple of threads on the internet that I managed to find, so I've started asking the questions to see how I can become a member. My profile pic is of a lunatic holding an AK47. I'm hoping that it impresses.'

'Won't the real owner find out that you're using his pic?' asked Trevor.

'Not really, there's thousands of these on the internet, tens of thousands of idiots holding guns. I reckon they all have tiny penises. Anyway, I altered Mr Small Dick's face using some AI software I have, so it changed his features slightly.'

'Okay, cool, so what now?' asked Kendra.

'Now I wait and see if I get the info I need to join them, which should come pretty soon as they are always online, this lot.'

'So, hang on, what makes your profile stand out so much?' asked Trevor. 'You mentioned there's thousands of these, why yours?'

'Because there's very few pictures of young white males holding AK-47's that live in the UK. It should make things interesting, don't you think?'

'Smug git,' Kendra said, nudging him in the ribs.

'Nothing wrong with being smug, Detective, if you're good at what you do,' Andy replied.

'Quit your boasting, boy, there's some sort of alarm flashing on your computer.'

His smugness quickly forgotten, Andy turned to the monitor.

'It's the camera in the yard. I turned the others off as they were being set off every few minutes by the tenants and passers-by. This way, we'd know for sure that there was movement by the bad guys. I'll switch them on now so we can have all-round views.'

Sure enough, Kendra saw two of Eastwood's men approach the pair of black Range Rovers. They had a cursory look underneath, before getting into the driver's seats and setting off. Seconds later, they double-parked outside the same entrance where one man stood guard, holding the door open for his colleague and Eastwood to make a swift exit from the building and straight into the second Range Rover. As soon as the men were all in the cars, the small convoy moved off northbound.

'Okay, I think it's safe to turn them on now, let's see where they take us,' Andy said, activating the GPS trackers.

Almost immediately the other monitor came to life, showing a map with two red dots moving northbound along Boleyn Road.

'They work great,' Andy said.

'All we can do now is note their course and destination and see where they go. Cup of tea, anyone?'

17

A WORRYING TWIST

'Well, it's about time,' Andy said as the GPS trackers finally came to a complete stop. It had been almost an hour since the Eastwood convoy had driven off and he was wondering whether their plan had failed.

'Well, don't keep us in suspense,' said Trevor, 'where the hell are they?'

'They've stopped in a car park at Cheshunt Football Club in Enfield, which is in North London. I'm pretty sure there's no game or training on this late at night, so I can only assume they are meeting someone there.'

'That looks quite remote there, doesn't it?' asked Kendra, noting that it was far from any residential area.

'It looks like an ideal place to meet, only one way in and out, so they'll see police or outsiders approaching by car very easily. There's a couple of buildings close to the likely meeting points. I'll do a search but there's nothing like having boots on the ground,' Andy said, finally looking Trevor in the eye.

Trevor picked up his phone and made a call.

'Mo, get yourself and Amir to Cheshunt Football Club in Enfield. It's pretty remote so your brother will have to do some magic again. We need you to move fast, I don't know how long they'll be there. I'll message the address, and call you on the way, okay? Good man,' Trevor said, and ended the call.

'They're making their way now,' he said, nodding.

'Well, if anyone can find out what these bastards are up to, Dad, it's Amir. He's like a ghost.'

'Let's hope they get there in time to see what it's all about,' Trevor said.

Mo and Amir arrived in Cheshunt just forty minutes later, having avoided any late-night traffic in East London. Amir had driven, so Mo had used the time to check his phone for maps of the area they were visiting.

'There's a bowls club and community sports club just north of the football pitches, so we should go and park there and walk over the fields to see what our Nazi friends are up to,' he said.

'Sounds good, bro, just tell me where to go,' Amir replied.

Within a few minutes they had parked near the sports club and were soon on foot crossing over the newly mowed practice football pitches. They skirted the training areas, which were in darkness, and kept to the hedgerow that led south towards the main football pitch and the outbuildings associated with the club.

It wasn't long before they noticed activity at a large modern barn-like building that was adjacent to the football pitch. They saw four men standing guard by the door leading into the barn and could hear voices from within.

'I'll stay here and keep an eye out, bro, you go and do your thing. Just stay safe, okay? Don't do anything stupid,' Mo said.

Amir rolled his eyes. 'Seriously, a late-night lecture while we're in the middle of a hedge looking for white suprema-cists?' He smiled and then snuck into the darkness, out of sight within seconds.

'That boy,' Mo muttered, smiling, proud of his younger sibling.

Amir laughed and joked a lot, but he was very serious about his parkour skills, which were amongst the best. He had trained himself to automatically plan any routes in his mind as he approached them, not waiting to get there and waste time. He had identified the route to get a view into the barn, preferably inside the barn itself. He navigated the hedges successfully and approached the northeast corner, the side furthest from the entrance where the guards were prowling.

The end of the building that Amir approached was different to the other end, with a corner missing, giving the appearance of an L-shape or dogleg, which kept him out of view of the guards.

Within seconds Amir was shimmying up the drainpipe, making his way towards the small first-floor window. It was a four-foot jump from the drainpipe to the windowsill, which he jumped silently and grabbed easily with minimal exer-tion. The window was closed, as expected, but he was prepared with his trusty shimmy tool, a metal ruler that he had refined especially for jobs like this. He worked the thin ruler into the gap and turned the latch the opposite way to unlock it. Sliding the sash-style window open, he crawled into what looked like a storage room, complete with shelves that were arrayed with many different types of dancing shoes, along with boxes of ribbons and other materials.

Amir found it amusing that Eastwood, a member of one of the most right-wing groups in the world, was meeting at a dance club.

Making his way to the door, he opened it just enough to see and hear any activity. The corridor was in darkness, so he knew that he was safe at this time. He could hear the murmur of voices downstairs, sounding like a very busy bar. He made his way towards the noise, hoping to avoid detection.

As he reached the metal stairwell, typical of industrial style buildings, he looked down and could see several groups of men talking, each with a drink in their hands. Much of the rest of the hall was out of his view, but there was no way of seeing the entire floor.

Suddenly, he heard a loud clink and the room fell silent. Amir, his phone on silent, turned on the voice recorder, anticipating that some useful intelligence was about to be disclosed.

'Listen up, gents. We appreciate you all making the effort to ditch your wives and mistresses for the night and join us.'

There was laughter and raised glasses as the attendees saluted the speaker.

'As you know, our group of dedicated supporters has waited a long time for someone to come along and kick the crap out of the establishment, bringing in a new, modern world order where the right people are in charge, finally. An order where our beloved country can spar with the best of them, and, if necessary, beat them, too.'

There were more raised glasses and loud hollers from the floor. 'Hear, hear!'

'So, it gives me a great deal of pleasure to introduce our benefactor, the man who has helped us grow, the man who has supported our cause for the past year, and the man who we hope will lead us into the next period of prosperity and power. Gentlemen, I give you our future Prime Minister, Mr Michael Eastwood!'

There was rapturous applause and more cheering from the raucous crowd. The response was deafening and didn't surprise Amir, who knew that a large group of like-minded racist thugs would be excitable at the prospect of a new world order – their order.

'Gentlemen, thank you, and please, that is more than I deserve,' came the voice of Michael Eastwood, out of sight to Amir but very much within earshot.

'Thank you again for such wonderful support, it gives me a great deal of hope for the future, which I grow more confident about with every passing day. Our enemies are making a rod for their own backs: the vicious robberies, the cruel burglaries, the brutal rapes, need I go on? Every single day we are being subjected to news about their evil, inhuman atrocities. Atrocities that are conducted against our people, our loved ones, our children.'

There were howls of abuse aimed towards the perpetrators, the volume increasing as the rabble worked themselves into a frenzy.

'I know, I know,' Eastwood continued, 'I feel the same, don't you worry. I have pledged myself to you and your group, to your party, and to your communities. I pledge to clear out the scum that are causing such misery and pain to our loved ones. I will purge them all. Whatever it takes!'

The crowd screamed more support towards Eastwood, hearing the words that they had been hoping for years to hear from a politician. To them, Eastwood was the Messiah, the man who would liberate them, the man who would destroy the enemy, the man who would give them back their country.

'I have started the process to become an elected official for the London Borough of Hackney. I will not shirk from my responsibilities, and I intend to fight head-on in one of the worst boroughs in London. With your support, I cannot fail. With your support, we will start small and grow in such a way that we will never be ignored again.'

There was more applause, raised glasses, and cheering to the rafters.

'My friends, I have started another process, whereby our brothers will follow my lead and register to join the electorate in their areas, covering the length and breadth of our beloved country. As of today, we have more than seventy officials, and we grow as a party day by day. We will be clever, we will better them all, and we will take our country back. Long live the British Patriots Party and long live the King!'

The cheering went on for several minutes as the crowd soaked in the atmosphere.

'We shall crush them all!' Eastwood shouted.

'Crush, crush, crush!' came the call from the crowd, as fanatical as anything Amir had seen.

The shouting went on for minutes, before the man who had introduced Eastwood spoke again.

'Your support and hunger for change is what drives our cause, gentlemen, so we thank you for everything. Please, enjoy the drinks and snacks we have provided, and we look forward to seeing you again in a few days. Long live the Party!'

'Long live the Party!' came the response, before the more usual murmur of drinkers in a bar resumed.

'Wow,' Amir mouthed, turning off his phone and walking slowly back to the storeroom and the small window. He left the door slightly ajar as an early warning indicator, always mindful of potential pitfalls.

As he went to exit via the window, he noticed one of the guards below, walking towards the corner of the building where he was, and ducking out of sight of his colleagues but below the window where Amir was waiting. The man looked around and unzipped his trousers, before relieving himself against the barn wall, directly below him. Amir couldn't leave until the man had finished, so he waited patiently.

Just then he heard a sound from the direction of the stairwell, and he realised that someone was coming up the stairs and along the corridor. The light came on, as the heavy-footed man walked towards what Amir assumed would be the toilet, next door. Only when he saw the man's shadow at the open door did he realise he may be in trouble. Thinking fast on his feet, he quickly and silently crawled out of the window and closed it as tightly as he could in the seconds he had left before the man entered the storeroom. Barely making it, he dropped out of sight.

The light came on in the storeroom as the man investigated the open door. Amir, gripping the windowsill with one hand with all his strength without making a sound, held his breath as the window was shut firmly and locked again – inches from where he hung.

From the hedgerow below, Mo also held his breath as he saw what was happening, his eyes back and forth from the guard below to his brother dangling precariously above the man's head.

He grabbed a rock from the ground and threw it as hard as he could towards the opposite side of the barn, where the other guards were standing. The rock struck a metal shed with a loud clang, stopping the guards' conversation in its tracks, and more importantly attracting the attention of the guard that was relieving himself. He quickly finished his business and hurried over to join his colleagues, who were cautiously approaching the shed. Amir seized the opportunity and scurried silently down the drainpipe and into the hedgerow and out of sight, where he joined his brother. Mo pointed towards the north and they stealthily began their retreat.

A few minutes later they made it back to the car without any further incident, thankful to have escaped detection.

'Bro, that was close, eh?' Amir said. 'My heart was pumping hard, and I don't think I could have held on much longer. Good job with the rock.'

'It's cool, bruv, if I can't look after my baby brother then I'm useless as a big brother, right?'

'And we're back to that,' Amir replied, rolling his eyes.

'So, what did you see? Was it worth it?'

'It certainly was, big brother, there were some very scary men in that building, and that bastard is aiming to be their leader. I recorded some things that we need to get to Trevor, so let's get back.'

'Good boy.' Mo patted him gently on the head.

'Knob,' Amir replied.

AMIR PASSED his phone to Mo, who uploaded the voice recording to Trevor as they made their way back to East London. He dialled the phone.

'Trevor, I just sent you a recording that Amir took from the meeting that Eastwood attended. The little boy did a great job, it's some scary shit,' he said. 'We managed to get out undetected, but it was close, so we're on our way back home now, okay?'

'Great job, guys, give the little man a pat on the back from me. I'll speak to you both tomorrow,' Trevor replied and ended the call.

'Don't get upset, Trevor told me to do this,' Mo said, reaching over to Amir and ruffling his hair. 'Good job, little man, he told me to say.'

'Seriously, don't make me swear at you again,' Amir replied, managing to keep the car in a straight line. 'Just for that, you're buying the kebabs tonight.'

'Lucky me,' Mo said. 'Just drive, will you?'

* * *

'HOLY SHIT, did I just hear correctly?' Andy exclaimed, having heard the recording Amir had taken.

'Hold on, I'm seriously confused here,' Trevor said. 'Let me get this straight: Eastwood, who is a Russian exile, is paying idiot gangsters like Brathwaite to rob people violently, so that he can cause a race war in order to take over the country with his Nazi party? Is that the gist of it?'

'Sounds like it, yes,' Kendra said.

'Bloody hell, do you think he can get away with something like that?'

'Dad, haven't you been watching the news? If Brexit can

happen, and Trump can rule America, and several right-wing parties are close to taking power in Europe, absolutely he can make it happen. There are enough people in this country who fall for this sort of shit and will vote for someone they think can make them safe.'

'But it will cause a civil war, I am pretty sure of that,' Andy added. 'This is a step too far for millions of people who will not just sit there and let themselves be deported or even dictated to. There will be blood on the streets, all over the country, before it is decided one way or the other.'

'Shit,' Trevor said, 'I thought the days of the National Front were over with, instead we have rich little bastards thinking they could be the next ruler of the country. I mean, have you seen the size of him? Bloody hell!'

'Like I said, Little Man Syndrome has caused wars before, and it will cause wars again. How do we stop this bastard before he gets really popular, and we won't be able to get close to him?' asked Andy.

'We need to do it fast, is what we need to do. I need to phone the boys and set up a meeting at the factory tomorrow. Can you both be there?'

Andy and Kendra both nodded. Kendra saw the concern on her father's face but also the determination to put an end to the potential carnage were Eastwood allowed to progress.

'He has caused a lot of damage, that shitbag,' said Kendra. 'So many people have been scarred for life, just so that he could turn people against the non-white communities. He deserves to go to hell.'

'Before we can think about what we are going to do to him, we have to come up with a realistic plan to grab the bastard, so let's catch up again tomorrow and hopefully we can work something out.'

'Agreed,' Andy said. 'I'll have a think about some options tonight.'

'I'm off home,' Trevor said. 'Kendra, do you want a lift to your flat?'

'Um, I need to go over some stuff with Andy, Dad, I'll get a cab when I'm done. I'll see you tomorrow, okay?'

'Right,' Trevor said, nodding. 'See you tomorrow,' he added, glaring at Andy.

'He's going to kill me, isn't he?' Andy said, putting his arm around Kendra's shoulder.

'Yes. Yes, he is.'

18

DISTRACTIONS

The team gathered at the factory the following morning. Trevor had asked Darren and his colleagues to attend, along with the twins, a handful of boxers that the twins were training, and Charmaine Alexander, who had brought along several young women.

'Thank you all for coming at such short notice, but you know by now that I only do this if I have good reason, right?'

'If you've brought us here to give me and Mo a surprise party then you're out of order, Trevor, we don't like people to know these things,' Amir said. There were several sniggers.

'It isn't your birthday, is it?' Trevor asked, surprised. 'Are you jesting again, Amir? Now is not the time, okay?'

'It's true, Trev,' Mo said, 'and I told him not to say anything.'

'Well, we have something to celebrate, then, so Mo and Amir will be buying the doughnuts later, thanks guys,' Trevor said, eliciting more laughter.

'Idiot,' Mo said, punching his brother in the arm.

'Okay, let's get back to business, thanks again, Amir. Kendra, do you want to tell them what's been happening?'

Sure,' she said, turning to face them all. 'As you know, we have taken out a nasty group of robbers who were terrorising East London, scarring victims for life and letting them know to spread the word. We wondered why they would do that, why they would want to be identified as the gang who branded their victims, and, in some cases, nearly killed them.'

She paused for a second. 'We now know that they were being paid to be as nasty as possible so that they would turn the majority of the population against people of colour, who they were told the robbers were paid to represent.'

'Why would they do that?' asked Darren, confused. He hadn't expected there to be anything more than just a nasty gang, so this sequence of events was surprising to him.

'It turns out that a short, blond, white, billionaire's son is paying the gangs to cause chaos and hatred so that he can get his horrendously racist white supremacist party into power, with the promise that they will rid the country of crimes like that,' continued Kendra.

'What?' came the collective response from a number of attendees stunned by the revelation.

'Yep, the short little bastard is paying to start a race war so that his party can take over, of course with him in charge. The irony is that he is the son of a Russian exile, a billionaire who was imprisoned for going against the government there. He's been in exile for many years, and his son, the Nazi, changed his name, for obvious reasons.'

'So, what are we doing, then?' asked Jimmy.

'That's why we're here, to come up with a plan to take the man down,' Trevor said. 'We know where he lives, and we know that he has at least four very well-trained thugs to look after him. They keep him close, so whatever we come up with must include neutralising the guards.'

'Does he like girls?' asked Charmaine, surprising everyone. There was a pause before anyone answered.

'Actually, yes he does,' Andy spoke, for the first time, 'he has been known to host parties with many more women than he could ever need and shares them with his guards.'

'I wasn't actually asking in that context, but it's good to know so the girls are aware. I ask because my girls are all very talented and can look after themselves in many ways. Personally, I think the only way to take these animals out from their penthouse is to use deceit and guile. Using women will both distract and deceive them.'

'I can personally vouch for Charmaine,' said Trevor. 'She regularly kicks my arse when we spar. She's shown me many ways a smaller opponent can still beat the hell out of you.'

'Have you got any ideas, Charmaine?' asked Kendra.

'For starters, if you can find a way to turn off their power or their water, we can send a couple of girls in to fix the problem, giving us entry to the penthouse. You'll need to speak to the security boss at the block, though, to make sure he calls the right number when the fault is reported.'

'He's a concierge, and I'm sure that a few quid will help him call the right number,' Trevor replied.

'So, the girls go in on the pretext of fixing the problem. If you can find a way of causing another diversion, we could split them up and make it easier to take them out,' Charmaine continued.

'That's a good idea,' Trevor said. 'But I'm not too comfortable sending just two of you up there, however tough you are.

I think we can make enough noise to send a couple of them downstairs, what do you reckon, Mo?'

Mo nodded. 'I already know how we can do that, so yeah, not a problem.'

'Alright, so we split the guards up, what next?' asked Kendra.

'Can you get hold of some drugs?' asked Charmaine.

The team looked around at each other, it was an amusing sight watching them decide who was going to come forward first.

'Really? Is it down to me again because you're all so damn shy?' said Amir. The rest laughed as he shook his head dramatically. 'What do you need, Charmaine?'

'Relax, Amir, I wasn't talking about cocaine or anything like that. Can you get hold of some of those drugs that they spike drinks with at the clubs, like Rohypnol? Or some of those strong tranquilisers that will knock someone out, maybe ketamine?'

Amir thought for a second. 'Don't think badly of me, but I know a man who can get this stuff, so leave it with me.'

'What are you thinking, Charmaine?' asked Trevor.

'If we can find a way of getting them to take a drink that we can spike, then it will be a lot easier to take care of them, right? Just trying to box clever here,' she replied.

'Sounds good to me, and then what?' asked Kendra.

'Once we take them out, we can remove them from the tower block a lot easier. If they have laundry baskets there, we can sneak them out and nobody will have a clue.'

'I've seen those large cage trolleys that the supermarkets use to move their stock around, will they do?' asked Trevor.

'We'll need to cover them up so that people can't see what we're moving, so if you can find a way of doing that, then yes.'

'I will try and do something about the CCTV, so there is no record of what we do,' Andy added.

'Great idea, good thinking,' Trevor said, his irritation towards Andy seemingly forgotten. 'So what else do we need to make this happen, people?'

'I'm now on the way to becoming a fully-fledged member of the Russian Imperial Movement,' said Andy, 'so I'm hoping to do some more damage with their computer as a result.' He purposely kept it vague so as not to divulge all his tricks and secrets.

'Where do we fit in, Trevor?' asked Darren.

'Mate, I think you'll be more than busy looking after these blokes when they wake up.'

'Also, I'll need a few of you to help us out with the diversion,' added Mo. 'We'll be using tasers, but they are big blokes, so we'll need some good old-fashioned muscle, too.'

'Cool, whatever you need,' said Darren.

'Okay, we're on a roll here. Can anyone think of anything we haven't covered?' Trevor said.

'How are we going to coordinate all this?' asked Charmaine. 'Because there's a lot happening, so the timing needs to be spot on.'

'Don't worry about that, Charmaine,' Trevor said. 'I have the best team on the job who will take care of all that.' He looked over at Kendra and Andy and nodded.

'Looks like Marge is in,' Andy muttered excitedly to Kendra. 'I told you she'd be great for us.'

'You're an idiot, Andy. Dad wasn't nodding because of us working together as a great team, he was nodding at us because he thinks we're a couple now and he's accepted it. You really need to pick up on these things, you know?'

'Really? Wait – what? A couple? He thinks we're a couple? But we haven't--you know.'

'You know I can be just as scary as my dad, don't you?' she said, narrowing her eyes at him.

'I believe you,' Andy replied, shying away.

'Now shush, Dad hasn't finished.'

'Right, so we all know what to do. Let's be on site by seven this evening, so that we can take advantage of the dark. Also, it's likely that they'll be getting ready to leave by eight, so we know they'll be there. We'll take two vans with us, so Charlie, can you sort them out, please? The rest of you, come and see me for kit on the way out, okay?'

The team dispersed in all directions as they split up to prepare for their roles. Trevor led a group of them to the storeroom, where he issued the taser guns and CS gas to Mo's team, along with armoured vests and zip ties.

It was a hive of activity, reminding Kendra of the many police operations she had been a part of. It was uncanny how similar it was, only this was not because of a warrant, or a power of arrest or anything legitimate like that. This was a very different matter altogether.

───

'Isn't this exciting, Detective?' Andy said as he finalised preparations in the camper van.

'You're not nervous at all, are you?'

'Not really, I've been too busy to worry. I've prepped Cyclops to get on the CCTV system in the tower block. I want to get there early so I can set up a loop instead of deleting footage this time.'

'Yeah, good idea, who knows if this will be investigated in future,' Kendra said.

'Exactly, now can we have a hug, for old times' sake?'

Andy's timing, as ever, was impeccable, as Trevor chose that very second to enter the van.

'Steady on, you one-eyed monster,' he said. 'There are some things that a Dad shouldn't see, okay?'

'Wait, isn't one-eyed monster another term for – '

'– penis,' Kendra finished. She covered her mouth to stop laughing.

'No need for that, is there?' Andy muttered, sitting down in the driver's seat.

Trevor sat next to him and said, 'Yes there is, now drive.'

19

TIME FOR ACTION

They arrived on scene thirty minutes early and parked up safely out of the way in the same car park in Gillette Street, primarily for Andy to sort out the CCTV loop, but also for Trevor to go and speak to the concierge once more. He made his way to the front entrance of the block via Kingsland High Street before entering the reception area. He had wanted to check the vicinity and ensure there were no obstructions or issues likely to hamper their plans, including confirming the existence of the cage trolleys near the exit points, of which there were many stacked by the wall, ready for use the following day.

'Hello again, sir, it's good to see you. Have you changed your mind and decided to buy?' the concierge said as Trevor approached and shook his hand.

'Hi, Harvey, it's good to see you again. Actually, I was hoping to have a few words in private, if you have time?'

'Sure,' Harvey said, looking around to check that it was still quiet. 'Let's go to my office.'

He led Trevor to a small office behind the reception desk and to the right, screened off by some large plastic planters.

'Please, sit,' indicated the concierge, as he sat behind a small desk.

'I need a small favour, Harvey, which will involve you calling me when one of your occupants contacts you to complain of some problems.'

'Oh? What problems?'

You know the water tanks and the pumps in the basement?'

'Yes, sir, I do.'

Trevor went on to say that he had seen doors leading to the basement area when he had reconnoitred the block. Andy had confirmed the location of the additional pumps that allowed water to reach all of the apartments, including the 15th floor, in the plans he had found online.

Harvey started to look concerned, trying to figure out where this conversation was leading.

'Harvey, I need to turn off the water to penthouse flat number 1, for an hour or so. When you get the call from them, complaining, I want you to call this number.' Trevor handed

Harvey a slip of paper with his number on it. 'Why?'

'Harvey, you told me yourself that there's stuff going on here that you don't like, remember? I'm guessing that your dealings with the occupants in that flat have not been great, and they're not your favourites, am I right?'

'He's a horrible shit, that one, him and his brutes. They don't like me or anyone of colour who lives here, they go out of their way to make life uncomfortable for us all.'

'I guessed as much. I can make that problem go away, but I need your help to do so. And I need you to destroy that piece of paper and forget you ever spoke to me, okay? That's really important because people will come asking.'

'Why are you doing this?' Harvey asked.

'Because they are much worse than you think. They want to get rid of us all, and they have been paying the local gangs to rob people and turn everyone against the minorities. We're going to take them away and send them back to the country they came from. It's the only way to deal with them.'

'So, nobody will die?' asked Harvey. His voice trembled as he became conflicted with the request.

'No, sir, you have my word that nobody will die. That's not how we operate.'

'Then I will help,' Harvey said, standing. He opened a small cabinet on the wall and removed a bunch of keys with an orange tag on it that said Utilities Room. There were a number of keys on the ring, each with its own tag, indicating its purpose.

He handed the key to Trevor and said, 'This has the key you need; the pumps are all clearly marked. Please let me have it back when you're done.'

'Thank you, Harvey,' Trevor said, shaking his hand. 'You are doing a good thing.'

'No, sir, it is I that must thank you, for doing the right thing by us all.'

A FEW MINUTES after leaving Harvey, Trevor made his way to the utilities room and entered using the key. He went down the stairs onto a long corridor that ran underneath the tower block. There were several doors on the left-hand side, each marked with their purpose, such as Boiler Room, Electrical

Systems, with hazard warnings on the doors, and one door on the right-hand side which said Pump Room. Using another key, he entered the vast room that housed several large pumps, each attached to a greater number of smaller pumps. They were noisy, emitting a loud hum that indicated they were working constantly, pumping water from the underground storage tanks to smaller water tanks located throughout the building, including those for the penthouses.

It took a minute to find the one marked Penthouse 1, its green light indicating that it was working correctly. Trevor switched it off, which turned the light red. He left the room immediately and went upstairs back to the reception area, where Harvey was waiting.

'Thanks, Harvey,' he said, handing back the keys. 'If you can turn the pump back on tomorrow, that would be great.'

'Understood.'

'I guess they'll be calling any time from now, so I shall speak to you soon.'

'THAT WAS QUICK, how did it go?' asked Kendra when Trevor re-joined them.

'The concierge is onside and gave me the key to the pump room, where I turned off their water pump. It won't be long before they notice and call down to complain.'

'Great, so what now?'

'Now we wait for the call. I'll contact Mo and get him ready for his part.'

When Mo picked up, he said, 'Just so you know, their water will be out soon, and they'll contact the concierge to complain. As soon as I get the call, I'll message you to put your part into operation. You're ready, right?'

'Seriously, old man? I was ready before the plan was put together, so don't insult me, please.'

'Less of the old, Mo, remember I can still kick your arse.'

'Yeah, but I might ask Charmaine to help me out next time, now I know she beats you up regularly.'

'You do that, but in the meantime, get yourselves ready for the message, okay?' He ended the call, shaking his head once again at the jokers he was having to deal with.

'Everyone is a comedian nowadays,' he said.

'Well, if there's a joke to be had, then—' Andy started to say.

'Each time I hit you will be harder than the last, remember that, okay?' Andy said no more.

Trevor dialled another number.

'Charmaine, are you ready for your stage debut? We'll be getting the call soon, so they will need some top plumbers to fix their problems.'

'Good to know,' she said. 'Me and Zoe will go in when the call comes from you. Amir dropped off some nasty drugs for us to use up there, so we're good to go.'

'Excellent, I'll speak to you soon.'

'It sounds like we're ready to go, Dad, right?'

'I hate this bit, I always feel as if I've forgotten something,' Trevor replied.

'I get that,' said Andy, 'especially since I lost my eye, sometimes I forget that I can't see on the left side and walk into things.' He paused. 'It's not the same thing, is it? Anyway, I've managed to add a loop into their CCTV system for the entrances, exits, the whole of the ground floor, the lift area and the penthouse floors, so as soon as we get the call, I can switch it on and it will loop until I turn it off again, hopefully not too long a wait.'

'Nice one, Andy,' Kendra said, 'now all we have to do is wait.'

It didn't take long; just fifteen minutes later, Trevor received the call from Harvey.

'Harvey, thanks for calling. Okay, call them back and say that someone will be with them within twenty minutes. And thanks again.'

'According to Harvey, Eastwood is not happy because his shower stopped working halfway and he doesn't want to run late for his appointment. I'll call Charmaine and Mo and get them ready. Andy, get ready to switch the CCTV over before anyone makes a move.'

'Rock and roll!' exclaimed Andy, his excitement clear. 'Things are about to get very interesting!'

'Calm down, Andy, otherwise you'll forget something,' Kendra said, 'and we'll never let you out again.'

Andy mimed zipping his mouth closed.

'Better,' she said.

TWENTY MINUTES LATER, Charmaine and Zoe entered the tower block's reception, wearing boiler suits, steel toe caps, and carrying a tool bag each. They were met at the desk by the smiling concierge.

'Thank you for coming so quickly,' Harvey said. 'Please come this way and I'll show you where you need to go.'

He led them to the lift around the corner, which needed activating with a special fob.

'This lift is only for the penthouse flats, nobody else can

access it. You will need this for repeated use,' he added, handing Charmaine a small fob on a keyring.

'Thank you. So we just knock at number one and they'll let us in, right?'

'That's right,' Harvey said, 'and thank you.'

He turned and made his way back to reception, hoping that the two women would stay safe.

'He was nice,' Zoe said as the lift arrived and the doors opened. The interior was a decent size and luxurious, with a cushioned bench at the opposite end, mirrors on both sides, velvet curtains bunched in each corner, and a dark blue carpet.

'Wow, nicest lift ever,' Zoe said as they stepped in. 'You're not nervous, are you?'

'A little, but I'll be fine. This is new to me, remember?'

'Zoe, if I didn't think you could do a great job, you wouldn't be here; remember that, okay?'

'Thanks, Charmaine, I appreciate it. Oh, here we go.'

The door pinged as it opened on the fifteenth floor. They emerged onto a luxurious circular hallway with more dark-blue carpet, gold-and-white wallpaper, and golden light fittings. There were three brushed-steel doors between the light sconces, two on one side and one on its own on the other, where Charmaine rang the doorbell on the wall under the number 1 plaque.

They waited until the door was opened by a huge, bearded man wearing black trousers, black shoes and a white shirt, the top two buttons undone.

'Who are you?' he asked. His voice was heavily accented.

'Mr Eastwood? We are the plumbers, you called about a problem with your water?' Charmaine said.

'I'm not Mr Eastwood, I work for him. Wait here.' He closed the door before Charmaine could say anything else.

'Rude,' Zoe said, shaking her head.

The door was opened again by the same brute, who said, 'This way.'

He led them into an airy, white hallway, with matt-white walls and a white carpet.

'Take boots off,' he told them.

'We are not allowed to take our boots off, sir, it is company health and safety policy,' replied Charmaine.

He looked at her, and she couldn't tell if he was confused or angry.

'Wait,' he said. He left them in the hallway and walked off. Charmaine nodded as she looked around and noticed works of art along the walls, skilfully matching the modern décor and seamlessly fitting into the style of the flat. The hall curved off to the left, obscuring their view of the layout.

The guard came back and tossed a tea towel to each of the women.

'Clean boots before you come further,' he said.

'Charming,' Zoe said, cleaning the bottom of the boots as instructed. Charmaine followed suit.

'Now, can we do our job, please? We've had a busy day and want to go home.'

'Come,' the man said, turning and walking off again. This time they followed. They passed two doors on the left and continued. They emerged from the curved hallway into a spacious open-plan room. Zoe gasped at the sight. On one side there was a seating area in front of a huge television that was currently showing a basketball match in silent mode. Further along was another seating area, where two more burly men were seated. They turned to look at the visitors.

One of them laughed and said something in a foreign language, eliciting a laugh from the other. Further along and just past another corridor was an oak dining table, with eight leather-backed and cushioned chairs, conveniently placed near the open-plan kitchen.

'It's about time,' said a voice behind them in flawless English, from the man who emerged from the second corridor. It was Eastwood. He was dressed in a plush white dressing gown and white slippers. His hair was still damp, and he was in a foul mood.

'Mr Eastwood?' asked Charmaine.

'Yes, that's me. What took you so long? And why didn't they send a couple of proper plumbers instead of a couple of girls?'

'Sir, I can assure you that we are both qualified,' Charmaine replied curtly. Eastwood laughed.

'What, you don't like what I said? What did I say wrong, boys?'

The two seated men laughed again, and the guard that had brought them in smiled as he stared.

'If you can show us where the mains stop valve is, we'll be able to see what the problem is,' she replied, ignoring his efforts to embarrass them.

'I'll do better than that,' Eastwood said, smiling broadly, 'I'll let Andrei show you.'

He walked back to the corridor and shouted, 'Andrei! Get your useless arse out here.'

Seconds later, the largest of the four guards, Andrei, appeared from the corridor, naked except for the towel he was holding around his waist. His hair was dripping wet.

'There you are, finally,' Eastwood said. 'This is Andrei, the man who probably caused all the problems with the water.

He loves to shower and would spend hours doing so if he didn't have a job to do. Which, by the way, he is useless at.'

He turned to the man and said, 'Go and show these nice girls where the mains valve is, will you?'

Andrei stood there, sheepishly looking back and forth between his boss and the women. 'Is it the one in the airing cupboard?' he asked.

'Yes, that one, well done. Now go and show them, you oaf.'

'Follow me,' Andrei said, straightening up and walking back towards the curved corridor they had first entered. He opened one of the two doors and switched a light on. It was a large airing cupboard, with shelving along one side and cupboards along the other. Andrei opened one of the cupboards to reveal the water pipes that came into the flat, with the stop valve clearly accessible.

'Thank you,' Charmaine said, turning to the giant guard. 'Is there any water coming through at all? Where is the nearest tap?'

'Next door,' he said. 'Utility room.' He opened the adjoining door to show them the utility room that housed a washing machine and dryer, a sink, and more cupboards and storage space.

'Can you please fetch me a kettle, or something I can put water in?' she asked.

'Wait here,' he said.

They heard laughter coming from the main room.

'Oh, good, are they making us some tea? Lucky us,' they heard Eastwood say, eliciting more laughter from his cronies.

Andrei hurried back with the kettle and handed it to Charmaine. 'Thank you.'

There was enough water still in the pipes to fill the kettle, albeit slowly.

'Come with me,' she said as she turned and headed back to the main room. As she entered it, the three guards and Eastwood turned to see what she was doing.

'See? Tea!' Eastwood said. More laughter.

Charmaine walked to the sink and set the kettle down. She turned on the tap and let the water trickle to nothing.

'Go and do the same in the bathrooms,' she told Zoe, nodding. Zoe walked off to do as she was instructed.

'What is the problem, then?' Eastwood asked.

'We have to empty the tank for the flat and check that it isn't a simple air pocket that has caused the problem. It is the most likely cause,' she said.

'And how long will that take?' He pointed to an imaginary wristwatch and said, 'I have to be out of here in thirty minutes.'

'I hope to be done by then, sir.'

Charmaine could see that the guards seemed to be distracted by something, turning to face the roof terrace and talking in a foreign language that Charmaine was sure was Russian.

Eastwood noticed her staring and turned to see his men walk to the doors and exit to the roof terrace.

'What the hell is going on?' he asked abruptly, storming towards them to find out. One of the men turned to him and said something in Russian.

'In English, you fool,' he replied.

They both then walked to the other guards and looked over the side of the roof terrace at something downstairs. Charmaine could hear a car alarm going off.

'Wait here,' Andrei said. 'I put clothes on,' he added, and walked off.

'You do that, please,' Charmaine muttered.

She looked at Zoe, who had entered the main room again, and nodded towards the two drinks that were on the table where the guards had been sitting. Zoe walked to the table and took out a small bottle of clear liquid. Making sure she wasn't spotted, she poured a small dose of the liquid into each glass.

While the men were still distracted, Charmaine also took out a small bottle and poured a generous amount of the liquid into the kettle she had just filled, quickly putting the bottle back in her pocket.

'What are you waiting for?' she heard Eastwood shouting. 'Go and do something, you useless buffoons!'

The two men that had been seated ran back into the flat and towards the door to go and investigate the disturbance downstairs.

'Idiots,' Eastwood said, coming back inside, leaving the other guard to continue looking down from the roof terrace.

'What are you looking at?' he shouted at the women. 'Did you come here to stare, or did you come here to do a job? Or is a man's job too difficult for you? Mark my words, I will be complaining about the shit service you are providing.'

'Sir, we are doing what we can. There seems to be a fault in the pumps delivering water to your flat. One of us has to go and check them out while the other stays here to check if they are working.'

'Well, get on with it, I told you I have to leave soon.'

'Go and check the pump, Zoe, and call me when you're there so I can see if there is any lag.'

'Will do,' Zoe said, and walked away.

'I have to call my boss and let him know what is going on,' Charmaine told Eastwood, dialling a number in her phone.

'Yes, yes,' he replied impatiently, sitting down at the dining table in anger.

'Hey, boss, we're in the penthouse at Fifty-Seven East and there's no water coming through. I sent Zoe to check but wanted you to know that if it's a faulty pump we won't be able to do anything tonight, okay?' she told Trevor, letting him know that all was going to plan and that Zoe was on her way back down.

'Okay, thanks, I'll call you when I know more,' she added, hanging up.

'What do you mean tomorrow?' Eastwood asked angrily, 'you can't fix it now?'

'If it's a faulty pump we can't get one until tomorrow, the stores are all shut now, sorry. Do you have any water to drink?'

'No, I have fruit juice, and those idiots don't drink water unless they have to. You mean we have nothing for coffee?'

'No, except for this kettle I filled. You have enough here for a few coffees, maybe even enough until tomorrow.'

Eastwood sighed and said, 'We wait for your friend, then.' It was a few minutes before her phone rang.

'Hi Zoe, what does it look like?' she asked. 'A-ha, okay then, come back up.'

'Sorry, Mr Eastwood, it looks like a faulty pump. We'll come back tomorrow, hopefully we can pick one up nice and early.'

He shook his head and reached for his phone. After dialling a number, he said, 'Frank, please accept and extend my apologies to the group, but I won't be able to make it tonight. I have a utility emergency that requires me being here, sorry. Thanks, and we'll speak tomorrow, okay?'

'Sorry about that,' Charmaine said. 'I hope it wasn't anything too important?'

'It's not your business, but it can wait. What the hell are those idiots up to?'

20

EFFICIENCY IN MOTION

Z oe had called Trevor immediately when the two guards had rushed out of the flat to investigate the car alarm, to confirm they were on the way down. She then waited for the lift, and when back downstairs, prepared a pair of cage trolleys for the next step of the operation. When ready, she called Zoe to let her know, before making her way back upstairs.

The two guards had seen flashing lights and heard the car alarm go off from the yard where Eastwood's cars were parked. When they got to the gate, they could see that it was still locked. They peered through the bars, but they couldn't see much going on, other than some lights flashing from under the covered area. The alarm was deafening, so one of the guards unlocked the heavy padlock and opened the gate, taking out a bunch of car keys in readiness. Once inside the yard they determined that it was the Aston Martin alarm that had been activated. And they could see why.

Leaning against the car bonnet, shouting into a phone held to his ear by his shoulder as he checked his fingernails, was a young man dressed in a black tracksuit with grey piping. He was laughing and joking on the phone as the two huge guards approached, perplexed by what they were seeing. The guard with the keys pointed the key fob at the car and switched off the alarm.

'That's better! Hang on, Moose, someone just turned up. Let me ask them,' the young man said casually, before hanging up.

'How are you doing, gents? Is this your motor?'

'Who the hell are you?' asked one of the guards, moving towards Amir. 'Get off the car before I beat you to death, you little shit.'

'Whoa, whoa, big man, there's no need for that. I'm here to buy the car from you, that's all. Would you rather I stole it?'

'Car not for sale, now get lost,' said the other guard, also moving closer.

'You haven't heard my offer yet, don't be so hasty to turn me down, gentlemen,' Amir replied.

The first guard moved towards Amir threateningly, as if to swat him from the car. Amir, expecting something like that, rolled back onto the bonnet and landed on his feet on the other side, leaving a nice big dent on the bonnet.

'You shit, I kill you,' the guard said, moving around to intercept. It was at this point that Darren popped up alongside Amir, having been hidden from the guards. He was holding one of Andy's trusted taser guns, which he immediately shot into the midriff of the approaching guard. The barbs bit deeply through the white shirt and the high-voltage charge shook the man to the core. To his credit, he didn't collapse like most would, but simply fell to one knee, reaching for the insulated wire with his trembling hand. Darren gave him another charge and stopped him dead in his tracks, and he collapsed to the floor like a gibbering wreck.

In the seconds that this was happening, the downed guard's colleague shouted angrily and ran towards the intruders, completely oblivious to the two further trespassers that had popped up alongside Darren, one of whom was also holding a taser gun, which he fired instantly. Rory's aim was not as accurate, and the barbs struck the rushing guard in the neck. The charge was severe enough to cause him major problems, as he shook violently, but his momentum caused him to crash into Darren, taking him off his feet and smashing him against the Mercedes S500 behind them.

The impact drove the air from Darren's lungs, and he let go of the taser gun, the wires tangling them both, and which then pulled at the skin of the first guard. The barbs were ripped violently from his stomach, drawing blood. The crisp white shirt was immediately drenched as a result.

'Quick, get some zip ties on them before they're fully conscious,' Amir shouted to Rory and Clive. 'You okay, Darren?'

Darren was dazed but unhurt, shaking his head to clear it as he got up.

They moved fast and both guards soon had two zip ties securing their wrists, the guys conscious of the guards' strength. Their belongings were taken, including phones and the car keys to Eastwood's fleet, which they would likely remove later. Amir called Mo, who brought one of the non-descript vans straight into the yard, where they quickly loaded their captors into the back and were gone within a few short minutes, the gate locked behind them and the yard silent.

'Make sure you secure their ankles, too, guys, and keep

an eye on them all the way to the factory, these bastards are strong as an ox and will try to get free,' Mo told Rory and Amir, who were tasked with looking after the guards in the back en route to the factory. Darren and Clive remained to assist with Charmaine and Zoe, as did Martin and Jimmy, who were in the other van along with driver Charlie.

'Two down and three to go,' Darren told Trevor on the phone.

'Great stuff. Let's hope that we finish this quickly and without incident,' replied Trevor, who was very wary and conscious of the potential that Eastwood's guards had.

'Amen to that,' Darren replied. 'I'll call when we know more.'

IN THE PENTHOUSE, Charmaine wandered away from Eastwood as she continued her role of impersonating a plumber, using the time to check each bathroom as part of the pretext. When she came back to the main room, she could see that he was agitated again, looking towards the door for his guards to return with an update.

'Have a look from the terrace and see if you can spot those idiots downstairs,' he instructed Andrei and the other guard, 'they are taking forever. At least the bloody alarm has gone off.'

The two guards went to do his bidding as he sat in an armchair, impatiently drumming his fingers on the arm rest. Charmaine could see that he was not a patient man, and that the smallest thing could set him off on a rant. It was time to test the water.

'Sir, are you okay? You look upset. Can I get you a drink or something?'

'I'm not upset, I'm angry. Since my evening is ruined, I may as well have a large scotch. It's on the sideboard behind you,' he said, gesturing with his hand.

It wasn't the way she'd imagined the plan working but it was still a good option.

'Of course,' she said, 'happy to help.'

'Make it a large one, it's been a shit day,' he added dismissively.

Charmaine turned her back to him as she prepared the drink, grabbing the expensive bottle of scotch from the side.

'Do you want ice in it?' She bit her tongue, angry that he would assume a stranger would do this for him, but for the plan to work, she would have to swallow her pride and get on with it, obediently and courteously.

'No, as it comes.'

She opened the bottle and grabbed a glass from the cabinet. She reached into her overalls and removed the small bottle containing the clear liquid that Amir had supplied her with. She quickly poured a measure into the glass of scotch and swirled the glass around to mix it, as she put the bottle back in its hiding place with the other hand.

'Here you go,' she said, passing him the drink. He took it and nodded his thanks, clearly reluctant to thank the help.

'What are you doing now?' he asked, taking a sip, 'and where is your friend?'

'She should be on her way back soon,' Charmaine said, 'and then we'll make sure everything is turned off before we leave and come back tomorrow. We shouldn't be more than another half hour or so.'

'Good, make sure you leave the place as clean as you

found it, okay? Don't give me more reasons to complain, this hasn't been a good service from you today.'

'Like I said, without the pump there's little we can do, but I understand your frustration.'

Drink up, you little shit, then you can complain as much as you like, she thought.

'Ah, here is the other one. Did you go for a walk or stop to talk to a friend? Nice of you to join us and do your job,' Eastwood said, laughing out loud, enjoying the condescending behaviour so typical of a man with a superiority complex.

'Sorry, I wanted to make sure I got the right pump number for tomorrow, did I miss something?' Zoe asked innocently as she walked into the room.

'No, all good here, we'll be off soon,' Charmaine said, nodding when she knew Eastwood wasn't looking.

'What are you fools doing out there?' he shouted to his remaining guards, 'what the hell is going on?'

Andrei and the other guard, Vlad, both came back inside.

'The alarm has gone off and we can't see anything, sir,' Andrei said, 'including Ras and Pietr.'

'They're probably on the way up now, or having a cigarette or something, stop worrying,'

Eastwood replied. 'You may as well get the cards ready; we're not going anywhere tonight and I fancy taking more of your wages back,' he added, laughing some more.

Andrei's shoulders slumped as he realised he'd be without money for another week, and went off to get the playing cards.

'Don't look so sad, Andrei, you will still have plenty food in your belly, a roof over your head, and all the drink that you want, what's not to love?' He laughed out loud again, as did the other guard.

'Get the drinks and snacks and prepare the table, Vlad, and we'll both make a bit of money tonight, eh?'

Vlad nodded and made his way over to where Charmaine still stood, by the sink, as she pretended to work on the taps. He took five glasses and placed them on a tray. He then grabbed half a bottle of vodka and an ice bucket from the side. At the fridge, he placed the bucket under a dispenser for the ice, filling it up with cubes for their drinks. That also went on the tray. He then took a couple of bowls and put them on the counter and started looking in the cabinets for what Charmaine assumed were snacks. When he knelt and started looking in the lower cupboards, she quickly retrieved the bottle of clear liquid and emptied it in the ice bucket when she was sure nobody was watching.

Vlad emerged with two bags of cashew nuts, which he duly emptied into the two bowls. He placed everything on the dining table just as Andrei returned with two unopened packs of playing cards. He unwrapped one of them and placed the deck on the table.

'Ready? Good, let's get started. The others can join us when they get back. Maybe you'll be out of the game by then, eh, Andrei?' Eastwood laughed yet again. His abuse of Andrei was relentless. Andrei remained tight-lipped and stoic, recognising that his fate was sealed.

'Come, sit. Vlad, you deal first,' he said, taking another gulp of scotch.

'You,' he said to Charmaine, 'bring the bottle.'

'Yes, sir.' She obliged. She wanted to smash it over his head, but she knew that the drug would start taking effect soon.

'Good, you know your place, maybe I won't complain as much, eh?'

'I'd best get back to work, sir, and we'll be out of your way.'

The three men sat at the table and began their game of Texas hold 'em, a fast-paced poker game with plenty of action. Within minutes they were all deeply immersed in the game, drinking, and snacking on the cashew nuts. Charmaine figured that Eastwood, with his slight build, would be the first to be affected, with the two much larger guards a few minutes behind. That was the potentially dangerous period where the unpredictable could happen.

In the meantime, she and Zoe met in one of the bathrooms.

'As soon as Eastwood zones out, I want you to call Trevor and get him to send some help upstairs, including the trolleys, okay?' Charmaine whispered.

'It's a shame,' said Zoe, 'I would give anything to kick that little bastard's arse. Don't worry about it, I'll be sure to make the call.'

'Okay, good, let's just keep out of the way for now until we know the drug has taken effect,' Charmaine added.

'How long should it take?' asked Zoe.

'Amir told me between twenty and thirty minutes, so it's bound to start soon with short arse, for sure.'

They went back to their pretence, all the while keeping their eyes on the game and on the three men's reactions.

Shortly afterwards, Vlad noticed something was wrong, as Eastwood's eyelids started to look as though they were on the verge of closing.

'Boss? Are you okay, boss?'

'What? Did I win?' Eastwood replied, clearly disoriented.

'How much did you drink, boss?'

Eastwood slumped forward onto the table, his face resting on the full house that he was about to show.

'Damn, even when he's drunk, he plays better than me,' Andrei complained, throwing his cards down in disgust.

'Let's move him to the couch so that he can sleep it off,' said Vlad.

The two men picked Eastwood up and took him to the large leather sofa, laying him down gently and making sure he was comfortable.

'How much did he drink?' Andrei asked. 'He normally goes for hours before this happens.' Vlad looked over to Charmaine, who was putting some tools away in her tool bag.

'Is he okay?' she asked innocently.

'How much did you give him to drink?'

'He asked me for a large one, so I gave him a large one, maybe half a glass, that's all,' she said.

Vlad stared for a moment before turning back to Eastwood, who was now snoring on the couch. He paid no attention when Zoe walked out of the room to make a quick call.

'Good work, both of you,' Trevor said, 'I'll send the guys up now, be ready to let them in, they won't knock and will wait for you.'

'Will do.'

Back in the room, the two guards stood over the snoring Eastwood, unsure of what to do other than keep him safe, as they had been trained to do.

'You should give him some coffee, if he's that drunk,' Charmaine said. 'And get him to move around.'

'He is knock out,' Andrei said, pointing to his prone boss. 'He will not drink or move.'

'Well, just a suggestion,' she said, shrugging.

'Let him sleep, she's right, but it will wait,' Vlad said.

'Where the hell are Ras and Pietr? Andrei, call them and get them back here now,' he continued.

Andrei nodded and went off to get his phone, which he had left in one of the bedrooms earlier in his rush to get ready.

Vlad sat down next to Eastwood, his brow furrowed. He yawned deeply, raising his hand to cover his mouth as he did so. He then shook his head as the fog started to come down on his vision. He stood, shook his head, and shouted, 'Andrei, where the hell are you?'

He headed towards the corridor that Andrei had gone to. When he got to the room that they shared, he saw Andrei laying on the bed, fast asleep, snoring as if his life depended on it. He walked over and shook him violently.

'Wake up, you lazy bastard, wake up!'

He continued to shake his head to stave off the sleepiness. It was then that the realisation dawned on him. He turned and stormed back towards the main room, swaying from the effects.

'What did you do, bitch?' he shouted, moving towards Charmaine, who calmly waited for the brute to reach her.

Vlad attempted a roundhouse punch that she easily ducked. He tried another, again missing completely, his disorientation worsening.

Charmaine then reached back with her right leg and kicked him in the groin as hard as she could. The steel toe-capped boots were merciless and the giant man dropped like a rock instantaneously, howling in pain.

'Well, that was fun,' she said, placing her hands on her hips and standing over the crying giant.

'I think it's time to get the guys,' Zoe said, moving towards the front door. When she opened it, she saw Darren and his three colleagues in the hallway, along with one of the large trolley cages.

The four men rushed into the flat as she held the door open, anticipating a fight inside. When they reached the main room, they saw that there were no challengers, with Eastwood asleep on the couch and one of the guards on the floor holding his groin, whimpering and on the verge of unconsciousness.

'What kept you, boys?' Charmaine said.

The visitors looked around in amusement as they realised there was no fight to be had.

'Credit where it's due, Charmaine, great job,' Darren said, nodding appreciatively.

'The other chap is in the bedroom asleep,' Zoe added.

'Okay, let's get to work, gang, secure the men and get them down to Charlie. Zoe, me and you will go through the flat and grab what we can: computers, valuables, whatever we can carry out of here,' Charmaine continued, taking charge.

They moved swiftly, firstly securing and taking Andrei down in the trolley to the waiting van, before returning and repeating the process with Vlad, who was also now fast asleep, and then Eastwood. Charmaine and Zoe took all the mobile phones from the occupants, placing them in the Faraday bags after first unlocking and then changing the settings for future access, before removing the computers from the flat: one standalone computer and two laptops. Eastwood had a number of expensive watches and several items of jewellery in his plush bedroom, and bundles of cash, amounting to tens of thousands of pounds, which were also taken. Finally, they took the firearms and all the Russian Imperial Movement paraphernalia, along with some posters from another wall, mocking the Russian president.

There was also a briefcase containing important documentation, including the deeds to several flats in the tower block, including the penthouse, and the vehicle logbooks.

The entire process took just thirty minutes. They then went around and wiped all the surfaces down to remove any fingerprints, which took another twenty. Charmaine took one last look around to make sure everything was as it should be, before closing the door behind her as she left.

'A good day's work, I'd say,' she said to Zoe, who waited with her.

She called and updated Trevor, who was overjoyed with their efforts. Charlie had driven the van with the three sleeping captives along with Jimmy and Martin to keep guard over them.

'Darren and Clive are taking the Mercedes and the Aston Martin; can you and Zoe take one of the Range Rovers back to the factory? Kendra will take the other one.'

'Sure thing,' she replied.

'Darren will meet you downstairs with the keys and you can all leave in convoy,' he added, 'and we'll meet you back at the factory.'

'Will do, see you there.'

A good day's work indeed.

21

THE FACTORY

Andy took a minute to return the CCTV coverage back to its usual settings, now that everyone had left the tower block. There was no coverage on the yard so it wouldn't cause any problems down the line. He went over everything twice to be sure, knowing that there could be an investigation later, as with the Qupi disappearance. If anyone checked local CCTV, they may see the cars on the move, but they would not be able to identify the drivers and would assume they were being driven by Eastwood's men. There would be no trace of evidence to implicate any of the team. These fine tweaks, learned from previous scares, would make them more efficient and thorough in their dealings to come.

Trevor picked up his phone.

'Thank you for your help, Harvey, we're all done, so please feel free to turn the pump back on. I'll pop over and see you soon, when things have calmed down a little, okay?'

'Thank you, Trevor, this place will be a lot nicer for what

you have done. A lot of people will be much happier for it. See you soon,' Harvey replied.

'In the meantime, if there is anything at all we can help with, please do not hesitate to get in touch. Just don't leave my number in your phone until this all blows over.'

'Understood, we shall speak again, my friend,' Harvey added.

'Okay, Mr Pike, let's get back to the factory, our work here is done,' he said, moving to the passenger seat in the front.

'Okay, let's do this,' Andy said. 'Can we have a chat about Kendra on the way back? I don't want there to be any misunderstanding or anything.'

'No.'

It was likely to be a long, silent, and very cold drive back. Andy was not accustomed to uncomfortable silences.

'You're not going to kill me, because you need me for all the tech stuff, so you're going to have to talk to me about it at some point,' Andy said, gulping, in hope more than expectation.

Trevor turned and glared at him.

'You're an idiot, you know that?' he suddenly said. 'I'm not angry that you're an item, I'm angry because you lied to me and tried to do everything behind my back. So no, luckily for you, I'm not going to kill you.'

'Phew!' Andy exclaimed, wiping his brow dramatically, 'lucky me.'

'It doesn't mean I won't beat you, though,' Trevor said. 'You're still an idiot,' he added, turning and facing forward again.

Andy started Marge and drove carefully out of the car park, smiling.

UPON RETURNING TO THE FACTORY, Trevor saw that both vans were parked up, meaning that the captives were all secure inside their respective holding rooms. The four vehicles were taken directly to Stav's garage. Trevor had asked him to check for and remove any tracking devices so that they could never be traced, and he had Andy double-check to make sure that nobody would ever be able to find out where the vehicles had been driven to. It was a healthy haul that would generate some revenue after Stav received his fair share. The boxing clubs would get more equipment and continue to thrive.

'How are our guests?' he asked Mo, who met him in the loading bay.

'The guards are still very groggy from the drugs, and Eastwood is still knocked out, so whatever Amir sourced did its job well.'

'Yeah, that stuff is scary, I'm not comfortable using it, but in this case, we didn't really have much of a choice.'

'Anyway, they are all secure, the bodyguards have been given extra restraints just in case, and we'll make sure to keep them groggy until they're moved,' added Mo.

'Good work, Mo, where are the rest of the guys?'

'Those that aren't looking after the guests are waiting for you in the canteen.'

The canteen was upstairs and was a basic kitchen area with four sets of tables and chairs for people to use when they were on a break. There was a TV and a couple of couches in the corner. When they got there, Trevor saw Darren and his team, Charmaine, and several of the girls including Zoe, and Kendra who was talking to Amir. They had all returned from Stav's, having been picked up by Amir in one of the vans.

'Well done, everyone, great job,' said Trevor as Kendra joined him and Andy at the front.

'It's all that extra training, innit?' Amir said from the back. 'Oh, wait.'

There was lots of laughter; Amir had that effect on everyone and made them all relax quickly.

'You were great, Amir, we couldn't have done it without you,' Kendra added, bowing, with Amir mirroring the move in return. More laughter.

'Okay folks, this is where we are at the moment,' Kendra continued. 'The nasty robber shits are on their way to a less than comfortable resort for a while. Now that we have baby Hitler here and his giant goons, we have to decide where to send them quickly. Once his contacts find out he is missing, it is likely to cause another investigation, so we have to be careful.'

'I'm not following, Kendra, what do you mean?' asked Darren.

'Eastwood's dad may be dead, and a big chunk of the company may be his, but he is still very well connected, and it is still a big, viable company. They will want to know where their main stockholder is and what will happen to the company and its assets if he is missing, including the flats in the tower block.'

'Gotcha, so we have to move fast,' Darren said.

'Exactly, before anyone gets wind of it. If we put everything in place now, it will be too late for them to do anything,' Kendra continued.

'So do you still need us?' Darren asked, 'because that doesn't sound like something we can help with.'

'We have one last job that we need your help with, Darren,' Trevor said, 'and then you can leave with our thanks and huge respect, you guys have been bloody amazing.'

'Nah, it's nothing,' Jimmy said, 'we've had a great time, haven't we, Izzy?'

There was lots of laughter when Izzy raised his middle finger at Jimmy, holding his side, which was still recovering from the knife wound.

'It was our pleasure, Trevor,' said Darren. 'Just make sure to let Frazer know that we did right by you, that's good enough for us.'

'I've already told him several times, don't you worry,' Trevor replied, 'and I've sent him a few presents for the gym as a gesture of thanks for all you've done.'

A few presents was an understatement; Trevor had spent tens of thousands of pounds on brand new equipment that would transform Frazer's gym. He had also sent some money to help expand his club and help more of the local youth in Walsall. It was the least he could do and wanted it to be a nice surprise for Darren and his team when they returned.

'That's great, thank you,' Darren said. 'So what else do you want us to do?'

'Okay, we have a small problem,' Kendra told Trevor and Andy when they were alone in the operations room.

'What the hell are we going to do with this lot?' Andy said.

'Yeah, I know we've spoken about where to send them, but the container is on its way elsewhere, so we need to find another way. Any suggestions?'

'The problem is, we can't send them by sea as Kendra has mentioned, and where I'd like to take them here is always under heavy guard, closed to the public and constantly under surveillance, so not an option,' Trevor added.

'So, what do we do, Dad?'

'How about we get them picked up?' Andy said, stating the obvious solution that hadn't been considered.

'How the hell do we do that? I just told you they're always being watched,' Trevor said.

'That's true, but they have dozens of operatives all over the country, it's just a case of finding the right person who will – firstly, believe us, and secondly, pick them up.'

'So, you know how to contact them?' Kendra asked.

'I reckon I could, yes,' he said, feigning an expression of innocence to hide his smugness.

'Crack on then, smart arse,' she said, punching him lightly in the arm.

'No need for violence, Detective,' Andy said, 'I'll get on that now.'

Kendra and Trevor left him to it. Andy knew that finding the right contact through the usual channels was almost impossible and likely to attract unwanted attention. He also knew that the only prospective chance of success would be for him to reach out to his contacts through the dark web, where he could find almost anything. He logged in as his alter ego and started his search in one of the chat rooms he had frequented successfully in the past. He greeted many of his known acquaintances there; ironically, he had no idea of who they really were, and asked them one at a time if they could have a private chat.

After three unsuccessful attempts he got lucky with the

fourth, who he knew as Grizzly777. 'It's gonna cost you, my friend,' Grizzly responded.

'Tell me your price,' Andy replied.

'Five thousand dollars,' came the reply.

Andy paused, knowing that there was no point in accepting too quickly; he had played this game many times.

'I'll give you two.'

'Four.'

'Three thousand, final offer,' Andy said.

'Done. Send it to my crypto account and I'll message you back,' came the reply.

'Send me your key and I'll do that now but stay online as I need the information now.'

'Deal, I've messaged the account key, I'll let you know when the payment comes through.'

Andy copied the key and transferred the currency in crypto coins. It would show up immediately.

'Okay, that was quick. Here's the contact number of the person you need to speak to. The name she uses is Anya. I have dealt with her before, and although that is unlikely to be her real name, I know that she is for real.'

'Thank you, my friend, hopefully we will catch up again soon,' Andy replied, copying the number and signing off.

He found Trevor and Kendra in the canteen and told them of his progress.

'Wow, that's great news, what do we do now?' Kendra asked.

'Now, I think, Miss March, that you should make the call and try and organise a pickup. May I suggest somewhere remote and therefore unlikely for us to be discovered or ambushed?'

'I know just the place,' Trevor said, 'and although it isn't as remote as you'd like to think, nobody will bother us.'

'Okay then, I'll get one of the burner phones and make the call,' Kendra said, getting up to retrieve the handset. 'Write down the time and location so I have it to hand,' she said as she walked off.

Kendra returned after a few minutes with the phone.

'Okay, here we go,' she said, dialling the number that Andy had given her. The phone rang several times before it was answered.

'Hello,' came the reply.

'Is this Anya?' asked Kendra.

'Who wants to know?'

'I was given your number by a trusted source. I have something I think you will be happy to receive, and I want to arrange for you to pick it up.'

'What are you talking about?'

'I have Michael Eastwood, also known as Mikhail Aleksei Vordorovsky the second, who, as you know, is not a fan of your president. I want you to pick him and four of his personal guards up and take them back home.'

There was silence on the other phone. Kendra had anticipated reluctance, so she had taken some photographs on the way back from the operations room. Before Anya replied, she sent the photographs to her.

'What I just sent you is young Mr Vordorovsky having a sleep, and his four guards resting, as our guests. There is no catch, you pick them up and you get them out of our country.'

There was another long pause before Anya eventually replied. 'Call this number back in five minutes,' she said.

'I guess she wants to ask her superiors what to do,' suggested Andy.

'I don't think they will turn down the opportunity to have Eastwood back after everything he has said about their president. Did you see the photoshopped image of him with the other man? It's disgusting. I want to beat him for that, let alone the president,' Andy said, 'and there's a lot more where that came from. I should print them off and add them to the parcel.'

The five minutes was soon up, and Kendra called back.

'Look, if it was easy, I would have dropped them off at your embassy, but you know it's being watched, so what is it going to be?'

'I accept your kind offer,' Anya said. 'Tell me where to pick the gift up from.'

Before replying, Kendra looked at the note her dad had written.

'Meet us in ninety minutes in the car park of the Hainault Forest Country Park car park, we'll be parked close to the lake. You'll need a large van for your gift.'

Anya simply hung up without responding.

'I guess that's how they do things,' Kendra said. 'We have a green light.'

'I'll get them prepped and ready to go,' said Trevor. 'It's going to be a tight squeeze in that van, and I want some of our guys in there with them, so I'll make sure they're given another dose of sleeping tablets. Can you call Charlie and have him ready the van?'

'Will do,' Kendra said, waving her dad off.

She turned to Andy and said, 'Once again, good job, Mr Pike.' She reached over and gave him a gentle kiss on the cheek.

'It was worth it, just for that,' he said.

Kendra put two fingers in her mouth and pretended to retch.

'Nice,' he said, shaking his head. 'Very nice.'

THEY ARRIVED at the site ten minutes early. The club was quiet, being a weekday, so they drove past the main car park and along one of the gravelled drives towards the lake. They were unlikely to be disturbed there. Charlie was driving, Trevor and Darren in the front with him. The five captives were in the back, sluggish from the drugs that kept them under control, with no idea of what was going on. Clive and Martin were there with them, their taser guns and CS gas ready for use. For that reason, they were wearing protective masks and gloves, just in case.

'Looks like they beat us to it,' Trevor said, spying a large white van parked next to the lake, its engine running.

'Stop here, Charlie, I'll go and speak with them.'

Trevor got out and headed for the waiting van, a long-wheelbase Mercedes Sprinter, more than big enough for the five men they were about to take. As he got close to the van, both doors opened and the occupants got out, the bulky driver clearly the muscle as well as the driver, and a young woman in a dark blue trouser suit. A side door slid open and two more heavy men stepped out, standing by the van. The woman held up her arm to keep the two men where they were for now.

'Anya, I presume?' Trevor said, stopping short. She nodded, clearly wary.

'We have something for you in the back,' he said. He indicated for them to walk with him. Darren was now standing by the passenger door, watching closely in case anything went wrong.

Trevor took them to the rear of the van, where he opened both doors widely so that the newcomers could see clearly inside. The five captives were all zip-tied by their wrists and still very groggy, so they didn't respond to the doors being opened.

'You were not wrong,' Anya finally said. 'I thought it was some sort of ruse, but here he is, in all his glory.'

Within a couple of minutes all five captives were safely moved to the rear of the white Mercedes and the doors closed.

'You may be able to use these,' Trevor said, handing over a folder with photos and evidence of Eastwood's misdemeanours.

'Thank you,' Anya said, taking it. She made to walk off but stopped and turned back to face Trevor.

'This has been a pleasant surprise,' she said. 'I am rarely surprised like this in your country. I like it.'

'I'm happy for you,' he said, a trace of irony in his voice, 'but let's not do this again, eh?' He got into the van, along with Darren, before driving off slowly back towards Fox Burrow Road and the exit.

'That was surreal, Trev,' Darren said as they drove off, 'we don't get shit like that in Walsall, mate.'

'Yeah, I didn't like dealing with them at all, but justice needed to be done, eh?'

'And then some.'

'Let's get back to the factory, I think we all deserve a drink and some pizzas, on me.'

'Mate, you sure know how to look after us. Pizzas and a

drink, it was worth coming south just for that.' Darren laughed.

'Don't knock it, mate. To clarify, when I say drink, I mean something non-alcoholic.' Darren laughed out loud.

'Like I said, well worth coming for.'

22

DISAPPEARANCE

Kendra was working the following morning, so she had to wait until late afternoon to meet up with Andy and her dad for a debrief and an update. In the office, she went through her usual routine and was quickly able to determine that no progress had been made with the investigation into the missing Albanian gang.

'They have literally vanished from the face of the earth,' Rick Watts had said when they met for a coffee. 'Usually you have a trace here or there, a rumour, something that gives you an indication. Not this time. I think even our friends from the NCA have given up.'

'How has the twat been the last few days?' she asked.

'He's actually been mellower each day that he hasn't found anything to have a go about, so in a way, it's ironic that it's made him less of a dick.'

'Sarge, that man will always be a dick, nothing will change that. He's probably seething inside now that he hasn't found anything that would get us all into trouble; he's getting ready to piss off with his tiny little tail tucked between his legs.'

'You're probably right. Anyway, I'm going to speak to the bosses and see if we can just put it to bed once and for all,' Watts said. 'There's too much tension around here and I want it gone so we can get on with our jobs.'

'I couldn't agree with you more. Just so you know, he doesn't like me one little bit, so don't be surprised if he doesn't try something funny. I'm surprised he hasn't, yet.'

'Yeah, don't worry about that, I know exactly what type of person he is. Like I said, hopefully he'll be gone any day.'

'Amen to that,' Kendra replied.

WATTS WAS true to his word and had the investigation closed that very afternoon, citing poor morale, a significant drop in detections, an increase in crime figures, and half-a-dozen complaints against the NCA – namely Eddie Duckmore's misogyny and overbearing conduct. When Watts made his case and showed the figures, it was decided immediately that the investigation would be closed until further evidence came to light that would justify re- opening it.

Her shift at an end, Kendra made her farewells and went to see Watts on her way out.

'Great job today, Sarge, it was the best outcome possible,' she said.

'It was, I think the complaints against Duckmore were the turning point. The boss upstairs has made an official complaint against him to the NCA. That could prove very interesting. Speak of the devil...' Watts paused as Duckmore and his sidekick Critchley appeared at his door.

'Just wanted to let you know that we're out of here now that the investigation has been closed. Glad to see the back of this place, to be honest,' he said, smirking at Kendra. 'Looking forward to getting back to some real police work, you know?'

Watts and Kendra both smiled, knowing that he hadn't been made aware of the complaints yet.

'Yeah, thanks for helping out, guys. Good luck,' Watts said.

'Can I have a quick word, Detective Sergeant?' asked Duckmore. 'In private?'

'Sure,' Watts said, knowing what was coming. 'Kendra, see you when you're next in.'

'Bye, Sarge,' she replied, walking out without acknowledging the visitors.

'See now, that's what I'm talking about, Rick,' Duckmore said, looking back at Kendra as she walked down the corridor and out of sight. 'The discipline in this place has been tough to take, especially from that young filly.'

Watts looked at him and rose from his chair, resting on his fists as he stared into Duckmore's face.

'Listen here, you nasty little shit, that Detective has more skills in her little finger than you will ever have in your entire shitty little career, and if I hear you talking about her like that again you'll have me to deal with. You don't want that, trust me.'

Duckmore was shocked and instinctively backed away.

'What did I say that was bad?' he asked, still oblivious to his dated ways.

'Piss off, both of you,' Watts shouted, 'and don't come back!'

Duckmore and Critchley backed out of that room quicker

than they had moved in years, retreating down the hall and leaving the building as soon as they could.

'I'll have that bastard one day,' Duckmore muttered. 'I'll have him.'

Kendra met with the rest of the team as they gathered at the factory, where Trevor had been true to his word and provided refreshments for everyone. It was a chance to bid farewell to Darren and his colleagues, which was a sad occasion for many of them, who had bonded with the Walsall crew.

'Listen up, everybody,' Trevor said, standing in front of those that had gathered, 'I just want to thank you all again for everything you have done these past few weeks. East London will be a much better place for it, now that robberies and burglaries have plummeted, and more importantly, we will not have another wannabe Hitler running our country, because that was looking very likely at one point, I tell you.'

'Man, it would have been tough round here, for sure,' Amir said, wiping his brow.

'Yes, Amir, it would have been,' Kendra said, 'for more people than you will ever know.'

'Darren, guys, all of you who came in to help us, what a great job you did. I couldn't be happier with the outcome, and only one little scratch to show for it,' Trevor continued, to the laughter, as Izzy again raised his middle finger to them all, but with a smile on his beaming face.

'Yes, Izzy, you're a hero. That goes for the rest of you, all of you contributed in some way. Charmaine, what you and Zoe did up in the flat was bloody marvellous, thank you both so much for doing what none of us even thought of doing.'

'The pleasure is all mine, Trevor, what you all have done for the club and the girls has been brilliant, so helping out like this helps pay you back a little.'

'There's nothing owed, Charmaine. You've proven yourselves many times now and are an important part of what we are doing, so it's we who are grateful.'

There were many cheers to that, and it helped cement their place in the team, giving them the support and confidence that came from being a part of something good.

'Well, you know where we are and what we can do, so don't be a stranger,' Charmaine added, waving in gratitude.

'Don't worry, we won't be. Right, as a final thank you, we have some farewell gifts for our friends from the West Midlands. Darren, like I said, I've already sent some equipment to your club and sorted Frazer out, who is happy as Larry with you all. Here's a bit of cash for you to spend in London before you go home, it's a couple of grand each, which will buy a few goodies for you.'

Kendra passed a small holdall to Darren, who took it and nodded in appreciation.

'You didn't need to do this, but we're grateful, right, guys?' His colleagues all acknowledged their thanks, smiling at the small windfall.

'It's nothing, brother, you deserve every penny. Charmaine, there's something for you and your girls too, you decide what to do with it, hopefully it will help you all a little.' Kendra passed another holdall to Charmaine.

'The rest of you miscreants are getting a slice of pizza and a can of coke,' he said, to much laughter from the rest.

'Damn, I thought I'd at least get another tracksuit,' Amir said, feigning disappointment.

'Stop your whinging, Amir, I've got something for you all

too, but it can wait. Tonight is a celebration of our friends who showed what can be achieved if we work as a team doing good in this often shitty world. Thank you all,' he finished, clapping along with the rest of them.

'That was great, Dad,' Kendra said, pulling him to one side with Andy. 'You deserve a big pat on the back too, you know, both of you. None of this would be possible without what you have both been doing, so thank you.'

'He's still going to kill me,' Andy said, stepping back from a potential jab from Trevor.

'Damn right I will, if I ever find out that you've done anything to upset my baby,' Trevor added.

'Ha! Honestly, she's likely to kill me in a more painful way than you ever can, so I think I'm damned whatever I do,' Andy replied. 'It's just as well that she's hotter than hell,' he added, one step too far.

He was too slow to avoid the punch as it hit his arm. He would have a dead arm for hours.

'I'm gonna go lie down in Marge, I think, call me if anything new comes up,' he said, swerving out of their way and leaving the room, rubbing his arm the entire time.

'He can be an idiot, but he's a good idiot. I'm glad he's on our side,' Trevor said.

'Thanks, Dad, me too.'

EPILOGUE

Central Africa

The container stayed shut until it reached its final destination, just as Bruno had instructed. It was lifted from its lorry by a crane and dumped unceremoniously in the sand outside the fort, where its contents would be removed before being hauled onto the back of the truck.

The stench was unbearable after a two-week journey by sea and another two days by land. The ten men inside covered their eyes from the brutal sun that awaited them as they cautiously left the stinking container. They had no idea where they were and would not be told for the duration of their stay.

'Welcome, Legionnaires,' said a tall, uniformed man with a small cane under his arm. 'I am Staff Sergeant Lamare. You will address me as Staff Sergeant Lamare at all times, even when you are off duty. Do we understand each other?'

Brathwaite was the first to speak, confused and still a little blind from the sun.

'What are you talking about, man? What is this place? Why we here?'

He never saw the cane coming as it struck him on the back of the leg, eliciting a high-pitched cry from the disorientated gangster.

'I will not tell you again, you will address me as Staff Sergeant Lamare at all times. Are we clear?'

'No, staff whatever, you are not clear. What the fuck are we doing here?'

Another welp was the result, this time striking the other leg. Brathwaite now rubbed the back of both legs, which were stinging like crazy.

'Okay, okay. Staff Sergeant Lamare, please tell us why we are here.'

'Better, but next time stand to attention, or your legs will be hurting for a long time, soldier, are we clear?'

'Yes, Staff Sergeant. Did you say soldier?'

The cane hit its mark again, and he screamed in frustration.

'You are all soldiers in the French Foreign legion, where you will be based here at our lovely fort in the desert. If you want to eat and drink, you will do exactly as you are told from today until the very last day that you serve with us.'

There was a pause as Brathwaite considered his next sentence carefully, reluctant to hear the answer.

'Staff Sergeant Lamare, why are we here?'

'You are here because you are the scum of the earth. You are lucky to be alive; what you have done back home deserves far worse. You are here for redemption, for payback, call it whatever you want, but you will pay for the crimes that you have committed.'

'Staff Sergeant Lamare, how long will we be here for?'

'You will be with us for twenty years.'

Brathwaite's shoulders slumped in total defeat, and he collapsed to his knees. He looked slowly around him; there was nothing but sand for as far as the eye could see in all directions, except for the dull sand-coloured fort that was to be their home for two long decades.

Three of his men passed out. The others cried.

Norilsk, Siberia

Four-and-a-half-thousand miles away the weather was not so welcoming. In fact, it was as brutal as it can be, with freezing winds and icy rain a daily constant. Brutal, unwelcoming conditions for most of the year, perfect punishment for those that had committed crimes against the state, or even for something as simple as making a silly comment against the government on social media. There was no sun shining when the latest batch of prisoners arrived at the gulag. These were special prisoners; all five of them had been especially selected for this gulag by the president of Russia himself.

All five men shuddered as they dropped from the lorry that had brought them the last hundred miles, a journey that had driven any hope of salvation from their minds. One in particular, the short blond man, shivered uncontrollably as he looked around at the surroundings. The icy rain struck his pale face mercilessly as he tried to make sense of his surroundings. Other than the giant grey granite wall that loomed above them, stretching either side for fifty-odd feet before the sleet hid the rest from view, there was nothing to see.

'This way!' the guard shouted gruffly, striking one of the larger men with the butt of his rifle.

The guard was clothed in a heavy long brown coat that reached his feet, and a gigantic fur hat that covered most of his face. You could barely see his eyes, but you could see enough to know that this man was not to be messed with. He turned and led them away, two further armed guards at the back of the five prisoners who had been shackled together by their ankles.

After a short walk, the guard led them into a narrow badly lit tunnel that brought them into a small courtyard. The gate was closed behind them and locked by one of the rear guards.

Eastwood looked around and could see more grey, this time the grey of the ugly building that surrounded the court-yard, with tiny barred windows at several levels.

The guard led them to the far corner where another gate stood open, waiting for them. This time they entered the building itself and walked along another badly lit corridor until they were allowed entry by yet another barred gate into a large holding room.

'You will wait,' the lead guard said, striding off.

The five prisoners sat down on the solitary bench that was fixed to the wall. There was one large table in the centre of the room, with a chair on either side. Two armed guards remained with them, their fur hats adjusted now so that the prisoners could see the stern bearded faces of the men who would likely shoot them if they so much as farted. The lead guard reappeared with a another dark-suited, gaunt man who carried a clipboard. He nodded to the two guards and one of them unlocked the ankle chains.

The gaunt man sat at the desk facing them. He looked at each man in turn for several seconds, before looking down at his clipboard and then addressing them.

'My name is Gorvski and I am the commander of this godforsaken place. You are here because you have collectively insulted the president of our glorious country, for which you will pay a very heavy price.'

'Sir, there has been a huge mistake, we have done no such thing,' Eastwood said, pleading to the man who had control of his fate. 'I am sure that we can resolve this quickly, I am a very wealthy man and can look after you in a manner that will change your life and your family's lives forever.'

Gorvski looked down at his clipboard and pulled out an envelope that was tucked behind the front sheet.

'My family is long dead, Mr Vordorovsky, killed by the capitalists that you love so much. I have no use for money, I want no luxuries, and I do not want my life to be changed by scum like you.'

He pulled out several sheets of printed paper that showed photoshopped images of the president lying naked with a man in one, holding hands with a different man in another, engaged in depraved carnal intercourse with two other men in a third, and finally engaged in something similar with a horse.

'For these alone you should be shot, but the president has decreed that you shall spend your days here, in this paradise, with me, for the rest of your miserable life. I shall pass you around the other men who will play with you as you seem to like being played with. You will suffer greatly here, you depraved animal.'

Eastwood was stunned and had no words. He slumped forward, his head in his hands, tears running down his frozen cheeks, as he realised that he was doomed and would be better off dead.

'As for you other men, you will also be my guests for a short period of time, we can use your muscle for some renovations we are carrying out. You can choose to defy me and serve the same fate as this piece of shit, or you can contribute and be well fed while you are here. Do not take my offer lightly, I very rarely make them.'

All four of Eastwood's personal guards stood and declared their loyalty to the commander of the gulag.

'It is as I thought. So, Mr Vordorovsky, it seems that you are without any allies here. You have nothing. You will always have nothing. So shall your miserable existence be, forever.'

He stood and glared at Eastwood one last time.

'Take them to their cells,' he said to his guards, and left the room.

The silence was broken by the whimpering of a small man who had lost everything.

London

Just a few short weeks after Eastwood's surreptitious disappearance from the tower block, a large family of Ethiopian refugees took up residence in the penthouse flat, overseen by the Refugee Council who had been gifted the property by their benefactor, the deeds having been signed over by

Michael Eastwood on behalf of the company that had owned the premises. Three further flats had been similarly gifted to a local vulnerable women's group.

Harvey took great pleasure in looking after the new residents, who collectively contributed to the uplift in spirits within the block.

It was several months before the company found out that Eastwood had been repatriated to Russia. They quietly redistributed his shareholding and wrote off the assets that he had taken control of, namely the tower block and a number of vehicles. It wasn't long before they had completely wiped out his involvement in the company, the board deliriously happy that they had wrestled full control back and could now move forward unencumbered by the rich spoiled brat son of the founder.

There were somewhat different celebrations at New Scotland Yard in London after a successful national operation that had led to the arrest of ninety-three white supremacists who had infiltrated and supported the British Patriots Party in an attempt to illegally influence local elections. The tip-off and intelligence had come anonymously in the form of a large folder containing all the personal information of the men, including the financial support they had received from their benefactor, now known to be of Russian descent and repatriated.

The Counter Terrorism Command had concluded there was nothing to be gained in asking the Russians to extradite him for attempted electoral fraud, bribery and corruption, and so kept the information from the public. It was a wake-up call for them and resulted in more attention towards far-right groups in the country.

Ironically, the wannabe Hitler's attempts to destroy the

country had the opposite effect, giving the public more peace of mind and security, with nobody having any idea that it was all because of a small group of individuals who wanted nothing more than for justice to be served.

THE END

'Road Trip'

Book 3 of the *'Summary Justice'* series
with DC Kendra March.

https://mybook.to/Road-Trip

Or read on...

BOOK 3 PREVIEW

They stood in silence, unmoving, two ranks of almost two dozen, like sentinels, waiting for their leader to address them. Dressed in all-black, all-weather motorcycle gear with blacked-out visors, they looked like extras in a sci-fi movie, playing the bad guys. It was the part they were born to play. You had to look closely to see the black shield-shaped patch on their right arms, each bearing a capital R in dark grey. The large empty warehouse in which they stood had been provided to them for their forthcoming mission, which their leader was about to explain.

His footsteps broke the silence as he approached from a side office, flanked by a pair of his most trusted and feared men. One sported a Māori warrior tattoo that covered half his face and neck. The other had several piercings in his nose, lips, ears, and between his eyes. Both were bald, both were fierce, and both were evil in appearance. It was exactly what their leader wanted from them, to instil fear into everyone they encountered, including colleagues. The leader himself was neither pierced nor tattooed but wore sunglasses indoors, in what was a poorly lit warehouse. He was dressed exactly as the others in all-black but wore a blood-red bandana around his neck. He stopped in front of those gathered before him and spoke.

'Listen up, people, it's finally happening!'

There were hoots and hollers from the small crowd in appreciation; it was the news they had been waiting for.

'Our benefactor has given us the go-ahead to start our operation,' he continued, 'so as of tomorrow, we shall cause as much mayhem as we possibly can.'

More cheers and the stomping of feet.

'Our benefactor has been generous. Not only has he provided us with this base of operations, but he has also given us the list of places he wants us to target. But best of all, he has filled our bank account with lots of lovely money, so we can buy all the drugs and guns we need to make this operation the most spectacular yet. Oh, and there'll be a ton of money left for us all personally if we do the job within a couple of months.'

This time there were whistles and shouts of 'beer' and 'drugs', amongst other things. Motorcycle helmets were raised in the air in approval and salute.

'You'll have whatever you want when we're done. Remember what I told you, people, when I picked you for this special team? You were unwanted pariahs, known as troublemakers, and to be avoided. Nobody wanted to work with you, nobody trusted you, nobody had faith in you – except for me! You are all perfect for this, and you are perfect for us. You are perfect for the Rejects, and we shall show them all exactly what we are worth!'

He raised his arms in the air as his minions cheered

raucously, his two lieutenants urging them on and raising their fists in the air.

'Rejects! Rejects! Rejects!'

Chapter 1

The campfire crackled, its sparks floating upwards, brilliantly bright against the night sky as they weaved magical shapes and raced upwards before spluttering and disappearing. The family sitting around the fire laughed and joked as their annual gathering gained momentum. They ate and drank well into the night, celebrating the seventieth birthday of Manfri, their much-loved *Rom Baro*, or Big Man, the tribal leader of the Romany family that had been gracing this campsite once a year for the past fifty-three years. It was a well-attended ritual and celebration; although their family had diverged so much over the decades, they could gather annually to reflect upon and cement their long, proud heritage.

Manfri stood, raising his glass. 'May you all live long and happy lives, dear ones.'

'Hear, hear,' came the shouts from many, before they went silent in respect for their elder.

'Some of you have travelled far to be here with us once again. Some of you have chosen a different path to that of your Romany traditions, which we all respect,' he added, to some boos and laughter.

'Not all of us!' shouted someone from the darkness..

'Yes, yes, we hear you back there, Patrick, always wanting to get a word in,' Manfri continued, 'but in all seriousness, the world has changed a great deal in my lifetime, and I see nothing wrong with that which some of our families have chosen. I respect their decisions – and let's face it, they aren't doing too badly, are they?'

'Yuppies, Rom Baro, that's what they be, yuppies!' Patrick shouted once more, to a of laughter.

'Come round to mine in Surrey and I'll let you drive my BMW, Patrick,' shouted another, 'and I'll let you wash in my swimming pool too, before you come into our lovely house,' he added, to continued hilarity.

The banter between those who still travelled the roads of England and those who had forsaken their caravans for brick-built homes and plant their roots anew had been going on for years. It had become part of the annual ritual, and everyone looked forward to it as it kept them grounded.

'As I was saying,' continued Manfri, 'you have come from far and wide to this place every year, at the same time, the same place, and it has become an important part of our family's custom, where we all look forward to seeing you again. Long may it continue!' He raised his glass again.

'Cheers and good health,' shouted many, for the umpteenth time that night.

'Finally, let us not forget our honoured guest, the man who has made us feel so welcome each year. You have been a friend to us all for many years now and are as part of this family as anyone else here. In these times of hatred and mistrust in the world, you are our shining beacon of hope. Knowing there are good people like you still around sustains us all. Please, all, raise your glasses to Mr. Rufus Donald.'

'Hear, hear,' shouted the entire family; there were almost

fifty people gathered around the fire: men, women and children.

'My friends,' said the elderly landowner, standing to address them all, 'I have looked forward to your coming here every year for a long time now, much as my father did before me. It is you that gives me hope, not the other way round. I see the love and respect you have for each other, the way you look after each other and make sure that at least once a year you connect.'

Several family members hugged as his words hit home.

'I only wish that I could see my children as often,' Rufus continued, sadly, 'but the ways of this modern world have taken priority for many people now, especially the younger generation who feel compelled to match—or better—each other's achievements in the material world. The life you have chosen is far better, in my humble opinion, and I wish you all the very best for the future. You will always be welcome here. You have my solemn word on this. Cheers!'

Rufus Donald raised his glass high as he toasted his much-loved guests.

There were rapturous cheers as the old man sat down, a smile hiding the sadness that he had just reminded himself of. Manfri, who had sat next to him, lay a hand on his shoulder.

'Thank you, my friend,' he said simply.

'There is nothing to thank me for, Manfri. You have been one of only a handful of what I can call genuine friends over the years, so you have my thanks and I will always make this place available to you. I have made it official that when I pass, my children will save the place for you each year.'

'I hope that won't be for a very long time, Rufus,' Manfri replied, raising his glass once more. Their glasses clinked loudly, and their drinks were downed in one, eliciting more cheers from the family.

A stockily-built man approached at sat next to them. 'You're slipping, Pa.'

'I'll still drink you under the table, young whelp,' Manfri replied.

'Rufus, you remember my eldest, Jacob? He stayed here many years ago because the life on the road became too much for him, remember?'

Rufus and Manfri both laughed as Jacob shook his head.

'Pa, you know I see Rufus regularly, right? You do this every year, as if it's going to embarrass me, and it never does.'

'Yes, but it makes us both laugh,' Manfri replied, clinking his glass against Rufus's again.

'Sorry, Jacob, I have to humour your Pa. He's one of my oldest and dearest friends and we have to look after each other in our old age, right?'

'Don't you worry, Rufus, it's this old man next to you who thinks he's a joker, you're fine. I take it from your toast that you have seen little of Peter and Emily?'

'Sadly, yes. Peter is a partner in the accountancy firm now, so he's working long unsociable hours, and doesn't even call much anymore. Emily started her own publishing company and also works stupid hours. She hired a nanny, so she doesn't even get to see her kids much, let alone her parents.'

'Don't be too harsh on them, Rufus,' Jacob said, resting a hand on the landlord's arm. 'The world has changed a lot recently, and it's tougher than ever. They're just trying to make a good life for themselves and their kids, you know?'

Rufus smiled and patted Jacob's arm.

'You reared a good one here, Manfri,' Rufus said, 'strong

and sensible. Tell me, Jacob, how is the boxing club coming along?'

'It's going great, thanks,' Jacob said. 'We're up on last year's numbers and training some good youngsters with potential. I reckon in a couple of years we'll have a champion from Norfolk. It's long overdue.'

'Hear, hear,' Manfri said, raising his glass.

'Now you know where he gets all his strength from,' added Jacob, pointing to his father. 'The number of times he raises that glass, it's no wonder he can still beat the living daylights out of us all.'

'Hear, hear,' Manfri repeated, raising his glass yet again.

Jacob and Rufus exchanged a knowing look and then both burst out laughing, spraying their drinks in the process.

'It's gonna be a long night,' Jacob said. 'Cheers!'

Before he could down the drink, Jacob paused.

'Do you hear that?'

'Hear what?' Manfri asked. 'Oh, that rumble? What *is* that?'

They listened for a few more seconds before the rumble became a roar and two dozen motorcycles entered the site. The chatter around the fire stopped dead as the family looked on in astonishment at the growing number of bikers who had now stopped in a long line facing them. The central rider raised his fist, and they switched all engines and lights off, leaving an eerie sight made visible only by the light of the fire.

'Who the hell are they?' asked Manfri, standing.

'Leave it to me, Pa, I'll go and see what they want,' Jacob said.

As he walked towards the riders, who remained silent and passive, the lead rider removed his helmet and strode out to meet him, with two of his riders in tow. As they walked, they too removed their helmets. They stopped ten feet from Jacob and stared at him. Jacob could see the leader's face. There was a piercing pair of eyes like nothing he had ever seen. Completely black. No whites.. As the firelight flickered across his face, it gave him a fiendish look as he tilted his head for effect. Jacob realised they were waiting for him to react first.

'Oh, I'm sorry,' he said sarcastically, 'are you waiting for me? Who are you and what do you want?'

The leader smiled and raised his arms, spreading them in the associated gesture of peace.

'We came to pay our respects,' he said, eliciting a laugh from his companions.

Jacob was not expecting that as a response, and he certainly didn't believe it.

'You've lost me, stranger. We don't know you and so there's no reason for you to pay any respects.'

'Ah, but there is,' said the leader, 'we came to tell you we'd heard good things about this site and wanted to find out for ourselves. We want to join your little party here and have some fun, we hear gypsies like yourselves are very welcoming. Isn't that right, lads?' He turned to his fellow riders and nodded, stirring them into replying with muffled 'yea's' and raised fists.

'Well, you heard correctly, we Romany are usually a fun-loving and welcoming lot, but there is no room for you here tonight, stranger. There are many other sites around here for you to stay on, and we wish you luck finding one.'

The leader stepped forward, closing the gap between he and Jacob to just three feet.

'That's not very welcoming, is it, friend?'

His two friends joined him at his side, all three staring at Jacob.

'Oh, I see. My apologies. Now that you're staring me out with your scary-ass faces, I should bow down to you and let you join us, right? You don't scare me, stranger, you don't scare any of us. We've lived for centuries putting up with scarier people than you clowns, so why don't you turn round and piss off back where you came from before you get the beating of your lives.'

The leader's companions made to move towards Jacob, who stood his ground and stared back.

'Everything alright there, Jacob?' asked Patrick, who had stepped from the crowd along with fifteen other men, all holding weapons.

The leader saw the women had also armed themselves and even some of the older children had, too. His riders could lose this fight; they'd certainly take a beating, and he'd lose a lot of the team finding out. It was too early to take that chance. He reached out his arms to stop his lieutenants and smiled a sinister smile.

'Nah, we're all good here, Patrick, thanks for asking,' Jacob shouted back, without taking his eyes off the interlopers. 'These nice people were just leaving, weren't you?'

The leader laughed, nodding in acceptance.

'We're leaving—for now.'

He and his men turned and walked back towards the rest of their team. The leader paused and turned to face Jacob once more.

'I'll see you soon, stranger.'

'Not if I can help it,' Jacob replied, waving sarcastically. 'Goodbye, now.'

The men went back to their bikes, putting their helmets

on. The leader raised his fist to signal the starting of their engines. The roar from two dozen motorbikes was mighty, and they sat there and revved them for several moments before they rode out of slowly out of the site and away.

'That wasn't much fun, Pa. We'll need to keep our wits about us with that lot.'

'Yes, son, we will,' Manfri replied, his thoughts troubled by the unexpected malevolence. He had seen many things in his long life, but nothing so evil.

'I've never seen them before, or even heard of a gang like that in these parts,' said Rufus. 'I'll spread the word and warn everyone. They could cause a lot of problems around here.'

'Hopefully, it's nothing,' Jacob said, knowing full well that he would be sure to see the riders again. 'Maybe they just don't like travellers and wanted a scrap. Who knows?'

'Whoever they are, you be very careful, you hear? I'm off to bed. I've had enough excitement for one night,' Rufus added, standing. He shook their hands and those of many others as he left.

'A good man, that,' Manfri said. 'It'll be a sad day for us all when he's no longer with us.'

'You heard him, Pa, he's left instructions with his kids to allow us entry here.'

'Yes, he did. As long as they own the land, but what if they decide that city life is for them, and they don't want to live here?'

'I hadn't thought of that, but let's not dwell on a problem that could be many years away, eh? Now, pass me that bottle before you finish it all by yourself, you greedy old man.'

THE RIDERS DIDN'T TAKE LONG to get back to the warehouse. As the leader took his helmet off, he called over his two lieutenants.

'Bring that bastard to me,' he told them. 'He needs to be taught a lesson.'

As it turned out, teaching was what they were best at.

———

ACKNOWLEDGMENTS

I'd like to start off by thanking you, the reader, first. The fact that you are reading this suggests that you have also read the first book in the 'Summary Justice' series, 'An Eye for an Eye', and enjoyed it enough to come back for more. I hope that you enjoyed this as much and continue to follow the exploits of the team in future books.

What I can tell you is that I am enjoying writing about them immensely, the characters are growing and becoming real people in my eyes, so it has been a truly pleasurable experience for me.

As with book 1, Editor Linda Nagle deserves praise for her excellent contribution, I am thankful to continue working with her and look forward many more such collaborations.

I must also give huge thanks go to my partner, Alison, for her help with the cover for this book and for her ongoing support.

I would be very interested to hear your thoughts on the books so far. Suggestions, praise, criticism, all of it is welcome. It will certainly help me to know so that I can do better, so please contact me at theo@theoharris.co.uk and I will do my utmost to respond.

TH

You can reach me at: theo@theoharris.co.uk

ABOUT THE AUTHOR

Theo Harris is an emerging author of crime action novels. He was born in London, raised in London, and became a cop in London.

Having served as a police officer in the Metropolitan Police service for thirty years, he witnessed and experienced the underbelly of a capital city that you are never supposed to see.

Theo was a specialist officer for twenty-seven of the thirty years and went on to work in departments that dealt with serious crimes of all types. His experience, knowledge and connections within the organisation have helped him with his storytelling, with a style of writing that readers can associate with.

Theo has many stories to tell, starting with the 'Summary Justice' series featuring DC Kendra March, and will follow with many more innovative, interesting, and fast-paced stories for many years to come.

For more information about upcoming books please visit theoharris.co.uk

Printed in Great Britain
by Amazon